HARPER BLISS

A Breathless Place

Other Harper Bliss Books

If You Kiss Me Like That
Two Hearts Trilogy
Next in Line for Love
A Lesson in Love
Life in Bits (with T.B. Markinson)
A Swing at Love (with Caroline Bliss)
No Greater Love than Mine
Once Upon a Princess (with Clare Lydon)
In the Distance There Is Light
The Road to You
Seasons of Love
Release the Stars
Once in a Lifetime
At the Water's Edge
The French Kissing Series
High Rise (The Complete Collection)

the Pink Bean Series

More Than Words
Crazy for You
Love Without Limits
No Other Love
Water Under Bridges
This Foreign Affair
Everything Between Us
Beneath the Surface
No Strings Attached

Published by Ladylit Publishing – a division of Q.P.S. Projects Limited - Hong Kong
ISBN-13 978-988-74415-8-8

CONTENT NOTE

Please be aware that this book discusses the topic of suicide which could trigger certain readers.

CHAPTER 1

I'll be dead in six months. In 183 days to be exact. I can't wait. But for now, the prospect alone brings me adequate comfort.

I stare at my computer screen. The cursor blinks mockingly on the white background of the Word document. It's supposed to be the first of many. If this is the speed I'm going to be working at, I might have to add a few days to my very last calendar. I don't want to do that. I've chosen the date carefully—as carefully as these things can be chosen.

One day after my sixtieth birthday, I will say my final goodbye. It turns out, if you want to die, there's a lot you need to take care of. And I want every last thing to be taken care of. My perfectionist streak will continue until my very last breath. The only problem is I'm not used to sorting out every little thing myself. I have people for that. My personal assistant Daisy handles all my administration. My chef Rian cooks most of my meals. Harry takes care of my home here in New York. My manager Ira has made sure every single one of my needs has been met for the past thirty-five years. But I haven't told him my greatest need yet.

How do you tell someone something like that? If there is an acceptable way, I haven't found it yet. And I've had years to think this through. It's been nearly a decade since the thought first crossed my mind. Furtively at first, as though it was afraid to become a full-grown idea, the inkling of such a possibility would creep up on me in unguarded moments. It took months before it dared to linger for more than a fleeting second. Before I dared to grasp it and examine it further. It took years until I became certain it was what I wanted. But my own certainty is just that. My own. It's not something I can easily inflict upon others. That's what I'm trying to explain in this letter—the first of many.

Dearest Ira, I type. Before I continue this letter, I need to decide whether I will tell him beforehand or not. It will determine what I write. I've been going back and forth on this. If I tell him ahead of the time, I don't need to write him a letter. But he will try to talk me out of it. Oh, how he will try. Ira might know me best of all, but he will still try, with all his might, with all the power he has over me, to change my mind. That's not a conversation I want to have. So I need to write this letter. But I guess I don't need to write it today. Although that's what I told myself yesterday as well. And the day before. I can't keep on postponing it.

I click out of the Word document and check the list I made of people who need to receive a letter on March 19, 2021. With the life I have lived, I figured there would be more, but there are only a few names on my list.

Maybe I should start by writing one joint letter to all of them. I can add personal touches later on, once I've gotten down the gist of what I want to say.

My phone rings. It's my private number. The one only a handful people have—the number Daisy doesn't screen for me. Speak of the devil. It's Ira.

"Izzy." He sounds out of breath. "I just got word Bruce fell off his horse."

"What?" Bruce is the biographer I've been working with for the past two years on my final project—although, of course, Bruce doesn't know it is my very last professional endeavor.

"It's bad. He's in a coma."

"Oh no." On a really bad day, I would have considered Bruce a lucky son of a bitch. "Is he going to be all right?"

"I don't know. It's too soon to tell. But..." I know Ira. The cogs in his brain are ever-turning. Business always comes first. That's why I pay him his fifteen percent. "I spoke to the publisher. They have a replacement in mind already."

"Are you kidding me?"

"The book was as good as done, Izzy. All the source material is there."

I huff out some air, making sure Ira hears my exasperated sigh on his end of the line. "Who are they suggesting?"

"Leila Zadeh." He sounds as though that name should impress me.

I rack my brain. I've heard the name before, but that's the only bell it rings.

"She writes a lot for *The Metropolitan*," Ira says.

"Bruce really can't be replaced. Not this late in the day."

"I know. You're right." The last one is Ira's favorite sentence. "But just meet with her. See how you get along. No pressure."

No pressure? Yeah right. "I don't know, Ira." I was never totally on board with the whole biography thing, anyway. To have someone delve deep into my life like that. I only went along with it because of my own secret plan. Because by the time my biography is released into the world, I will be long gone. Ira sold me on the idea of leaving a different kind of legacy.

But Bruce was such a likable man. Easy to talk to. Unassuming. Never pushy, although his hands-off approach seemed to work in the end. Poor Bruce. "Which hospital is Bruce in? Is he getting the best care possible?"

"Of course." Ira's voice is calm. "We can go see him as soon as it's allowed."

"Send me a dossier on this.... What's her name again? Then I'll decide."

"Coming your way right now." A silence falls. "Are you okay, Izzy?" Ira asks after a while.

"All the time I spent with Bruce and I never knew he rode horses."

"Hm." I can hear Ira swallow. "It was his job to find out everything about you. Not the other way around."

A minute after we've rung off, I get a reminder on my cell phone for my workout. It's hot instructor time in my virtual gym. Ramona's the only reason I still show up every day. Ramona and the addictive blend of endorphins and arousal she elicits from me.

After the news about Bruce, I need the distraction. On my computer screen, I get a notice I've received a new email. It's from Ira and the subject reads *Leila Zadeh*.

That will have to wait until after Ramona has made me sweat and forget.

Dear Friends,

At first, this may be very difficult to comprehend, but I'm confident that, in the end, you will understand why I had to do this. Maybe not fully. Maybe not how I feel in my very bones that this is the only way things could go for me. But you will get it. That's why I'm writing you this letter.

I've thought about this for a very long time. For years and years. Taking my own life is not a decision I've made lightly; you can be absolutely sure of that. It's one I've looked at from every possible angle. I studied the outcome of every other possibility, although, let's be frank, between dead and alive, the options are quite limited. Or maybe that's not entirely true. There's only one way to be dead. But there are many ways to be alive.

You can be alive-alive, like you, Ira. You take every bull by the horns, you take on every challenge, no matter how difficult, and ride the fuck out of it. I do love that about you, but that's not an option for me. Since the surgery, I've been cautiously-alive. Well, depressed-alive at first. But the depression did lift.

I want you to know I'm not doing this because I'm depressed. When I was depressed, I went to see Doctor March and he helped me through the worst of that. This is not a matter of depression. This is a matter of actively choosing death over life.

I've led a privileged, astounding life. The kind of life people grow up dreaming of. It's truly been a wonder. It's a marvel, the way things have gone for me, back to when I was so young. Yes, there was pressure, and fame isn't something that comes without adversity and its very own challenges. But it's been truly great. If I was at all religious, I would say I've been blessed. Despite what happened, I have been very blessed.

It's also because so many wonderful things have happened to me that I'm now able to say, firmly, that, for me, it's been enough. You may think I don't have the right to say that, but I would disagree. This is my life. Why can't I do what I want with it, even if it means cutting it short? Besides, you can hardly call my life short. Maybe sixty is short for some, but I sometimes feel like I've lived many lives in those sixty years. I've been the singer—that alone has been enough to fill so many lifetimes. I've been the me I've become after my career ended. All in all, it's been a crazy, hectic, often ecstatic ride. A ride of which, nonetheless, I've had enough.

CHAPTER 2

When the bell rings, Harry, who insists on calling himself my house manager, goes to the front door to let in Leila Zadeh. After reading through the materials Ira sent, I decided to meet with her. Because I want to at least have the option of finishing the biography. The clock is ticking. 180 days left.

From the accompanying photos, I gathered Leila Zadeh is a glamor puss, so I dressed to match her. Off-white casual suit. Shiny earrings. Even a hint of lipstick. But when Harry brings Leila into the den, I greet a woman wearing jeans and a loose-fitting blouse.

"Miss Adler." She beams me a wide smile. "What an honor to meet you."

Here we go with the deference I used to bask in but have come to despise. Because I now know how little it means. "And you." I shake her hand. She has a firm grip. Not a hint of nervous sweat on her palm.

"What a lovely home you have." Leila's jet-black hair is pulled back in a tight chignon. Her eyes are equally black as coal. Her lips are painted fire-engine red. "And you look absolutely stunning, of course."

Holy moly. Enough already with the inane flattery. Didn't Ira brief her? Maybe he did, but maybe she's decided to disregard him. Who knows, she might even mean what she says. But *stunning* isn't a word I've associated with myself for a long time. Maybe because stunning people aren't in the habit of wanting to die.

"Can I get you anything to drink? Coffee? Tea? Something stronger?"

"Whatever you're having." She glances at the cocktail glass on the coffee table.

Busted. Not that it isn't amaretto-sour-o'clock somewhere. I nod at Harry, who hurries off to prepare my guest's drink.

We sit, and I cast my glance over Leila Zadeh again. From her file, I know she's fifty-nine, just like me. She slings one leg over the other. She's all soft curves and her lips seem to be stretched into a perpetual smile. Her skin is the color of molten gold.

"I'm truly thrilled you agreed to meet me. It's shocking news about Bruce, of course."

"Do you know him well?" I continue my study of her. The skin around her eyes is creased. Probably because she smiles so much.

"Quite well. We worked together a number of times. I'm, um, well-acquainted with this project as well."

"Are you?" I quirk up my eyebrows. I'm well aware Leila knows much more about me than I do about her—it seems to always be the case whenever I meet someone new.

"Let's say I've done a very deep dive into all things Isabel Adler in the past few days." She rests a kind gaze on me. "It's been fascinating, to say the least."

Harry knocks discreetly on the door, then walks in with a

tray carrying Leila's cocktail. He offers it to her and as he turns away from her, he shoots me a quick wink.

Maybe I should include Harry in my list of letter receivers as well. He hasn't worked for me that long, but I have grown very fond of him. He doesn't behave as though he has a broomstick shoved up his ass like my previous 'house manager' did. He doesn't take himself nor this job too seriously and brings a lightness that, on most days, my house sorely lacks.

"So you've read all of Bruce's notes already?" Leila's made it sound as though her continuing the project is a done deal already.

"Notes?" she says. "What I've received from his editor are not mere notes. It's a proper first draft. Only the last few chapters are missing."

Bruce has been holding out on me. Last I spoke to him, he told me things were progressing slowly but surely. Maybe he wanted to finish the last few chapters before he gave me more than that. The last few chapters that span the last horrible decade of my life. I know I haven't shared enough of my emotions for Bruce to be able to work it all into a cohesive narrative, without him having to invent things about me, or attribute feelings to me I might not have felt.

Bruce has been quite exasperated with me the past few months. I know that much. I was slowly working my way up to sharing with him the most difficult part of my life —and now he's being replaced.

"I'm a touch confused, Miss Zadeh." From her background information, I know she's not married. "I thought you coming here today was more like... an audition." I'm well aware of how condescending I sound. It's a test—although it's also true. "Whereas you're making it sound as though it's a given you will be taking over as my biographer." Who gave her

Bruce's draft, anyway? I'll have to ask Ira as soon as Leila leaves. Those notes contain very sensitive information about my life.

"Oh," she says, her perfectly-painted lips forming a circle of surprise. "Well, I'm not really in the habit of auditioning for jobs any longer. I usually get asked."

Now I can't help but smile. Leila Zadeh doesn't back down easily. At least I like that about her.

"I studied your résumé," I say. "Impressive." I fix her with a stare—I try to keep it cool even though I am rather amused by her. "Although it hasn't exactly made me feel as though you and I are on equal footing. You know everything I told Bruce about myself, whereas I only know about your many professional achievements."

She takes a sip from the cocktail, places the glass down carefully, then opens her palms. "Consider me an open book, Miss Adler. I'll share whatever it is you want to know."

I shake my head. "I didn't even know Bruce rode horses. For some reason, I feel so guilty about that." I take a quick sip from my drink as well. "I never asked him anything about himself. He just isn't the kind of person that invites that sort of inquisitiveness." Nice one, Izzy. If this is my way of saying I wasn't the least bit interested in Bruce's personal life, I must be succeeding.

Leila nods as though she understands what I'm trying to say. "His style is to disappear into the background. From what I've read, it appears to have worked."

I chuckle. These damn journalists. They'll play you until you've spilled your dirtiest, most hidden little secret. "What's your style?"

"I'm more... prominent." Her lips lift into a smile. "More present." With attention-drawing lipstick like that, I bet she is.

"If you were to get the job." I can't help myself. It's as

though I need to be patronizing with her. I don't know why. "How would you proceed?"

Her widening smile is bracketed by small creases in her skin. "I would start by trying to fill in the missing pieces." She stares me straight in the face. "I would need to ask you about losing your voice."

Bam. Leila Zadeh doesn't mince words. She's the opposite of Bruce. I nod, then drink again. I can drink as much as I like now. It's not as though I still have a singing voice to look after. Neither will I need my liver to perform optimally so my body thrives for decades to come.

"After we've gotten to know each other better, of course." She slants her head. "In fact, I might start by inviting you to dinner at my house so we can establish a more intimate rapport. This is a huge project, and finishing it is not a job I underestimate just because I was brought in this late in the day." She narrows her eyes. "That will also give you the chance to subject me to some in-depth questioning of your own."

Dinner at her house? What is she talking about? I'm not looking for a friend here. Before this meeting started, I was only moderately interested in having my biography finished. "That's really not necessary, Miss Zadeh."

"Please, call me Leila." Her voice has dropped into a super smooth register. "And I wish you would take me up on my offer. Take some time to think it over, of course. But my gut tells me we can be a good match to bring this project to a satisfactory close." As she hesitates, the tip of her tongue flicks across her bottom lip. She reaches for her drink. "And do bring the recipe to this with you." She expels a brief sigh. "Simply delicious."

Entirely unlike Bruce, Leila's modus operandi is gutsy charm. I can't say I'm unmoved by it. On the contrary. Her deference when she just arrived was just a ploy, or maybe a habit, or maybe even something she had to force herself to act until she got the lay of the land. What does she think of me right now? I already have more questions than I had before I started talking to her.

"I'll let you know. I need to talk to my manager."

She shifts her weight, uncrosses her legs, then recrosses them in the other direction. "Look, Miss Adler—"

"Isabel. Please."

"Isabel." Her gaze on me is so dark, it's a little unsettling. "I know a thing or two about loss. I think I can give a voice to your pain."

Her straightforwardness makes me glad I'm sitting down. I'm not used to someone speaking to me like this. Only Vivian and Ira would ever address me in this forward manner, and I've known both of them for decades. Leila just walked in the door.

"We'll see." My hackles are all the way up. I haven't decided to work with her. I don't have to show her how I feel just yet. Although the thought of opening up to a woman like Leila isn't unappealing.

"Will you let me know about dinner?" She pushes herself out of the chair Bruce spent hours in. "Call. Text. Email. Whatever suits you best."

Because I'm still sitting down, she gazes at me from above. When I rise to my full length, I'm a few inches taller than her. I've always been the tallest woman in any room. She offers her hand and I shake it. There's still no trace of nerves on her bone-dry palm.

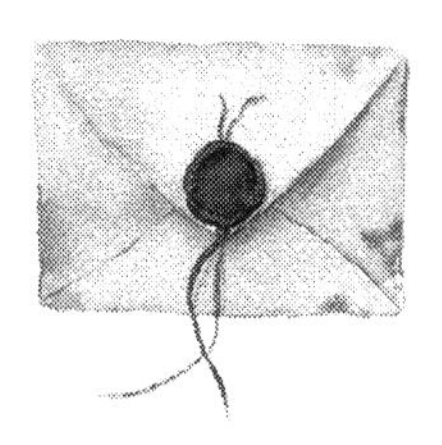

Not being able to sing any longer is not a terminal illness. It's not like cancer or any other physical disease that, ultimately, causes your heart to stop beating. But you have to understand that not being able to use my singing voice to express myself for such a long time, has felt like a long, slow death. Maybe it's wrong to liken it to a terminal illness, but that's how it seemed. Like a part of me was dying all along. And that being the case, then why shouldn't I die? The truth is I feel like I don't have much left to live for. Please don't take this personally—although there's no way you won't. You must know I love and care for you deeply. But that doesn't mean I should extend my life for you.

I know all of this is one big taboo, and I've done my best so you don't have to deal with the fallout of this too much. I've taken everything into consideration. Everything I could possibly think of. Every probable scenario and every potential question that might pop up. I've left clear and detailed instructions for what needs to happen after my death—when you read this. Of course, you'll be sad. That's normal. You might even be heartbroken for a while. I'm sorry to have to put you through this. But always remember: I wanted this. I was not someone with decades of life left in me. I didn't have an enormous quantity of joy left inside me to be experienced—to be unearthed. In fact, the biggest joy I experienced in the past few years was when I was putting together this plan. The plan for my death. The relief was instant. Not that I haven't had doubts. Of course I have. Which is why I made myself take the time to truly think it over, to come at it from every possible angle. To make sure you know this was not a rash decision.

CHAPTER 3

"She's read the first draft already, Ira." I give him a once-over. It strikes me that, to me, he's looked exactly the same for the past thirty-five years, although he must have changed. His hairline must have receded because he's practically bald now. But when you see someone nearly every day, these incremental changes just creep up on you. "I didn't even know there *was* a first draft."

Ira waves his hand. "Eh. They must have cooked something up at the publisher's as soon as they heard about Bruce's accident. Some sort of contingency plan. Let's not forget, we are under contract with them. And a large part of next year's bottom line is riding on that book for them."

"Fuck the contract. I'll buy them out if I have to."

"Did you like Leila for the job?" Ira ignores me the way he usually does when I go a touch diva on him.

"It looked to me as though she liked herself very much for the job."

"Just give me a yes or no, Izzy."

"I haven't decided yet. She invited me to dinner."

He whistles through his teeth. "Are you going?"

"I don't know." Secretly, I've already decided to go, but a part of me doesn't seem ready to admit that out loud yet.

"I think you should," Ira says. Of course, Ira wants me to go. The pickings of being Isabel Adler's manager have been rather slim of late—not that Ira isn't smart enough to have made his fortune off me a long time ago. But men like him can never have enough money in the bank. The pursuit of evermore dollars is what gets him up in the morning. "And not for the reason you think I want you to go." He lifts an eyebrow, inviting me to inquire further. Through it all, Ira has become much more of a friend than a manager. I do have to give him that.

"And what's that?" I smile at him. He pushes his glasses up the bridge of his nose. He's wearing his trademark navy polo shirt again, the sleeves tight around his biceps.

"It's a chance to get yourself out of this house." He looks around. "Don't get me wrong. It's a lovely house, but must you spend all your time in it?"

"I go out plenty." It's a blatant lie and we both know it.

"Okay, sure. In that case, next time you want to talk to me in person, why don't you come to my office? If you're out and about so much, it should be easy enough for you to drop by."

"Fuck off, Ira."

He shrugs. "That's what I thought."

"I'll go." I make it sound as though I'll go to Leila's house to please Ira, my long-plagued manager, when the truth is, now that I've slept on it, I quite liked her. Her energy was arresting. It filled the room. Her dark gaze was slightly mesmerizing. And I have been psyching myself up to tell the story of the last ten years of my life, in all its brief brutality, to Bruce. I'm not sure yet whether I'll be able to tell Leila—maybe my voice will fail me all over again—but I don't mind trying.

At this point in my life, with 179 days to go, I literally have nothing left to lose. Because that's the thing when you decide to die. So many former issues stop being important at all. In the end, I don't care what Leila Zadeh thinks of me. I no longer care what anyone thinks of me. Whether they feel sorry for me or want to give me a good kick up the ass or have forgotten about my existence entirely. None of it matters. Because in less than six months, I'll be gone.

"Good. Evie had nothing but good things to say about her," Ira says. Evie is his new assistant. Although, she must have been around a while for me to actually remember her name. "Zadeh won a Pulitzer for her essay on gender pay disparity in the theater."

"I know." I've won thirty-six Grammys that now have zero meaning to me. Or was it thirty-seven? I don't even know. It sounds conceited. And it is. But so many things are how they are, and usually for a good reason.

"Let me know how it goes. This book's going to be massive. People are absolutely dying to hear from you." Ira usually isn't one to put this kind of pressure on me openly. He's more of a stealthy manipulator.

"Do you have another agenda I don't know about?" I ask.

He shakes his head, then stops abruptly. "Actually, I do." He takes off his glasses. "There's something different about you that I can't put my finger on. I'm hoping that working with someone new might... I don't know. Spark something in you."

"What's there to spark?" It's funny he uses the word 'spark'. I've always associated it with how alive I always felt on stage. It's exactly that spark of vitality I've been missing for nearly a decade.

"Meeting someone new can have that effect on you," he says.

"Oh, that's right. You're the expert, of course. What did

Evie spark in you when you first met her?" I give him a facetious look. I've never been Ira's easiest client, not even when I made him millions every year and my antics were easier for him to stomach.

"A lot." Ira has always been a good sport. That's probably why I've kept him on for such a long time. Neither of us is going to change now. But I'm glad Ira feels the spark so often. I used to envy him for that, but I don't anymore. "And it's wonderful."

"I'll keep you posted, but don't go expecting too many sparks, okay?"

"At least she's better looking than Bruce." Ira paints on a smile. "Not wanting to speak ill of the ill, of course." We got word yesterday Bruce has woken up from his coma, but his recovery will be a long road.

Truth be told, I never even considered whether Bruce was handsome or not. Maybe that says it all. Leila's beauty, on the other hand, is pretty obvious. Uh-oh. Something begins to dawn on me.

"Am I to believe you didn't have any hand in her selection?" I study Ira's face for a reaction he might not be able to hide.

He holds up his hands. "I didn't. I would tell you if I did. She was on the short list two years ago, before we decided on Bruce."

"She was?" Surely, I would have remembered that. Unless it was kept from me.

"Or maybe it was the long list and she was otherwise engaged. I don't remember. If it's that important, I'll look it up for you."

I wave him off. It's not important. My phone buzzes its daily reminder. It's Ramona time. I feel like I need her more today, as if I have more energy to burn. I already know I will work extra hard for Ramona later.

I say goodbye to Ira and let Harry show him out. Before changing into my workout gear, I text Leila that I will take her up on her invitation.

I'm writing this almost six months before I will actually die. I could offer you proof of that, but it seems futile to put my energy into that right now. My point is that I've wanted this for a long time. Not that I've been dragging myself through the last months of my life, but I've known for years that this time would come.

And yes, it's unfair I've been able to live toward this date and you haven't. Please, don't go blaming yourself for not noticing anything. I made sure that you didn't. It's not your fault. If any of you even think that for a split second, let me assure you that you're on the wrong track. There's nothing you could have done. This is me. This is where the events of my life have taken me. To illustrate this in more detail, let me tell you about my 50/50 theory.

Even before the surgery, I lived by this theory, out of necessity. The big difference between Before and After is that Before, I had my Voice, by which I mean my singing voice. I've always been fragile, delicate, perhaps a touch too sensitive for this world. I'm sure that isn't news to you. Because of this, I came to realize that life is a 50/50 game. 50% of the time, I was happy or close enough. The other 50%, I decidedly wasn't. I don't believe I'm special when it comes to this. I think this is probably how it breaks down for most people. Or maybe not. I haven't exactly done a survey on this. I can only speak for myself. I've always promised myself that if I was having too many 49% days, I would do something about it. And by something, I mean this. I don't want to live a 49% life. Honestly, 50/50 is already hard enough.

I hope I'm explaining this adequately. Maybe not. To put it very simply: for a very long time, I was happy half the time. And that was enough. Because I had my Voice. I could sing. I was grateful for that gift. For all it gave me. The fame. The money. Although, honestly, I could have done without both, because I now know that they don't mean a single thing. The insurance payout still leaves a very bad taste in my mouth. Millions in return for what? I would give literally all I have—I would go millions into debt—for one more night on stage. Because I know what that *means to me and I know what money means to me. They don't compare.*

After the surgery, I had a long string of well-below 49% days, which was to be expected, of course. If there's one thing you can't accuse me of, it's that I didn't try. Because I tried every single thing. You know this. I didn't give up easily because my Voice is worth fighting for. I would even dare say it's the single most precious thing about me. It's not just my Voice; it's not just an organ that allows me to produce sound. When my Voice left me, a part of my soul, of what makes me quintessentially me, left me as well. Without what my Voice can do for me, I'm not the same Isabel Adler. I'm someone else.

CHAPTER 4

The first thing I notice, as though it has already become the feature that allows me to pick her out of any crowd, is her lipstick. Surely I must have come across this shade on many a woman in my life, but on Leila, it looks extra special. It makes her face come completely alive. Maybe it's what it suggests—a fierce, unquestionable love of life—that, ironically, draws me to it with such force.

Leila's wearing jeans again, but this time with a low-cut V-neck sweater. In my book, it doesn't really pass as dressed up, but at least I didn't go to too much effort myself this time.

After she closes the door, she bends toward me and plants the lightest, briefest, quickest kiss on my cheek. I'm not even sure it qualifies as a kiss, so barely-there is it. But a whiff of her scent lingers, a summery, fruity perfume I find myself inhaling greedily.

Yesterday, after my daily workout with Ramona left me sweaty and horny again, a thought I've been consistently pushing away snuck up on me. I can't say if it was triggered by Ramona or by Leila's visit—by the memory of her bright red lipstick and her pitch-black gaze on me. Either way, it wasn't a new thought, just one I've chosen to ignore, even though it's not the time for me to be ignoring persistent thoughts any longer.

As I follow Leila into the lounge, it hits me again.

I need to be with another woman one more time before I die.

It's a dicey idea, however. I'm not someone who can simply go out and pick someone up. The height of my fame was many years ago, but doing something like that is still out of the question. Even if I'm not instantly recognized, photographed, and posted all over social media, just the notion of being out on the prowl would make me too self-conscious to try anything.

I've considered going the 'professional' route, to pay a woman for her discretion, but that scenario is simply too unappealing to me. There are too many psychological hurdles to overcome and for what, this late in the game? The mental effort it would require doesn't feel like it would be worth the reward.

The truth is that my options in this field are very limited because of who I am. The truth is also that, at the moment, my gaze is drawn and glued to the shape of Leila's ass in her jeans.

"Sorry?" She said something that I missed.

Leila has turned to me, removing her shapely behind from my line of sight, and she flashes me that smile again.

"I make a mean martini," she says. "Dirty as they come."

Oh, dear. No, no, no, Izzy. No way, don't even go there. But the idea seems to explode in my brain, its particles merging with my own. My entire psyche is taken up with the prospect of kissing those red lips. But that's not why I'm here at all. It's most certainly not the intention I left my house with.

Something about seeing her has triggered this friskiness. And I should really stop doing Ramona's classes. I have no use for a shipshape cardiovascular system anymore. Only male virtual instructors for me from now on. *Yeah right.*

"I'd love one." I stand around not sure what to do with myself. Leila is wearing 4-inch heels—one of the only luxuries I've never been able to afford for myself because of my towering height—and her face is almost level with mine.

"I'll be back in a moment. Make yourself comfortable." She briefly touches my arm and hurries off to what I think is the kitchen. Great. She's a toucher. I should be happy she hasn't hugged me yet.

Check yourself, Isabel. This is getting out of control quickly. I don't know what has gotten into me. It's like someone flicked a switch deep inside me—a really well-hidden one. Now that it's been switched on though, and I'm suddenly aflame with desire, the off-function doesn't seem to work anymore.

I take a deep breath. I'm not going to sleep with my biographer. Unless, of course, I don't allow her to become my biographer. But no, I shouldn't think that way. I've barely spent thirty minutes with her. I'm just a touch aroused. It will pass. It reminds me of the hot flashes I used to have. They passed as well. Everything will be fine.

I look around her living room. It's cozy in that borderline messy kind of way. I can feel myself calming down. Another thing about knowing you're going to die soon is that extreme moments of aliveness can sneak up on you, as though to remind you that you're not dead yet. And what makes you feel more alive than being physically intimate with someone else? To be connected in that way with a gorgeous woman. Because, let's be honest, Leila Zadeh is really rather beautiful. I'd dare say even in a slightly overwhelming way. She's all elegance and pillowy lips and brooding gazes. And I haven't had sex in a very long time. It's not a kind of intimacy I feel I can still allow myself, which is the reason I try to banish any thought from my mind as soon as it asserts itself. I'm not sure I can even let someone in like that any longer.

Leila returns with two glasses, interrupting my stream of thought. I'm glad for both the interruption and the drink.

"Shall we sit?" she asks.

Silly me. I'm still standing around awkwardly, so lost in thought was I.

We settle into two armchairs with our martinis. I take a sip. That's dirty indeed. Not to mention super strong.

"I'm so glad you came, Isabel." She fixes her gaze on me and it unsettles me instantly. It's as though, now that I've had the thought of sleeping with her, I can't un-think it, and it's everywhere. It hangs heavy—and sultry—in the air between us, even though she knows nothing about it. Taking another sip isn't going to help one bit, I know that much, but I do it anyway. What else am I going to do?

"Ira told me I should get out of the house more, so here I am," I blurt out.

When she laughs it's like a warm bubble escaping from her throat with the sole purpose of delighting me. Oh, Jesus, Mary, *and* Joseph. I need to get a grip. I consider using the trick I use to bring me back to earth, quickly and efficiently, in situations like this. It's not a trick I enjoy deploying however and I might wait to see if it's really necessary that I use it.

"Can we speak candidly?" Her fingernails are painted the same color as her lips. They flash bright red as she twirls the stem of her glass around.

"Of course." But not too candidly, Leila. Trust me. You don't want that right now.

"I wonder what your life is like now. What a regular day looks like for you."

Why not dispense with the niceties already? I guess she didn't win that Pulitzer for beating around the bush.

"Are you asking me what I do all day?" I follow up with a chuckle.

"You say you don't get out much and, well, I gather you're not working on any new music. What do you do?"

I guess planning my death is too forthright an answer. "I work out a lot." It sounds so silly, I have to laugh at myself.

"I can see that." Was that a hint of admiration in her tone?

"Cocktail-o'clock comes around quite early as well." I try a smile.

"Okay, you can be coy with me, Isabel. I probably should have gone in with much softer gloves. My bad." She cocks her head. "Besides, you're here to learn more about me." She opens her arms, as though that's all it takes. It draws my gaze to her cleavage. For a split second, I have trouble pulling my stare away from that spectacular sight.

"I haven't prepared any interview questions." I drink again. "I just thought I'd see how we got along."

Leila nods while she purses her lips. "I've been a journalist for so long, it's difficult to have the tables turned on me, so I quite appreciate that."

"Do you live here alone?" I glance around the room. I don't see any pictures of Leila with a significant other. Or any of what might be her family, for that matter.

"I do." The skin around her eyes creases as she smiles at me. "I'm rather fond of my own company." She says it without any qualms, which makes me like her even more. "I wouldn't call myself a loner, but I have always very much preferred coming home to an empty house. I have never understood why that prospect terrifies so many people. I like the quiet. The tranquility. It restores me after a hectic day or a raucous night out."

I lift an eyebrow. "Do you have many of those?"

She shakes her head. "Not really. Just a boozy dinner once in a while." She drinks, as though indicating that tonight might just turn into that.

"You spend a lot of your time working?"

"When I get sucked into a project, it's hard to step away. And it just so happens that it's a passion I can afford. To really dig deep." She cocks her head. "I haven't had the chance to tell you this yet, Isabel, but I'm so thrilled to be working with you." She grins as though she knows very well that she just jumped the gun again. "The contract isn't signed yet, I'm well aware, but, regardless of whether that happens, it's such a treat for me to have you as a visitor in my home. It really is. Your music..." She pauses. "Is it okay to talk about that? It doesn't... trigger anything for you?"

"Of course it's okay." What else would people talk about with me if not about my music? My sparkling personality?

"Your songs have meant so much to me over the years." She pulls her lips into a smile again. "I sound like a fangirl, but I don't care. I'm an admirer."

Not much left to admire. But I've had ten years to learn how to deal with these kinds of conversations. It's funny to remember how I used to have trouble taking an actual compliment, back in the day when I had the kind of voice that warranted them. These days, I'm practically gagging for them.

"Thank you. I appreciate it," I say. "Even though I can no longer make new music, or perform my old songs, it's good to hear they still mean something to people." Hm. I hadn't meant to say that. While this is how I feel sometimes, it's not my most common sentiment about having lost my voice. My instrument. My most meaningful way of expressing myself.

"Would you tell me that even if it weren't the case?" Has she just read my mind? I didn't see an award for reading people's thoughts on her mantelpiece. "I just want you to know that you don't need to put on a brave face when you're with me. What happened to you must have been horrible. To lose that incredible gift you had."

Way to rub it in, Leila. Thanks for that. I take another sip from my martini. I relish the slight burn it leaves in my throat.

"Ten years should be enough to put that into perspective." Another lie. Another facet of the brave face I've perfected over those ten long years.

Leila shakes her head. "No, I don't believe that. I told you when we met earlier this week that I did a deep dive on you. Understandably, there aren't any interviews with you since it happened. So I can't claim to base my assumption on fact or on something you said in an interview, but I've thought a lot about the profound ramifications this must have had. How it must have changed you. Not that it's even comparable, but I've likened it to losing all ten of my fingers." She stares at her fingers for a brief moment.

I'm too stricken with what she's saying to have any lewd thoughts about them.

"And not being able to write anymore." She puffs some air from her cheeks. "I can't even begin to imagine the horror."

I know I'm supposed to say something, but it's been a while—since I quit therapy about five years ago, probably—since someone has been so frank, so utterly forthright with me.

"It's what makes you such an intriguing subject. I devoured Bruce's first draft. Your life has just been..." Her gaze skitters away for a moment then returns. "I'm sorry. I'm being so insensitive."

"No, really. The way you're dealing with this is actually a breath of fresh air to me. I'm so sick of all the tiptoeing around it." I fail to mention that I have a lot to do with the fact that barely anyone I know dares to mention my surgery any longer because they're afraid of my reaction. "I'm a singer who lost her voice. There's no two ways about it. It happened and now I can no longer sing." And I would rather die than go on living like that.

It turns out I don't need to deploy my special psychological trick to stop my friskiness in its tracks. There's no need to visualize the moment the surgeon came into my room and delivered the news that the surgery had been unsuccessful. And that, in fact, the operation had made it worse and I would never sing again.

CHAPTER 5

We've moved to the dining table. Leila has prepared grilled lamb and *tahdig* and it's finger-lickingly delicious. I still don't know that much about her, but at least I know she can cook.

"The other day," I start, "you said you knew a thing or two about loss. What did you mean by that?"

"I've lost people I loved very much."

I nod and keep quiet, hoping she will continue.

She puts her cutlery down and then, literally, licks her index finger. She sucks it between her lips and I have to keep my mouth from falling open. Is she doing this on purpose or is this just how she eats? It's not really the right timing because of my question, so maybe this is just how she is. Maybe I've learned much more about her already than I realize—all the things that words can't convey.

"When I was eighteen, I left my family in Iran to study here. That was just before the revolution. I only ever saw my father again. The rest of them..." She swallows hard. "Well, they've been gone a long time."

Damn. I usually win at comparing grief, but I have no

recourse against war and dictatorial regimes. "Is your father still with us?" I ask.

Leila shakes her head. "He died more than twenty years ago."

"I'm so sorry, Leila."

"I was lucky," she says. "Because I came to the United States. So, like most people on this earth, I've been both lucky and unlucky." She flashes me one of her all-obliterating smiles, but it doesn't seem to reach her eyes completely this time.

I don't regret asking the question, but the atmosphere has certainly taken a turn. "You never started a family of your own?"

"There were times when I wanted to, but then it never happened. Something always got in the way. Be it work or a breakup or... I don't know. Looking back, I should know. I mean, I feel like I should have more answers about how my life has gone. But I don't. Perhaps because I don't need answers. Perhaps because..." She exhales audibly. "...there was a time when I wanted nothing but answers to questions that were simply unanswerable. Grieving for the loss of my family was hard, especially because I had to do it all alone, out here, but it did teach me that some things happen for no reason at all. That life is just utter shit sometimes. And that asking questions will only wear you down more."

I'm trying to form a picture of Leila's life in my mind. She has already admitted to being a loner. To not wanting a family. She's just told me about her unspeakable loss. I can see where her drive comes from. Where she got the zeal to chase that Pulitzer. But what I can't fathom is why a journalist of her standing would take on a project like my biography, after what she's worked on previously and has gone through in her own life.

"Is that my cue to shut up?" I try a small joke.

"Of course not. I make a living asking people questions. I'm going to be digging into a painful period of your life—at least I hope so."

"Why?" I try to remember the title of the essay she won a Pulitzer for, but I can't. "Why my story?"

"Are you kidding me?" Her tone is completely free of irony. "Are you seriously asking me that?"

"I'm just a singer."

"No. You're Isabel Adler. You're not just *a* singer. You've been out of the game for ten years, yet no one has taken your crown. Sure, new singers with pipes like yours come along every so often, but while every single one of them aspires to be like you, none of them has managed to rise to your level. There is—was—something so unique about you. You always came across like you wanted it all so much more than anyone else, but yet there was always this vulnerability about you. As though, somehow, you knew—you carried it in you and you ever so subtly telegraphed it—that it could all end in one moment."

And then it did, I think. As always, it's human nature to be drawn to the tragedy.

"What happened to you is one of the biggest stories of this century." She takes a sip of wine. "I don't look down on entertainment, you know. Not even a little bit. As I said, your music has meant a lot to me at various times of my life."

I dare say you got yourself the job, Leila Zadeh. The pure passion that emanates from this woman is contagious.

I open my mouth to speak but close it when I see Leila hasn't finished yet.

"I was there in Central Park for your legendary twenty-fifth anniversary concert." She fixes her gaze on me. "I think I might even have fallen in love with you a little bit that evening. Me and thousands of other people. What a magical night."

"That was quite something." The memory washes over me like a tidal wave. The roar of the crowd. The chanting of my name long after I'd left the stage. The golden-orange sunset as the evening progressed. My voice at the very height of its power, seasoned but with no signs of cracking any time soon. The audience eating out of the palm of my hand. But most of all—and what I miss the most—the amazing energy a few well-held notes could create. What it meant for me to sing those songs and to get back so much love from the people listening to them. The elation. The enchantment. The utter joy it sparked in me.

"How long ago was that? Fifteen years?" Leila asks.

"Almost."

"I can understand why you would ask me that question, Isabel," Leila says. "But the truth is it would just be an enormous honor for me. It already is a huge one to have you in my house. To share a meal with you. To talk to you. It's an amazing opportunity. But... it's my nature to want to peek behind the curtain. To find out what makes you tick and what makes you angry. To get to know the real, human side of you would be a privilege."

"You're a very gifted cook." I nod at my empty plate. "And you serve excellent cocktails and wine." As though those are my main criteria for hiring a new biographer. "I hope it's not the last time I get invited to dinner." I hope she doesn't expect me to return the favor. Although, actually, I should. I should invite her to my house and cook her a meal. I haven't done that for anyone in too long.

"Thank you." One of her dark eyebrows is quirked up as she glances at me.

And let's not forget you're very easy on the eye. I can't help but smile again. She can think it's because of all the praise she just heaped on me. It is also because of that. One thing I've never been immune to is glowing reviews, even if they relate to long-past achievements.

"I'll get Ira to send you the necessary paperwork tomorrow."

Leila's face lights all the way up. It's truly a marvel to behold. Her dark eyes sparkle; her bright lips glitter. Something inside my belly stirs again. Do I really want this woman turning my soul inside out? But yes, of course I do. I may be attracted to her—I believe that's been well established tonight—but that doesn't mean I have to act on it. After all, I haven't acted on any twinges of desire during the last two and a half years. That's how long it's been since I've held another woman in my arms. Perhaps I believed that part of myself dead already. I now know that it's not.

"Thank you so very much, Isabel. You won't regret it. I promise you that." Apart from her charismatic looks and her abundant intelligence, I also admire Leila's confidence. She sits there as though she didn't doubt, not for one single second, she'd get the job.

"Here's hoping that *you* won't regret it then." I hold her gaze.

"There's not a lot of chance of that."

"If you're so interested in finishing my biography now, how come you didn't get it instead of Bruce?" I've spent so much time with Bruce in the past two years. I'm trying to imagine having spent all those hours, recounting my life to Leila.

"I was very interested at the time. I really was, but I had to choose between the fight to write your biography—and it would have been a fight because so many writers wanted to do it—and three weeks of being embedded with the Secretary-General of the UN for an in-depth profile. I'm sorry. It's just how life is sometimes. Certain opportunities pass you by. I hope you're not too offended by that."

"My ego has taken bigger hits." I'm well acquainted with how life can throw you the most impossible curveballs.

Leila offers me a sweet smile. "How about dessert?"

"Sounds like a plan."

"Join me in the kitchen?" She starts gathering the plates. I give her a hand. She looks at me as though she hadn't expected me to lift a finger. It gives me a tiny tinge of pleasure to be able to surprise her already.

"How long did it take Bruce to win your confidence?" she asks while rinsing the plates.

I have to think about that one. Bruce went about things so surreptitiously, it just happened. "You're not Bruce." I watch how she works. Leila's elegance is about to get the better of me again.

"Do you have any demands or restrictions I should know about?" She wipes her hands on a towel.

I'll be dead by the time this book comes out. I've known this since Bruce started interviewing me. It made me unusually open with him. I think I can extend Leila the same courtesy. Anything legal Ira will deal with in the contract.

"None." I do like the way my voice sounded when I said that.

"Then I very much look forward to working with you." She pins her gaze on me and, for a split second, I wonder if I will have to start a letter to Leila as well. I don't know why. I've only just met her. I had never intended to write Bruce a farewell note. But Leila is not Bruce. She may only just have gotten the job, but I already know that much.

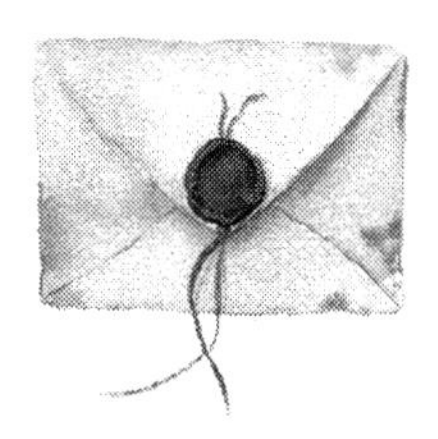

I miss the person I was. I have mourned her for a long time. Despite my 50/50 proclivity, which I believe I was born with, being able to sing was my lifeline. It was, in many ways, my life. It made me forget about all the rest. It was my therapy. My best friend. My way of laying it all out there. My means of processing all my emotions. Without it, everything just seems so pointless.

That's not to say that I don't care for anything else in my life. I care about you guys. But, and this is perhaps the crux of the matter, I wouldn't wish it upon my worst enemy to spend an hour in my mess of a head. It never stops. The doubts. The constant back-and-forth. The feeling that I lost everything in that split second the surgeon put his scalpel exactly where he did.

Until recently—until I made the one, final decision I'm writing to you about now—I woke up every single morning, still hoping some sort of magic might have occurred during the night. Every morning, I forced myself to sing the first few words of "Somewhere I've Never Been", and every morning, I was faced with the same massive disappointment. And every morning, it drained a little bit more life out of me. It has slowly been gutting me from the inside. Slowly chipping away at what made me me. And now, I tend to believe, even if I were to miraculously get my voice back, I could never be the performer I once was. Because I know what it's like to be without the power, without the strength my voice has given me. It has always been like an extra limb. An extra something special to help me through whatever life has thrown at me.

Despite the hours and hours of therapy. Despite all the medication I've tried. The Zen retreats. The silent retreats. The yoga and meditation retreats. The holistic healers. The energy healers. The battery of doctors I've seen. The follow-up surgeries that didn't change a thing. Despite everything I've tried in order to reverse the situation, I'm still without a voice. This is how I express myself now. Through a letter. No sound. Only silence. And without a voice, I might as well change my name. Without my voice, I'm no longer Isabel Adler.

Stronger people than me might choose to live. Yet I prefer not to call myself weak. Although taking one's own life is often thought of as the ultimate act of weakness, I don't believe that's what this is.

The only way I can explain it is by assuring you that I've lived all the life that I've had in me. I sometimes imagine that instead of the surgery going wrong, the anesthesia did, and I died on the operating table. If that had been the case, I wouldn't have had the past ten years. But because I did, I can tell you that I'm glad that I had them, although, I'm not going to lie—what's the point now, anyway? If I had died during surgery and if I had never had to wake up to the news of losing my singing voice, that would have been okay with me. I don't think any one of you can begrudge me that. But I didn't die. I lived and I thought and considered and debated and, ultimately, concluded, that this is the right path for me. Because at least, over this, I have power. This destiny I can control.

Some might say that I had so much to live for, but I disagree. Anyway, I don't want to be endlessly repeating myself here. By now, you should have a good enough idea of why I did it, why I chose to no longer live.

CHAPTER 6

Vivian looks so pale compared to Leila. I don't know why I'm even thinking that. Vivian's so bony and sinewy, whereas Leila is curvy and soft, with the kind of bosom I'd want to put my head down on after another long day of being this person that no longer feels like me.

"What's with you?" Vivian asks. "You seem miles away."

"Thinking about my biography."

"Speaking of. I need to read every single word about me before that book goes to print. Agreed?" She paints on that half-smile of hers.

"I've already agreed to that a million times, Viv." After the hundredth time she expressed her worry about being mentioned in the book, I had Ira draw up a contract, giving her full veto right over the chapters she appears in. Since I won't be here anymore then, I don't want my best friend to have any regrets over my last big project. It feels like the least I can do for her.

"When can I read it?"

"Even I haven't read it."

"I can read it for you." The half-smile has morphed into a full one.

"I'm seeing my new biographer tomorrow. I'll ask her when I can read what Bruce had written so far. I promise you that you will be the first person I send it to." I cock my head. "What are you so worried about, anyway? Did you tell Bruce something you weren't supposed to?"

"What's 'not supposed to' in the context of a biography?" She shrugs. "Everything I told him was certainly true, but, um... Maybe some things should not be printed in black and white in a book. Recorded for the ages, so to speak. Jackson will read that book one day. I might have said some things that, in hindsight, I shouldn't have."

"Like what?"

"Just stuff that happened between us. I didn't give it much thought after Bruce interviewed me, but now he's out of the picture, and this new person is coming in, it got me thinking about what I revealed."

"I'm sure she'll want to talk to you for some follow-up. Just tell her what you don't want to be included in the book." I narrow my eyes. "Better yet, tell me now." Vivian's not only my best friend. She's also my ex. We were together a very long time ago, when it wasn't *opportune* for popular singers to be in a same-sex relationship.

"I might have vented a bit about how frustrating it was for me at the time," she says.

"That's perfectly understandable." And not new information to me. Before Bruce interviewed her, Vivian and I had a long conversation about what she could talk about and what should remain private. We agreed anything sexually intimate was off-limits, but all the rest she could share.

"I might even have said some things that might be hurtful to you."

"Oh, come on, Viv. We've said all there is to say between us. We're still friends after everything that has happened. What could you possibly have divulged that would hurt me now?"

She sips from her glass of white wine. In my cellar, I have an entire shelf stacked full of the sauvignon blanc that Vivian loves so much. She's the only one who drinks it. "It's not new information, of course. It's just dragging up the past. Remembering things that I would have preferred to forget about forever. And now they're going to be in your biography because that Bruce is quite the sneaky bastard. Before I even knew it, he'd got me to tell him stuff I haven't told anyone. Ever."

I grin. "That sounds like Bruce all right."

"What about this new woman? Is she like that?"

I shake my head. "I don't think so, but the truth is that I don't know."

"Keep me posted." She glances at her watch. "I need to go soon. Jackson has a game." She gives me that look. "You sure you don't want to join me?"

Another thing we've been over a million times. "Tell my precious godson that I love him very much, but I can't come to his basketball game. You both know why." I don't know why Vivian keeps on trying.

"Put on some sunglasses and a hat and no one will recognize you, Iz." What she leaves unspoken is that it's been so long since I was in the public eye, most people have forgotten about me anyway.

"That may be so, but you never know. I'm not in the mood for that." Going to one of my godson's games is an item on my *Things To Do Before* list, but I can't tell Vivian and Jackson about that. And there's time.

"Suit yourself." Vivian gets up. "Don't forget dinner on

Friday."

"Have I ever forgotten?" I blow her a kiss.

"Bring a bottle," she says.

This conversation between us that we always repeat remains a huge source of comfort for me.

I nod and hug her goodbye. Now that I've actually started on the letter, it's become surprisingly harder. Even this everyday hug feels like it's more. Because this may be comforting to me, but it must also be something special for Vivian. It's her I worry about the most. Even though we're exes, we still have a kind of co-dependency going on between us. I rely on her for certain things—social interaction and a sense of family—and she relies on me for other things. At least I think she does—and not just the endless supply of white wine I keep her in.

Ira will bounce back. Jackson's still young, and we aren't as close as we might have been under different circumstances. He was only four when I had my surgery. All the years it took me to put myself together again, or rather while I tried and failed, I didn't give him the attention my only godson, the only child of meaning in my life, deserved. I make a mental note to go to one of his games soon. What Vivian said is true. If I properly disguise myself, no one will realize it's me.

Daisy and Harry will move on. But Vivian, she's my biggest worry. Because she stuck by me. Not only after I lost my voice, but also after we broke up. After she couldn't take being the secret girlfriend of one of the world's most famous performers anymore. We have decades of trust between us, and a deep intimacy, and the kind of bond that can only be forged through being there for each other no matter what.

Vivian is the weak spot in my plan. I've racked my brain for ways to somehow cushion the blow for her. She'll inherit plenty of money but, as I've come to realize, money means nothing. I would give my entire fortune for one more night on stage. For a few hours of doing what I've always done best. Sing my heart out.

Now that I can no longer sing, my heart is useless. It still beats, of course. It keeps me alive. But to what end? This is precisely what Vivian won't understand. Trying, after I'm gone, to make her see why I did what I did is the only thing I can do. Until I'm satisfied with how I've put my decision into words, I won't go through with it. Because the point is not to inflict pain on the people that I love, even though it's inevitable that they will suffer. The point is to, very simply, stop existing.

I have tried and tried to fall in love with life again. To feel that spark again. But it never happened. Everyone in the world may disagree, though I doubt that would be the case, but I believe this has earned me the right to die. Part of me has been dead for a long time. But please know, feel it in your heart of hearts, that it wasn't a lack of your love and attention that made me decide to do this. If anything, if it hadn't been for you, I might have done this years ago.

Because I didn't just owe it to myself to investigate my desire to die until, no metaphorical stone left unturned, I was absolutely certain of my choice, but I also owed it to you. You will be the ones that will have to let me go without having had a choice in the matter. And, in doing this, I will take control of a big part of your life, at least for a while. This is the part of this whole thing that is the hardest. Imagining your grief, your loss. Which is why I keep repeating that this is what I wanted. This is the opposite of a premature death. This is my choice. I know it's not your choice, this grief is not your choice, the way this will make you doubt yourself and feel like you didn't do enough, is not your choice. That's on me. And I'm so very sorry. I wish I could do this without making you feel this way. Maybe some of you can even follow my reasoning and, for you, the pain of my loss is not exacerbated by guilt. I truly hope so. If not, please be very, very aware that the life I had left after the surgery, those ten years without my voice, was worth living because of you, because of your love and your loyalty to me. I know I've often been difficult, although I did always try to do my best. I want to thank you for that. For your patience and your kindness and your love. Thank you from the bottom of my heart.

I also want you to know that I didn't suffer and, this should come as no surprise, I chose a painless death. Why shouldn't I? Even though the doctors will confirm this, I also want you to hear it from me. Although, of course, I'm writing this before I'm dead. I'm not coming to you from beyond the grave. Sorry. You're probably not up for some gallows humor at this point, but maybe you will be when you re-read this letter later.

But I do want you to see that the prospect of dying has inspired a certain lightness in me. Unlike most people, I'm wholly unafraid of death. I can't really explain it to myself either, but it doesn't scare me. All I know about death, which is the same as anyone else, I presume, is that I will cease to exist. It's exactly that ceasing that offers me the greatest comfort. I will go to sleep and never wake up. Maybe that makes it sound as though I got up not wanting to go through another day, but that has not been the case. Not anymore. Ironically, choosing to die has given me back a certain joie de vivre. I know it sounds a touch ridiculous, but let me tell you, my friends, there's nothing that will make you feel more alive than your imminent death. It's one of life's great contradictions. I don't know how I will feel on the day. It's impossible to predict. Light or darkness? I don't know. But one thing you can be sure of is that if, on the day, I wasn't 100% certain of what I wanted to do, you wouldn't be reading this letter. I won't die against my will. Nor will I live against my will. If you're reading this, it's because I believed, with every fiber of my being, that no longer being alive was the absolute best choice for me.

CHAPTER 7

"I've been thinking about you," Leila says. I can't read from her face what reaction she's after exactly, but if it's the smallest of shivers up my spine, she's right on the money. "I'd forgotten how completely immersive biographies are. You're all I think about now, Isabel."

Since I last saw her, Leila's never been far from my mind either, but I don't tell her that.

"I don't envy the carnage in your head," I quip.

She shakes her head. "I don't even know what you mean by that. Your life has just been so fascinating. I do regret not having been involved from the start, but what an opportunity to still be a part of this." She paints on a solemn expression. "With all due respect to Bruce, of course. Poor guy. Not only does he need to recover from the accident, but he also has to live with the fact that he won't be finishing a project he has worked on for years."

"True, although that might be the least of his worries right now. I think he's more invested in learning how to walk again than writing the last few chapters of the book."

"I guess health always comes first." She gives me a meaningful look.

"It does." I don't take the bait just yet. I'm sure Leila can do much better than this. I peer at her over the rim of my coffee cup. She looks so good in that armchair, as though it's her rightful place in my house. As though the chair was bought and put in that exact spot just so she could sit in it. It's a ridiculous thought—and not the only one of that ilk that I've been having when it comes to her.

When I'm not in her company, I can keep my lusty predilections for her at bay, but as soon as she enters my physical space, it's as if she sucks me into her force field. I can't help but focus on her lips for a second too long. I can't help but steal a glance at her hands and wonder what her fingers would feel like when they skim my body. But I did this to myself. I said yes. So here she is.

"I wanted to ask you something a little out of left field." She returns my gaze.

"Sure." Isn't that what she's here for?

"The other day, I asked you what a typical day for you consists of. It was hard for you to answer that question, which is understandable. So, I was thinking..." Her cheek lifts into a small smile. "Can I shadow you for twenty-four hours? I wish I could promise that you won't notice I'm there, but that would be foolish." She arches up her eyebrows. "But it would give me a much greater sense of who you are and what you do." She holds up her hand, as though prematurely wanting to ward off my protest. "I know it's very intimate. And I know you'll never fully be yourself while I'm around. Yet, it would be immensely helpful for me to get a better sense of you."

That's out of left field all right. "You want to move in for a day?" It's not so much the intrusion on my privacy that I'm worried about but all the sightings of her red lips I will need to endure.

Red lips pursed, she nods.

"I need to think about it."

"I figured that would be your first instinct, but..." She inclines her head a little. "I brought an overnight bag." She points at what I thought was just a laptop case.

"Wait..." Is she trying to blindside me? "You want to stay the night?"

Oh no. She really shouldn't.

"Yes. I'd like to stay after this conversation. So you don't have the chance to prepare for my arrival."

I chuckle nervously. "Wow. I wasn't expecting that."

"That was the idea. To catch you completely off guard."

"You're putting me in a tough spot here, Leila."

"I know, but I'd like to think I'm doing it for a good reason."

"If I say no, it might put us on the wrong foot. If I say yes, I might be doing something that I don't want to."

"Permission to argue my case?" Her eyes glitter. She's enjoying this. The cheek of this woman.

"I get the feeling that trying to stop you would only be futile."

"For the record, I don't want to force you to do anything you don't want to. Obviously, I need to consider *and* I'm responsible for my position in your life. I will always be respectful to you, Isabel. If you say no, that's perfectly fine. Really."

"Even if I say no, it will give you some valuable information about me."

"Correct." She manages not to sound too triumphant. "But, admittedly, when writing about someone's life, boundaries tend to blur. It comes with the territory. You're going to have to let me in, if you want this book to reflect who you truly are. And I get the impression you want that. You let Bruce in, although, I venture to guess that Bruce had his own way of accomplishing that. My way is different. Not confrontational per se, but I am more in your face."

I wonder if Leila is aware that, apart from Ira and Vivian—the people that I'm close to—no one has spoken to me like this in decades. It's what drew me to accept her as Bruce's replacement in the first place. She does things her way—the only way for her—regardless of her subject.

"I should..." I start to say what I always say. *I should call Ira.* Do we need some sort of written agreement to make this happen? Over the years, it has become a reflex. I'm also acutely aware that saying that I need to call Ira sounds very much like I need to call my father to ask him for permission to have a slumber party. Instead, I say, "Fine." I nod, more to encourage myself than to convey that I can deal with unexpected situations like this. "Let's do it. You can stay. I'll have Harry prepare a room for you." I can't help but grin at this. "Unless we need to share a room."

She gives a loud belly laugh. "That won't be necessary." She casts her gaze about. "It will however be an absolute delight to spend more time in this house." Her eyes come to rest on me. "And with you, of course."

She's part smooth-talker, part risk-taker, part... I don't know what yet. Maybe I'll find out in the next twenty-four hours. Leila might be here to observe me, but nothing's stopping me from doing the exact same thing to her. Already. I can't wait to see what she looks like in the morning, before she applies that lipstick, when her hair is messy instead of pulled back like that. Before she puts herself together.

"It's my turn to cook you dinner, anyway."

"Would you cook dinner for yourself if I wasn't here?"

I tap a finger against my chin. I hadn't planned on it. I used to enjoy cooking. It relaxed me—grounded me after a long world tour without access to a proper kitchen. But more and more as the years have progressed, I've found it easier to let someone else cook for me. Just another small pleasure I've taken away from myself.

"I might have." It's a lie, but Leila doesn't have to know that.

"Then I'd be delighted to taste your cooking."

"You're not going to keep on asking me, with everything that I do, whether I'd be doing it if you weren't here, are you?"

"No." She sinks her teeth into her bottom lip. "That would defeat the entire purpose."

I look at my watch ostentatiously. "Then I guess your twenty-four hours of unfettered access start now."

"I'd best make every second count then." She shifts her weight around and, perhaps for the first time today, I can spot a little bit of nervousness in her as well. Maybe she's nervous as hell but just very good at hiding it.

I know all about that. When you have to go out on stage every single day, there's a lot you have to fake. Except for one thing: the joy of singing. No matter how lousy I felt, for whichever reason—bad hangover, fight with Vivian, PMS—my voice was always there for me. The only time I ever came close to firing Ira, was when he suggested, after the surgery, I learn to lip-synch. To fake my voice. To pretend I was singing while I couldn't even hit the most basic note.

"And the interview hasn't even started yet."

"Maybe not formally, but I suggest you consider the next twenty-four hours as one long interview, even when we're not talking." She slings one leg over the other and sinks into the chair a bit farther. She's not going anywhere.

Well played, Leila, I think. Now, which game will I play with you?

CHAPTER 8

"Can I ask you the million-dollar question now?" Leila says. She sounds casual, as though she hasn't been interrogating me, in her own subtle way, for the past three hours. But it is true that she hasn't touched on *the subject* yet. She has held back. Undoubtedly waiting for me to finish that last glass of wine.

"What's for dessert?" I joke. "Of course you can ask me that."

She pats her belly, clearly not caring that it's not flat. "Okay, fine, what's for dessert?"

"You made it, so you should know." I must have had more wine than I thought because I'm finding this exchange a little too hilarious.

"You made me make it, Isabel."

"Please, call me Izzy." I take a large gulp of water. "Isabel just sounds so... formal."

"Maybe dessert can wait a bit, *Izzy*."

"Sure."

She takes a sip of wine, then leans over the table. "When did you last have a partner?"

I burst out laughing. Leila sure knows how to defy my expectations. "That's your million-dollar question?"

"Hmm." She plants her elbows on the table and looks at me.

"I haven't exactly been prime partner material these past ten years."

"You haven't been with anyone since..." She leaves her sentence open.

"Well, I have, but I haven't pursued a long-term relationship." I drink some more water. This is dangerous territory for me while tipsy. I can skirt her more probing questions, but only if I have my wits about me. I don't want to accidentally misspeak and give her the real reason why I haven't stayed with anyone since I made my decision.

"Why not? For a lot of people, being in a long-term relationship gives them a sense of purpose. I dare say it even makes them happy."

"I'm not 'a lot of people.'" I slant over the table a fraction. "What about you? Why are you single?"

She gives a one-shouldered shrug. "I've never bought into the whole couple-hood charade."

"What does that mean?"

"It means that I'm of the opinion that marriage is an archaic institution, invented by men, for the benefit of men, so they could own women. You know, give the women their name and have them give birth to their offspring and such." She shakes her head. "I wrote an article about it a while ago. I'll email it to you."

"You don't believe in long-term relationships?" I try to hold her gaze, but it's difficult. I can pretty much anticipate her reply and I'm not sure it's what I want to hear—although this should have no bearing on me whatsoever.

"I'm more of a serial monogamist," she says matter-of-factly, as though the majority of the world's population has gotten it totally wrong for centuries.

"What was your longest relationship?" I do my best to not sound too inquisitive.

She leans back. She looks as though she needs to delve deep into her memory to conjure up this fact about her life. "Almost three years," she says after a while.

"How long ago was that?"

She chuckles. "Damn, Izzy. Who knew you were such the cutthroat interviewer?"

Looks like I did a shabby job of hiding my curiosity about her personal life. "You can hardly blame me. Your job is to scrutinize my life."

"I know." She beams me a smile. "That was a few years ago. About four, I think."

I wait a beat to ask my next question. "And since then?"

"Since then..." Leila sounds more like she's musing now, like she's reminiscing about the past. "I've had a few flings. Even a few short relationships, but nothing that lasted."

"Because you didn't want them to last or for another reason?"

She reaches for her empty glass and twirls the stem between her fingers. "Various reasons." She finds my gaze. "I've just never really felt that need to share my life with someone else. How about I just live it? With myself?" The moderate, low tone of her voice makes it sound so plausible.

"It's not because you prioritized work or..." I swallow what I'm about to say next. I don't want to ask about her family now. The moment isn't right.

"I know how facetious this is going to sound, but there are very few people whose company I prefer over my own. It's as simple as that. I've never felt like I'm not leading a full, satisfying life. Yes, I have my work, which I love. I have my friends.

I have this amazing city as my playground. I have the occasional lover." She lifts a shoulder. "What more do I need?"

If I was auditioning for women to spend that very last night of passion with, I'm not sure I could find anyone more suitable than Leila. She wants to be unattached. She's not looking for love. And she's exceedingly hot. It's not just about how she looks, but even more so about how she carries herself and how she addresses me—and how she talks about herself.

"You're asking the woman who made a career out of singing the most dramatic love songs?" This warrants a chuckle from both of us.

"You can't possibly have believed every lyric you sang?"

"When I sang it, I believed it. It's hard to explain, but I think being able to lose myself fully in the lyrics of a song always allowed me to give a more heartfelt performance."

"You must have suffered a lot of heartbreak then."

"No, I haven't, actually. That's the thing with music. You don't need to have lived through it to feel it."

"Do you still listen to music a lot now?"

"On and off. Sometimes I crave it, because what's life without music? But often, I find it hard. I want to sing along, for instance, and I can't. Or someone new comes along with an amazing voice and then I'm just floored with jealousy."

"Jealousy?" She knits her eyebrows together—two narrow, black lines approaching each other.

"I don't know how else to describe the feeling." I bring two fingers to my chest. "It sits here, annoying the hell out of me."

"No music. No lovers. So how do you get your kicks?"

I don't, I think. "I never said 'no lovers,'" I blurt out instead.

"Right. Apologies for assuming." She shifts in her chair.

"Truth be told, the last time I went to bed with someone was more than two years ago." Saying it out loud like that, which is not something I often do, makes me feel pathetic.

Leila nods as though she fully understands my predicament. How did we land on this topic? I guess this is why she wanted to stay with me for a full day.

"How would someone like you go about it, though? You can't just go to a bar or get onto an app and do some swiping..."

"Is that what you do?" I half-say, half-chuckle.

"I've tried it. But it's not my preferred way of meeting someone." She lifts her eyes to meet mine again. "I prefer a casual meeting, like being introduced by unsuspecting friends. That's usually how it happens for me, but I imagine that for you it must be different. Or has it changed a lot the past few years?"

"It's probably one of the things that appear much harder in my head than they actually are."

"The person you were with two years ago? How did you meet... her?"

"You read Bruce's draft. You know it's a her."

"I've known these things to change or fluctuate over time and I've wrongly assumed before." She shoots me more of a grin than a smile.

"I met her through my ex, Vivian."

"Oh yes, Vivian." Not for the first time, the skin around her eyes crinkles, as though she's suddenly very pleased about something. "I'd love to talk to her one of these days."

"That can be arranged."

"So... Is the reason why you haven't been with anyone else since then because Vivian ran out of people to introduce you to or because you've prioritized other things?"

"Both, I guess." I give a small shake of my head. "Vivian keeps telling me I could go out and meet someone, but I'm not so sure. Also, it would make me feel too self-conscious, and what's sexy about that?" I pout. "Maybe I just decided that it's all just too much hassle for what I ultimately get out of it."

Leila rubs a finger over her chin. "But you do enjoy flirting."

I slant my head. "Who doesn't?" I sound a million times suaver than I feel. Is she flirting? Or is she merely asking me questions so she can write my story better? And where's the line between the two? I never had this issue with Bruce.

"I've often found that the flirting is better than what comes after." Leila laughs. "Paradoxically, although I'm not opposed to the idea, I find one-night stands often disappointing. I'm a much bigger fan of the several-nights stand. Or even just the second-night stand, when the first time is out of the way, and I know what the other woman wants."

"Why is it called a stand, anyway? It makes no sense." Behind the mask I draw with my words, I can only conclude that if we weren't really flirting yet before, we definitely are now, since she has mentioned she sleeps with women.

She gives me that hearty laugh again. "I will investigate that for you, Izzy. I'll let you know." She falls back against the chair. "Now how about that dessert I made?"

I'm dizzy from the mixed signals. Or maybe I'm just confusing everything. Maybe my attraction to her is getting the better of me. How long has she been here now? And how much longer is she staying?

I get up to fetch the chocolate mousse she prepared earlier.

CHAPTER 9

We've both kicked off our shoes and have retreated to the TV room, although I haven't switched the TV on. Even though I was slightly opposed to it, having Leila in my house for a day is a treat. It's an out-of-the-ordinary event and, of course, it helps that she's so easy to get along with. And very easy on the eye.

Leila pulls her legs up underneath her and cradles the tumbler of whisky in her palms.

"Tough job you have," I joke.

"Getting tipsy with Isabel Adler." Her lipstick isn't so bright anymore and a slightly darker rim has appeared underneath her eyes.

"You do prefer your own company, so..."

"Touché." She straightens her leg and stabs me gently in the calf with her toe. "I don't mind your company at all." Because of how the evening has gone so far, I would have expected her to look me straight in the eye when she said that, but her gaze wanders and doesn't land on me.

"I guess I can stomach your presence for the required twenty-four hours." Her proximity shakes something in me and I have to stop myself from putting a hand on her leg. Maybe another reason why I haven't been with someone in such a long time is because it reminds me of what I miss. The simple pleasure of sitting on the couch with someone. Of chatting. Of an inadvertent touch that doesn't need to mean anything.

"Where's your houseman?" Her head tilts a fraction.

"Harry? He's my house *manager*," I correct her, "and I imagine he's gone to bed."

"It's like he isn't here, yet he is. Doesn't it spook you sometimes?"

I've had employees live with me for such a long time that I'm completely used to it—perhaps a little too used. But still, after all these years, I don't want to sound like a spoiled brat. "Not anymore."

"You made such a mess in that kitchen, yet it was completely clean after dinner. Did Harry do that?"

"If you need a list of my staff for the book, I can have my assistant get you one."

Leila shakes her head. "That's one of the reasons I asked to stay here. To experience what it's like to have people take care of you twenty-four seven."

"What do you mean? I did all that cooking myself. You were there." I grin.

"You know what I mean. It's just a bit weird. We've been talking all evening and, more than once, I completely forgot that I was in *the* Isabel Adler's house."

"I daresay you wouldn't have thought that for a second if you'd come to my house ten years ago. I was very different then. My life was very different."

"You're so much more down to earth than I had expected." She takes a sip and pulls a face when the liquor slides down her throat. "Christ, this is strong stuff." She swallows again.

"But not just that... I had also expected you to be much more bitter about what happened. That's kind of your reputation now. That you've become this embittered hermit, surrounded by an aura of mystery because you're hardly ever spotted outside anymore. But there's so much warmth in your home. In *you*. That has taken me by surprise the most."

Damn. For all the loops Leila has already thrown me, this one actually touches me somewhere deep inside. Her words are not only surprising but moving as well. A double whammy of emotion. Nothing I ever got from Bruce.

"Thank you," I mutter.

"No, seriously, Izzy. Thank you for letting me into your home and your life so quickly. It means so much to me. And not just because of the book."

"What do you mean?"

"I'm not the only writer who wanted this gig, obviously. And I'm very grateful that you chose me to continue this project. I realize the last decade has been very hard on you, but you're still Isabel Adler. You still get millions of plays on Spotify every month, quite a few of those from me, by the way. But to come here and get to know you and get a glimpse of who you really are, that's where the real excitement is for me."

Because I have no idea how to respond to that, I sip from my drink. There used to be a time when I would have reacted in an aloof manner. I would have clung to my name and past achievements and considered them more than plenty to have this kind of praise from a gorgeous woman heaped upon me. But since, most days, I no longer feel like I inhabit what the name Isabel Adler stands for, what Leila has just said means so goddamn much to me.

"That's very nice of you to say," I mutter under my breath. For obvious reasons, I'm also no longer as skilled at taking compliments.

"It's also nice to be able to say it." She narrows her eyes as though she's just had a brain wave. "Hey, if you're looking, I could hook you up with someone." She waggles her eyebrows, completely ruining the moment. Maybe that last drink was one too many. "I know someone whose life would literally be made if I introduced you to her."

"Seriously? You're about to start pimping me out now?" I try for lightness in my voice.

"Just helping." She jabs her toe into my calf again. "It's been two years, Izzy. Don't you want to?"

Of course I want to, I scream inwardly. But not with someone you know. Not with some random woman you might introduce me to. Not with someone who's not you. Oh shit. There we go again.

"What?" she asks.

"What?" I ask, very maturely, in return.

"Why are you looking at me as though I've just robbed your house?" She chuckles. "Did I go too far?" She holds up the tumbler. "You can blame this. Damn. I would stay here just for the post-dinner fifty-year-old Scotch you serve."

"Don't you think it would be inappropriate for you to introduce me to someone for that... purpose?"

"Depends." The grin that forms on her lips is nothing short of devilish.

Oh sweet Mary and Joseph. It takes all I have for me to not lean over and kiss it right off her face.

"How much do you like blondes?" She bursts out with laughter.

"These days I'm more drawn to darker types." I can't help myself. Her foot is so close to my thigh, it's as though I can feel it. I haven't touched her. I most certainly haven't kissed her, despite the desire to do so waging a violent revolution inside me.

"Oh." Something sparks in her eyes. Or maybe it's the way she holds her head when she says it and how the light catches in them. She pins her gaze on me. "I'm sure I can rustle up a dark beauty for you." She narrows her eyes. It feels as though her gaze is emitting a force field of heat and I'm the sole recipient of it. My cheeks flush. I feel like I need to pull my blouse away from my skin, that's how hot my flesh burns—like I'm having a damn hot flash again, although my doctor assured me I was well and truly done with those. If it's not my hormones, it must be Leila.

"As I said." I only manage those three words. My throat is too dry. I sip from my Scotch, which doesn't really help. "Inappropriate."

"I didn't see anything in the contract about us not being allowed to become friends." The lift in her eyebrows is ever so slight.

"Of course we can be friends."

She sits up a bit straighter and tucks her leg underneath her again. "Would you consider Bruce a friend?"

Her tone is different. Whatever moment passed between us, it's gone. My cheeks and skin cool off. Inside, I'm still burning.

"Not really a friend. More of an acquaintance. We didn't have... nights like this."

Leila nods. She tilts her glass and finishes her drink. "Enjoyable though it was, I fear I have reached my limit of good food, amazing booze, and your excellent company, of course." She brings her feet to the floor, and it's as though the gesture ends the evening. "In fact, when it comes to the booze, I might have had a bit too much. I'm a real sucker for the up-up-up-market stuff." The skin around her eyes crinkles again, but I can see how tired she is.

"So I gather." I straighten my posture. "Maybe it's my ploy

to soften you up tonight and leave you with a hangover tomorrow, so you don't question me too mercilessly."

She turns to fully face me. "Nah. I know you're not like that, Izzy."

"Come on." I get up and hold out my hand to her. For an instant, it feels like I'm asking my lover to go upstairs with me. She looks at my hand, stares at it as though whether to accept it or not is something that requires careful consideration, but then lets me tug her out of the couch.

In silence, I escort her to her bedroom.

"Thank you," is all she says, her voice a mere whisper, as though it has already gone to sleep, before closing the door in my face.

CHAPTER 10

I've already had three cups of coffee by the time Leila peeks her head into the kitchen. She's trying to look bashful, but she's also grinning.

"Am I still welcome here?" she asks, her body hiding behind the corner.

"Don't be silly." I hold up a mug and Rian fills it with coffee.

When Leila spots Rian, she gets a mortified look on her face. She shuffles into the kitchen gingerly, as though she's been caught red-handed at something, and sits at the place that's been set for her.

"Morning," Leila says to Rian first, then to me.

"How are you feeling?" I ask.

"Surprisingly chipper." There's that grin again, although it's not at full wattage yet. "That good stuff you serve must not be so lethal after all."

"Up for some breakfast?" I return her grin. "Eggs? Pancakes? French toast? Granola? Fruit?"

"Maybe I'll just start with some coffee."

Rian hurries off, even though she doesn't have anything to prepare.

Leila takes a sip and emits a low groan from her throat. "I'm not sure I can go back to my own house." She finds my gaze. "It's surprisingly easy to get used to this." She lets her head fall back briefly. "That bed I slept in." She fake whistles. "And the impossible softness of those sheets."

"Only the best for my biographer."

She tilts her head. "Apologies for anything inappropriate I said last night."

"You don't remember?" She wasn't that drunk.

"Oh, I remember everything, but, you know, I might still have offended you and not been aware of it at the time."

It makes me wonder if she remembers the flirting. And the moment right before we went to bed. Or maybe, to her, it was all nothing. Maybe that will be my task for the day. Observe her while she observes me.

"You have nothing to worry about," I assure Leila. "Although you were planning on..." I hold my tongue. I realize I'm speaking to her as I would to a friend.

"What? Pimp you out?" She looks at me over the rim of her coffee mug.

"There's that."

"But you're not too keen on blonds at the moment." She puts down her mug, and her tongue flicks over her upper lip, which is painted the same shade of red again.

"Right." Are we picking up where we left off last night? Without the effects of intoxication?

"Vivian's blond, isn't she?" Leila asks, deflating my expectations instantly. It was just wishful thinking.

"Vivian's hair has been many colors."

"I read about your break-up in Bruce's draft." Leila seems to be in work mode this morning. It makes sense because her work is my life. It's difficult to draw any sort of line. But I must remember any interest she shows in me is purely work-related. She's being paid to be interested in me. To ask me personal questions. To make me feel at home in her presence. "Was it at your request that he glossed over it quite quickly?"

I really need to get my hands on that draft. Why don't I have a copy yet?

"Please excuse me." I know it's rude, but I need to text Ira right this minute. I need a copy couriered over to me today. When I look up from my cell, I say, "I haven't read the draft yet, so I have no idea what Bruce wrote about Vivian and me breaking up."

"I'd print you a copy if I could, but someone at the publisher's would have my head on a platter for that. Can you believe that? We were given a print version only, with water-marked pages, so if any of them should leak, the publisher will know who leaked them."

"You could lend me your copy. I'm sure no one will consider giving me a copy of my own biography a leak."

"You're absolutely right, Izzy. I'm sorry. I should have given it to you already."

"I understand why you didn't. You only signed the contract a few days ago." I shrug it off. I'm used to people not being their normal self around me and I'm most certainly willing to give Leila the benefit of the doubt.

"If I give it to you after breakfast, will you be reading all day?" She looks at the empty plate in front of her.

"God no. For some reason, I'm both curious and terrified to read it." I call for Rian. "Truth be told, I would have Ira read it first. Or no, I wouldn't even bother to read the first draft, which is why I haven't received it yet." No one knows this, of course, but I wasn't even sure I would be reading it at all. On the one hand, it might be nice to read the story of my life a week or so before I end it. On the other hand, the reason why I want to die is so that I don't have to deal with life any longer. It's a two-edged sword.

Rian shows up to take Leila's breakfast order. She asks for scrambled eggs, buttered toast, and some fruit for after. And more coffee, please.

"You don't have to read it just because I'm taking over from Bruce." She briefly sucks on the inside of her cheek. "When I negotiated the contract, I asked for the right to rewrite Bruce's draft. I can't just tack on my own chapters. That wouldn't make for a good reading experience. You could just wait for my version."

My cell buzzes. Ira informs me he will drop off the draft later today. "I'll see."

"What's on the schedule today?" she asks.

To keep myself fully in touch with my decision which, in all honesty, is quite hard to fathom while Leila sits next to me like this, I work on my mammoth goodbye letter a little bit every single day. Even if it's only to add a sentence or tweak a paragraph, like I used to do when I was in the midst of writing a song. Of course, I can't do that today. Not only can I not allow Leila into my office in case she sees what I'm working on, but it doesn't feel like the right thing to do when I have a house guest—especially when that guest is my biographer.

"Ira will stop by around eleven. I usually do my workout around one, depending on the schedule."

"Whose schedule? Yours?" Leila is still a journalist, of course.

"I use Olympian, a virtual gym."

"You don't have a personal trainer?"

"No. I can't bear them any longer. I used to have several." I shake my head. "Here's a nugget for you. When we were renegotiating my record deal after my first two albums, the record company wanted to have a clause in my contract making it compulsory that I work out, so that I didn't put on too much weight." I scoff because it's easy to do so now. "This was the eighties, of course. It might as well have been prehistoric times when it came to the rights of a female artist." Or their cash cow, after my second album went double platinum.

"I wish that surprised me, but it doesn't at all." Leila shakes her head. "Did you manage to negotiate it out of the contract?"

"Only after I hired Ira."

"So now you follow the schedule of your virtual gym and take their classes?" Her face lights up. "Perfect anonymity."

Rian brings over Leila's eggs. "Anything else for you, Izzy?" she asks.

"No, thanks." Now that it's less than six months before I die, I no longer pay any attention to what I eat. If Leila weren't here, I'd be having some chocolate to end my meal, or perhaps a slice of fresh sourdough bread with peanut butter, but not today. It does irk me that Leila's presence has such an influence over me. But it's only for one day. She'll be gone in a few hours. Tomorrow, I can have all the sugar I want.

"What's your favorite class?" Leila asks after Rian has left.

"Wasn't that in Bruce's draft?" I'm just teasing. I never shared any of this with Bruce.

"Not a word."

"High Intensity Intervals and some lifting." With Ramona. Yum. "I also like to run. On my treadmill. Not outside." Even when I go to my house in Vermont, where there's literally no one around, apart from my staff, and which is surrounded by woodland, I hardly ever run outside, just in case I bump into someone who might recognize me.

Leila's forkful of eggs halts midway between her plate and mouth. She gets that look, focused but warm, that I already recognize. "Are you planning to go outside today?"

"Yes." My nod is almost triumphant. "I always have dinner at Vivian's on Friday. Her son, Jackson, is my godson."

"When I asked you to dinner at my place, it didn't seem to bother you that you had to leave your house for it."

I bet Bruce devoted more than a few paragraphs to my propensity for staying inside. Or maybe not, as he had yet to start writing about the last decade of my life.

"Going to your house for dinner didn't pose any threat to me. It merely involved me getting into a car and getting out at your door."

She doesn't say anything. Having been interviewed hundreds of times, I know she's trying to let me fill the silence.

"What I fear the most..." I sound like I'm speaking to the therapist I stopped seeing a while ago. "Is being recognized and asked a bunch of questions I don't want to reply to."

"Like what?"

I expel a sigh because this question also annoys me. "When's your next record coming out, Izzy? How does it feel to no longer be able to sing? Or, worst of all, how are you doing..."

"How are you doing?" Leila's tone is soft, but her repetition still irritates me. She doesn't know what it's like to have possessed something that could move a crowd of thousands, could still an entire stadium of people to the point where, between notes, you could hear a pin drop, and then lose it forever.

"I don't want to talk about this."

"You do realize that's why I'm here? To talk about that particular part of your life." Her lips suddenly don't look so kissable anymore.

"How could I forget?" I know I sound facetious, possibly even like a too-spoiled superstar, but I don't care.

"Hey." Leila lays down her fork and leans over the table.

She gently puts her hand on my arm. "I know it's really hard for you, Izzy. I'm not here to push you. Okay?"

I look at her hand. Emotions war within me. Her touch moves something inside me—the untouched, suppressed horny part of me, no doubt—while her words make me want to shrug her hand right off.

Leila removes her hand and leans back. "Can I work out with you?" she asks.

I can't help but laugh. "That was the clumsiest change of subject ever."

"But it made you laugh." Her eyes sparkle again. They definitely have the capacity to dazzle me, but I can't let them.

"It did," I admit. "And the answer is no. My workout is private." There's no point in me working out beside Leila. The stress of doing it with her in the room would defeat the whole purpose. Although I am curious what she looks like in running gear.

"Phew." She chuckles. "I'm so glad you didn't say yes. I'm more of a gentle yoga person myself. Anything too high intensity, I gladly stay away from."

She's making me laugh again. It's not enough that this woman is gorgeous and smart and an excellent, though at times slightly manipulative conversationalist. She has to make me laugh as well.

"In that case, I might change my mind."

She just shakes her head, as though she knows all too well that I won't do anything of the sort, and goes back to eating her eggs.

CHAPTER 11

"She asked to stay here," I say to Ira, my voice chock-full of indignation I don't feel. But when I'm with Ira, I automatically go into complaining mode. It's a remnant of my time as a proper diva. "To observe me for twenty-four hours."

"I'm just surprised you agreed to that," Ira says matter-of-factly. "That doesn't sound like you at all."

This gives me pause. Mainly because he's right. It's very unlike me to just let someone in like that.

"Either way, she's been here for almost a full day, Ira."

"Do you want me to ask her to leave?" He studies my face.

Leave? Oh, no. "That's all right. I just thought you should be aware."

"She tells me almost after the fact." He rubs the stubble on his chin. "I don't want to get all up in your private business." Another one of Ira's favorite phrases. "But... is something going on between the two of you? I know she's, *you know*."

"Pfff," I huff out. "Of course not. Just because we both like women, you think something should be going on?" It sounds so utterly false coming from my mouth, but I know Ira will buy it.

He holds up his hands. "All right. Sorry. Had to ask."

I shake my head, even though his comment didn't really offend me. On the contrary. I can hardly deny that an ever-growing part of me would like it very much if something were going on between Leila and me. Maybe she doesn't see it that way, but in my book, we have most definitely flirted.

"What's she doing now?"

"She's in her room, making some notes." That's what she told me she would do while I talked to Ira.

"When is she going?"

"In a few hours, I guess." Again, that conflicting feeling of both wanting her to stay and wanting her to leave.

"Has it been helpful?"

"You should really ask her."

"I just might. I wanted to check in with her, anyway. It's good that she's here. Saves me a phone call."

He fiddles with the big brass ring he always wears on the index finger of his left hand.

"You're twisting your ring," I say.

"I am." He fixes me with the Ira stare.

"Why?"

"I don't know, Izzy. I still haven't been able to put my finger on it, but there's something different about you. Something that precedes introducing you to Leila, so it can't be her. Although that doesn't mean she can't contribute to it." He lets go of his often-plagued ring. "Clearly, you have no intention of telling me, so I'll have to figure it out for myself."

Good luck, I think. Unless he starts delving through my hard drive and discovers the letter I've been working on, he won't find out a single thing about my intentions. But kudos to Ira for sensing that something in me has changed. He's always had a nose for sussing out secrets, for unearthing details that people prefer to keep buried.

"Maybe your famous Ira-intuition is wrong this time around." I offer him my broadest smile, which won't help me convince him. I do feel guilty looking at him. Ira's been so loyal to me. He spends so much time on me and no request I ever make is too big for him. My death will hit the people I love in different ways rather than with differing degrees of hardship, I suspect.

Ira still makes good money off me, but money's not what the core of our relationship is about these days. It hasn't been for a long time. When he finds out I'm dead, I expect that Ira will be devastated. He won't have seen it coming. And then, perhaps, he will remember moments like these, when he intuited something about me, and he will think of ways he could have prevented it, even though there weren't any. But it will make him feel guilty nonetheless. I make a mental note to address this in my letter. He has to know that he couldn't have done anything to save me. That it was all just down to me. It's very important that he understand this.

"There's nothing wrong with my intuition," he says in that tone I've only ever seen men adopt. He's so certain—and he has every right to be, but I can't tell him that. "But it doesn't matter. I'll find out sooner rather than later." He stands up. "I'm going to find Miss Zadeh." He gives me a look again. "I take it things are going well with her?"

"Swimmingly." I'm just trying to wind him up now. "Seriously." I do feel like I owe him some honesty. "She's great. She's very intelligent and quite sly, at times. But wonderful company."

"Good." I can see him thinking it before he says it. "Hey, it's not because nothing has happened so far, that it won't." That, too, is how Ira is. He follows up with a mirthful chuckle.

Ira has just given me another reason to keep my increasing Leila-related friskiness in check. I don't want to give him the satisfaction of hearing him say that he told me so.

"Yeah. Yeah." I wave him out of my office. After he has left, and I hear him stomping up the stairs with Harry, I look at the closed door for a while longer, thinking of ways to soften the blow of my death for my manager and friend. I come up empty.

CHAPTER 12

I'm beginning to think, if I'm going to spend the last 175 days of my life seeing a lot of Leila, that I should include her in my farewell letter.

At first, the thought makes me shudder. A shiver chases up my spine. The prospect of Leila reading my letter seems somehow inconceivable to me. Until I sit with the thought for a bit and I conclude that, although the letter is only addressed to a few specific people, anyone could read it. I make a note for myself, in a document rather morbidly named TEOI.docx—The End Of Izzy—to leave very clear instructions as to who is allowed to read the letter and who isn't. I've already composed the one that should be posted on my website and social media channels, the one that will, inevitably, become the press release announcing my death.

"You're miles away," Leila says. She's still here. Doesn't she have anywhere to be? From my own experience, I know very well that people who prefer their own company, rarely have. But I have somewhere to be tonight. I would like a few hours on my own to unwind before I go to Vivian's.

"You're not," I say, unsure whether I mean it as a joke or

not. From the very beginning, Leila has sparked a slew of contradictory feelings inside me.

She nods, a solemn expression on her face. "Before I leave, I'd like to ask you one last thing."

"That's why you're here." If it's one last thing, I will happily oblige.

"Do you still write music?"

"No." Damn it. She has caught me off guard again.

"Is it too hard?"

"What do you think?"

"With all due respect..."

Oh, how I love sentences starting with that old chestnut. I expel a sigh before she can even continue, just so she realizes that I know that whatever she's going to say next won't be respectful at all.

"It's been ten years, Izzy. I get that losing your voice, your instrument, was a catastrophe at the time. But you're so much more than a singer. Surely, during the past decade, you've had plenty of time to reassess. To take stock of your other talents, your songwriting for instance, and to do something with that."

"Write songs for other people to sing?" I'm aware my speaking voice has lost all life as well. "I don't think so."

"Why?"

I raise my eyebrows. "I don't want that."

"Okay, but..." That hyper-focused look is back on her face. There's not much left, however, of the warmth she has bestowed on me the past twenty-four hours. Maybe because she's about to leave, she feels like she can push a whole lot harder. "If you don't want anyone else singing your songs, have you tried singing... differently?"

"Differently?" I tap the tip of my shoe against the floor.

"I was just going through the medical notes I have access to. From what I understand, which might not be the full extent of it, you could still sing. In a lower register and within a limited range, but all the skills you have, all the technique you honed over the years, must allow you to still... sing."

"Oh, really? Do you want me to sing for you, Leila? Do you want to hear what's left of my voice?" I clear my throat, fully intending to let her hear the pitiful croak that my vocal cords manage to produce, but I can't do it.

"No, Izzy. That's not what I meant. I was just asking the question."

Yeah, yeah. That's what she's here for.

"Listen to me very carefully because I'm only ever going to tell you this one time." I glare at her. "I. Can. No. Longer. Sing. Okay? No matter what you've gleaned from my medical file or what you've been told. Got it?"

"Sure." Leila appears frighteningly unperturbed by my outburst. Maybe she was expecting it. Maybe she checked with Ira earlier if she could ask me this question and he predicted my reaction to a T. "I'm sorry, Izzy. I know this is hard, but it is my job to ask. To see how you react."

"I know." My shoulders sag. "I also know that the past ten years should be an important part of a book about my life, because my life changed so drastically, but... half the time, it doesn't feel like my life anymore."

Leila sits there nodding. I can't decide if she looks scrumptious or haughty. Maybe a bit of both. Either way, as long as I have thoughts like this about her, I can't be angry at her for asking me the difficult questions. I also can't help but wonder if she has ingratiated herself with me for the sole purpose of being able to ask me questions like the one she just did, without me kicking her out. She clearly hasn't gotten the memo that I'm not always an easy person to deal with. Of course, previously, I would never have been asked a question like that.

"Are you contracted to do publicity interviews for your biography?" she asks.

That's another thing about Leila. I can never predict what she's going to say next. Then again, I have been out of touch with people in general and it's a skill I haven't much practiced.

"No. I made sure there's no contractual obligation for me to do the talk show circuit. Or go on Oprah's SuperSoul Sunday." I snicker.

"Makes sense." A flicker of warmth is back in her gaze. "Because you'd be bound to get some questions that would annoy the hell out of you."

When I signed the contract with the publisher, more than two years ago, the plan for my death was a lot vaguer than it is now, yet it was already there. I always knew I wouldn't be around to physically promote the book. Just as I've always known that my unexpected death will make the book sell better than any of my albums, even at the very height of my career. I hope for Leila's sake that she negotiated a high enough percentage of the royalties in return for her work. If so, completing this book about me might make her a good few bucks.

When I don't reply, Leila puts her notebook away. "Maybe I've overstayed my welcome." She smiles as though she knows very well that she could never really do that.

"Can I ask *you* a question?" Of course, now I want her to stay a little longer.

"Sure." She uncrosses and recrosses her legs in that way that drives me a little crazy. Slow enough to get my full attention. Measured enough to telegraph that she knows she has a role to play here. "Please, Izzy, be my guest."

"Are you trying to be my friend because you think it will benefit your work or because you genuinely like me?"

Underneath her upper lip, she runs her tongue over her teeth. "Can it be a bit of both?"

This, too, is such a breath of fresh air. While she has told me in very clear terms that she likes my music, she's in no way intimidated by me. Sometimes, I think that's another thing that keeps me from going outside and meeting people. That they will only be able to see me as the fragile human I've become, with my broken vocal cords and shattered resolve. That they will no longer see the woman I once was. That I will meet nothing but pity in their glance instead of the exuberant admiration I grew used to. When I lost my voice, I lost so much more than my ability to sing, to express my emotions through music. I lost my identity. But when I'm with Leila, when she's not asking me the hard questions, she makes me feel as though none of that really matters.

"I guess it can be a bit of both." I nod. "I appreciate your honesty. I really do."

"What else am I going to be but honest with the likes of you, Izzy?" She stands. She must really be going now. Argh. There's that feeling again. That duality irritating the hell out of me. But she'll come back. She has to. Then this whole game can start over again.

Instead of letting Harry walk her out, I escort her to the front door myself.

"Thank you so much for having me." She looks me in the eye. "I know it wasn't easy for you." Her lips lift into a hint of a smile. "But it has been truly enlightening."

Has it? Now she's making me doubt what I have told her. Although whatever was so enlightening might not have been derived from what I said, but from my actions, from just being around her.

"Is it okay if I hug you?" she asks.

Oh yes. "Sure." I manage to sound casual, as though I don't

care whether we hug goodbye or not. Although, judging by how my heart is beating double-time as she opens her arms for me, I must care a great deal. I step into her embrace. She smells of my soap. It only takes my breath away a tiny bit. Not enough for her to notice. She presses me against her. Even though she's wearing her coat, it's impossible not to feel the swell of her breasts. Oh goodness, I could stand in this embrace a good while longer, but she's already letting go.

For a split second, I consider pulling her toward me again for a kiss on the cheek, but I decide against it. Maybe I should let her introduce me to her blond friend, just so that I can expel this agitation inside me. This frenetic energy that she stirs in me. But that wouldn't be right either.

"See you soon," Leila says.

Can't wait, I think, as I close the door behind her.

The first thing I do after she has left is ask my assistant to send Leila a couple of bottles of that Scotch she was so wild about last night.

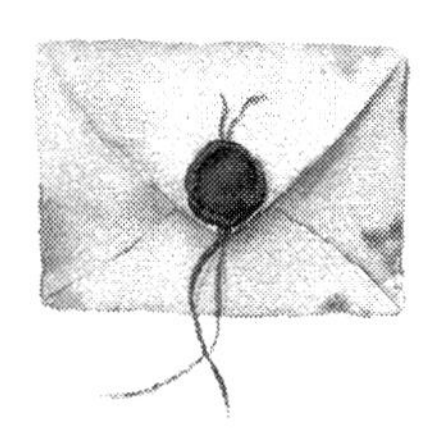

Even though I know this will be a hard pill for you to swallow, I'd like to offer some perspective. Millions of people die every day on this planet. Or, to say it with a cliché, death is the only certainty we have in life.

The biggest uncertainty is that we don't know when or how we will die. I have chosen to take that uncertainty away. Not because the not knowing was driving me crazy, but because I didn't want to wait anymore. Because I've had enough. But please try to look at it this way. If I'd had a terminal physical illness, you would be able to accept this better. Because you would comfort yourself with the knowledge that all avenues for getting better had been exhausted. The doctors did all they could. Second and third opinions were given. I would like to urge you to look at my death through the same prism, even though I didn't die of a physical illness.

If it makes it at all easier for you, you can consider my death the result of a terminal mental illness. Because what I'm suffering from, there is no cure for. And excuse my use of the word 'suffering'. I don't want to put the image in your head of me being in pain, although I'm no stranger to pain of any kind. But I did find a way to live with it. Until I came to the conclusion that 'living with it' is not the same as 'living'. Not in the way I see all of you live your lives. Although I have no more idea of what has been going on inside your heads than you have of what's been going on in mine. As people, we are never fully knowable to someone else.

I have surely found that, as time progressed after the surgery, I made myself consciously less knowable. If this hurt you, I apologize. If you used to be able to read me better and then found you couldn't, that was my doing. That was how I wanted it. Because I didn't want you figuring this out beforehand. I didn't want to have this discussion with you. Maybe that makes me a coward. Maybe so many people will think of me as a coward for taking my own life. But I will never know.

What I do know is that, for me, this is not the coward's way out. Sometimes, you just have to leave. Slip away. Cease to exist. Never come back. That's what I've chosen. I could write and write about this—I seem to have taken a shine to it—but the outcome will never change. I can say it in a dozen different ways, but it won't change how I feel. Just as I know that, no matter how much I love you and I would like to know what happens next in your lives, you wouldn't be able to change my mind. Yes, a part of that is stubbornness. But the other, more important part, is simply awareness. In this, also, I'm so privileged. To be able to go to my end in this manner, knowing exactly how many days I have left and how I will spend them.

The one thing I am dreadfully sorry about is that I was not able to give you the same awareness. I had to do this secretly. I had to keep it to myself and make it my very own private project. That makes what I did my most selfish act to date—and I've had a few in my day. (Right, Ira?) This is selfish. I won't even try to deny that. My death is only about me. I'm going through with it despite knowing the pain it will cause to the very few who truly know and love me. For that, I do ask forgiveness. I'm sorry. As I said before, it's all me. It's not you. How could it be?

Throughout the blessed and not-so-blessed parts of my life, all of you have been equally amazing. Thank you for that. Of course, writing this letter is a lousy way of saying it, but thank you nonetheless.

CHAPTER 13

"Are you sure you don't want me to read you a bedtime story?" I joke. The days when Jackson even allowed me in his room are long gone.

He rolls his eyes at me.

"Can I at least get a hug?"

"Jax. Come on," Vivian says, using her stern mom voice.

"I read an article the other day in which they said making kids hug people when they don't want to can be considered child abuse," Jackson quips.

"Since when do you read actual articles instead of watching YouTube videos?" Vivian asks.

"Tssss," Jackson scoffs. He walks up to me and puts his arm around my shoulder.

I roll my head backward. "How can this ever be considered abuse," I say.

"Love you, Izzy," he says. Who knows whether he means it? He's been saying it his entire life. Jackson is fourteen now and he clearly has much better things to do with his time than have an after-dinner chat with his mom and godmother.

"Lights out by eleven," Vivian says when he kisses her on the cheek. "I will come and check."

"Newsflash," he says. "It's Friday. The weekend. As in, I don't have to get up early and go to school tomorrow."

"You heard me." Vivian doesn't waver.

With a loud sigh, he disappears from the dining room.

"Wiseass," Vivian whispers when he's out of earshot. "He must have gotten that from his father."

I give her the look I always give her when she blames one of Jackson's not-so-fine qualities on his father.

In response, she pours more wine. It makes me think of the bottles of Scotch I had sent to Leila. I made it an express delivery so it would arrive at her house before the weekend, but I haven't heard anything from her. Either she hasn't received it—she could be out on a hot date, who knows?—or she doesn't bother with thank-yous for random gifts.

"I brought something for you." I retrieve a rectangular package from my bag and deposit it on the table. It's still wrapped in the same brown paper it was delivered in this afternoon. "So you can check for any mentions of you."

Vivian's eyes grow wide. "The book?" She reaches for it. "How exciting. Have you read it?"

I shake my head. "I thought I would leave that pleasure to you."

She purses her lips. "You're afraid, aren't you?"

I give her a slow nod. "It's not the final version. It's Bruce's first draft, which Leila might still rewrite, and it needs the last chapters added."

"Got it." Vivian pushes her plate away. "Can I open it now?"

"Sure."

She slips a finger underneath the sticky tape holding the wrapping together and tears it open. There it is. The book recounting my life. My biography. It doesn't have a title yet. On the title page, it just drily says: "Isabel Adler Biography by Bruce Winkleman". Poor Bruce. He will have to share the credit.

"Don't start reading it now, please."

"Don't worry." Vivian quickly thumbs through it. "That should keep me entertained over the weekend."

"Leila will want to talk to you."

"Okay. Good. That will give me a chance to tell her what I'd like to be changed about me."

"There might not be anything. Bruce might have painted you like the partner and then ex-partner from heaven."

"Yeah right." She casts her gaze to me. "It's funny to hear you say that, though. I never think of you as my ex anymore. You're just my best friend now, you know?"

"What? No rekindling of the old flame?" God. Vivian. If Ira is devastated after my death, Vivian will be destroyed. I swallow a lump out of my throat.

"Are you all right, Iz?" She cocks her head. "That was a joke, right?"

"Yeah." I take a quick sip of water. "Of course it was. Dry throat."

She promptly refills my wine glass.

"You want to hear something funny?" I ask.

"Why wouldn't I?" She runs a hand through her slicked-back hair. Vivian has always been so effortlessly stylish. If the record company people had let me, I would have been so proud to walk any red carpet with her on my arm.

"Leila, um, said she wanted to introduce me to a friend of hers, for..."

"For?" Her barely-there eyebrows shoot up.

"A hookup. She wanted to set me up with one of her friends for a hookup."

"That's forward of her." Vivian narrows her eyes and studies me.

"She's a very forward person."

"And? What did you say?" Vivian's tone of voice indicates that she can very easily guess my response.

"No, of course. What do you take me for?"

"A human with basic human needs."

"You're one to talk." Deflection has always been an easy tool for me. It used to be that hardly anyone dared to talk back to me. Vivian was never one of those people, however. "You've been single forever."

When Vivian doesn't immediately reply, I examine her face. "Are you trying to tell me something?"

"I've met someone." A grin breaks on her face. "I've been seeing her for a few weeks now."

"A few weeks? And you never said?"

"I'm sorry. I just really wanted to keep it to myself. I didn't tell anyone for fear of jinxing it."

"I'm your best friend." I sound more offended than I am. Although I do rely on Vivian to be the person through which I can do some of the last vicarious living of my existence. "Who is very happy for you," I quickly correct myself. "Tell me everything."

"She's a wood sculptor." She lets out a sigh that could either indicate jealousy or admiration. Or maybe a bit of both. "You should see her stuff, Iz. It's phenomenal."

"Name. Age. Other significant details…" I'm genuinely excited for Vivian.

"Her name's Jade. She's a *touch* younger than I am."

"How much?"

Vivian shrugs it off as unimportant, which tells me that the age difference between them is probably significant. It wouldn't be the first time.

"She lives and works in Greenpoint. She's the next big thing in the New York City art scene." She reaches for her cell phone. "And she's absolutely gorgeous." She swipes a few times then shows me her screen.

"I agree, Viv. She's gorgeous. She's also... what? Twenty-eight? Twenty-nine?" The woman staring back at me from Vivian's phone screen can't be older than thirty.

"Thirty-one," she says.

I drink just to occupy my mouth. Who am I to judge my best friend? "Okay."

"Oh, and this should give you a thrill. Up until recently, she was an instructor at Olympian."

I have to keep myself from gasping. "She's a colleague of Ramona?"

"Oh yeah." Vivian smiles triumphantly, as though she's just presented me Ramona on a silver platter. "Well, used to be. She quit a while back to focus fully on her art, but she sure knows Ramona. They're friends. I thoroughly quizzed her about the whole thing."

Way to get my attention off their age difference. "I can't believe you didn't tell me."

"I've been dying to, but what if it didn't work out? I didn't want to get your hopes up as well."

"My hopes for what exactly?"

"If you want to, I can have you in a room with Hot Ramona this very weekend. Just sayin'."

"To what end?" Despite myself, my cheeks flush.

"I don't know, Iz. To confess your bottomless lust for her." She bursts into laughter. "Get the private workout of your life." This makes her laugh even harder.

"I don't want to meet Ramona." Hm. Or do I? Considering my limited life span, it might be a nice parting gift to myself.

"Let me know if you change your mind. I have the key." Vivian waggles her eyebrows.

"Have you met Ramona?"

"No. We haven't met each other's friends yet. Might start doing so soon, though. Maybe next Friday when you come over? Would you be up for meeting Jade?"

"Just Jade, though? Not Ramona?" I'm not sure I could take that so I need to double-check.

"Just Jade," Vivian confirms.

"Of course. I'd love to meet her."

"Great." The smile on Vivian's face is nothing short of ecstatic. She must have it bad. Oh, to fall in love like that one last time. But falling in love is strictly off-limits for me. "And don't worry, Iz. These millennials have no clue who you are," she adds a bit too matter-of-factly, although I know she means well.

"Wonderful." My voice drips with sarcasm.

"You know what I mean."

"I do. It's fine. I won't be subjected to some sort of interrogation over dinner." I smile at my friend. "Has Jax met her?"

"This weekend."

"Your son meeting your new girlfriend sounds much more exciting than reading that." I point at the stack of papers that make up my biography.

"I believe I can deal with both."

"Ah, Viv. I'm so happy for you."

"I think it could really be something. I know she's much younger than me and I know it sounds like the biggest cliché in the world, but she has an old soul, you know? She's a true artist. She's fucking incredible." Her eyes almost glaze over with lusty glee.

If I believed in any deity, I would pray to them right now and ask them to make sure this works out. It would give me such pleasure to see Vivian fall in love in the 175 days I have left. And it would give me great comfort to know that, after my death, she will have someone to be with.

"I know I'm all loved-up and seeing the world through rose-tinted glasses and all of that," Vivian says. "But maybe you should take Leila up on her offer to introduce you to her hot friend. At least I assume she's hot." The grin on her face has gone all goofy. "You just never know, Iz. She might very well be the one you've been waiting for."

"Nuh-huh. I'm not looking for anything like that." Because Vivian's in such a good mood, I chance it. "I might be looking for a hookup, though."

"Well, then. All the more reason."

"Yeah, maybe..."

"What? Did she show you a picture?" Her eyes light up. "Or would you like me to get some info on Ramona?"

I chuckle. Imagine that. Ramona likes wearing tops that show off both her abs and her cleavage. I feel like I know too much about her body already. Anyway. No.

"I... seem to be having a bit of trouble getting my mind off Leila." There. I've said it. I've admitted it to another person. Please, oh please, let that be enough. Let that take all the power out of my appetite for Leila.

"Ah... Well, you never did talk that much about Bruce and I googled Leila after you told me about her the other day." Vivian sounds as though she had fully expected me to say this. Has falling in love given her mind-reading abilities? "She's a bit mature for my taste, but yeah, I can totally see it." She chuckles.

"She's definitely not a millennial."

"You like her..." She nods slowly, as though trying to absorb the information. Or maybe she's just trying to think of something to say.

"Things between us have gotten so personal so quickly. And she's so different from Bruce. Not just because she's a woman. Her style is much more invasive and to-the-point. But she's just really..." I weigh my words because I don't want to sound exactly like Vivian just did when she described the wonderful Jade. "Lovely to be around." Most of the time.

"So? What's stopping you?"

"It feels somehow inappropriate," is all I manage to say.

"Why? Because she's writing this book about you?"

"Yeah."

"Come on, Izzy. From what you've told me, she'll mostly work on the last part of the book and... well, she kind of has to get to know you the best she can in the time she has. In a situation like that, feelings can arise. It's only natural." She drinks some more and fixes me with a stare. "Or are you afraid she's not interested in you in the same way?"

"I have to tell her all about the hardest decade of my life. It's not exactly a pretty picture."

"Have you picked up on any vibes from her?"

"It's really hard to say. How do I know which vibes are hers and which are mine?" I know I'm not making any sense.

"You just know." Vivian nods slowly. "Do you need me to ascertain this for you? Shall I casually drop by next time she's at your house?" Vivian's eyes light up. She lives for this kind of stuff.

I chuckle. Her enthusiasm is quite contagious. And, admittedly, even before I came here, I already couldn't wait to see Leila again. One thing's for sure, though, talking to Vivian about my feelings for Leila will not be stopping them in their tracks any time soon.

"That won't be necessary."

"Okay, let me make sure I'm getting this right. Leila wants

to set you up with her friend while you would like to hook up with Leila. Or do you want more than just a hookup?"

"No."

"Why not?" She shakes her head. "I mean, you keep saying that, Izzy, and you give me a bunch of convoluted reasons, but I don't understand. Are you so afraid of falling in love again?"

"Maybe you're not the right person to talk to about that in your newly loved up condition."

"Oh, really? Who else are you going to talk to about it? Ira?"

I can't tell Vivian why I can't fall in love. The most I could possibly afford is a flash-in-the-pan crush. Something that fizzles out almost as soon as it starts. Maybe Leila is the right person for that, what with her being an admitted commitment-phobe.

"You're right. Sorry, Viv."

"Maybe you should look at all the time you spend with her as foreplay. All leading up to that one night you will have with her when the book is done." She paints on an annoyingly triumphant smirk.

"What? Like a big romantic night of goodbye sex?"

"I never used the word 'romantic'."

"Look, I'm attracted to her and if I'm being completely honest, I do get a certain vibe from her. It's tripping me up a bit because I don't know what to do about it."

"Oh, Iz, of course you were going to be attracted to her. You suddenly find yourself with a beautiful woman in your house who is asking you deeply personal questions. A woman skilled at listening and making her interviewees feel comfortable and special. You haven't been properly touched in years. Whatever you do, don't beat yourself up over that. Just let it play out."

"I want to, but it's hard... There's no balance in our relationship. We mean very different things to each other."

"So what?" Vivian shrugs. "Stop overthinking it. Just enjoy it." She leans over the table. "What have you got to lose?"

Good question. I've lost so much already. Along with my voice, my joy, and my professional confidence, I've also lost the ability to date other women in a relaxed, normal manner. The difference with Leila is that I don't have to date her. I already see her at regular intervals.

"You're right. Again." Being in love has injected Vivian with so much wisdom, it would appear.

"It won't hurt you to take my advice once in a while, you know." Vivian raises her glass to me.

Just then, I get a text on my cell. It's the number only very few people have. Instinctively, I know it will be from Leila. Who else could it be? It's not just a text message. It's a picture of Leila with a glass of Scotch, one of the bottles I sent her sitting on the table next to her. She holds up the glass as if to say cheers. I show Vivian the picture.

"Showering her with gifts already?" She shakes her head slowly. "Oh, Izzy."

"What?"

I'm still staring at Leila's picture when Vivian says, "I thought *I* had it bad."

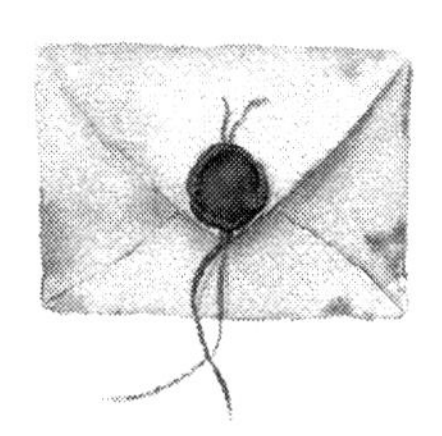

You might think I have died before my time, just as so many other people have done. But I don't see it that way. My last, ultimate act of control has been to decide when my time was up. The constitution says we have an inalienable right to life, but if we do, then why don't we have the same right to die? Why would anyone else, most likely some doctor, or, even worse, some civil servant or—the horror—some politician get to decide on that? I see this very much as my right to choose. And I've made my choice.

I know I'm also doing a lot of guessing at what you might be thinking. It's only natural. I've spent the past years thinking through so many different scenarios. Here's a thought I've often entertained whenever I heard about someone taking their own life: if only they'd had someone to talk to. Someone to take away their pain. If only they could have, somehow, realized that all their suffering was unnecessary. That things could and would get better.

Right now, as I write this, I'm ashamed of ever having thought something like that. Something so self-righteous and presumptuous. Because some pain is unbearable, no matter how much talking you do or how much a person might be aware of the options of help of any kind. People take their own lives for lots of reasons. I'm taking mine because going on living is costing me too much emotionally. I'm not the same person I was ten years ago. How could I be? I won't say I'm a shell of the woman—the singer, the performer—I used to be, but I know that's what I will turn into eventually. I've tried and I tried, but I haven't been able to find anything to replace the joy of making music. It has always been at the very core of my life. It's such a big part of my identity that without it, I don't feel like me.

Maybe it's some sort of big test for me to try to find who I am without my voice, but, frankly, I'm tired. And I don't feel like taking another test. The good days no longer outweigh the bad, and that is most certainly my own doing, because, I'm sure everyone will agree, I could perhaps have done more to find something to truly enjoy again. But I didn't want to any longer. Because I can't live without what I used to have. Ironically, I could probably say all of this much more efficiently in a song. I could probably convey my emotions effortlessly. But if I could do that, I would most certainly, without a shadow of a doubt, still be alive. And you wouldn't be reading this.

CHAPTER 14

It's Tuesday when I see Leila again. 171 days left. Vivian's words have been spinning around and around in my head. Judging by the number of pictures Leila has sent me over the weekend, she must have made a good dent in one of those bottles of Scotch already.

When she sits in front of me, however, she looks fresh as a daisy, her usual makeup applied.

"I promise I won't stay as long this time," she says. "Although I do still miss that heavenly bed."

My first thought is that I should send her a new mattress and sheets, but I quickly realize that would be a bit much as far as gestures go.

"How was your weekend?" she asks.

"Fine. Nothing unusual happened." I don't tell her that my workouts with Ramona had an entirely different dimension to them because I now have the prospect of meeting her in an organic way—as opposed to how I used to meet people I wanted to get to know. All I had to do was tell Ira their name and he would summon them for me. I shudder at the thought. "Yours?"

"I've been working on the book. Rewriting some of Bruce's chapters and I've even made a start on the ones that need to be added."

"Vivian's been reading the draft." I pick up my phone. "She's been texting me non-stop." A more accurate description would be off-and-on. It was very easy for me to deduce when she was spending time with Jade because then the texting abruptly stopped for a few hours.

"What are her thoughts?"

"It's a bit of a mindfuck for her, apparently. She was there for almost everything that happened in the first ten years, when I shot to fame. She says it's a real trip down memory lane."

"You haven't read it?"

"I'm waiting for your draft."

Leila smiles at me but I don't really know what it means. Because what I've also done over the weekend, much against Vivian's advice, is think over the whole thing between Leila and me, whatever it might be, to absolute death. Up to the point that I don't know what to think, let alone what to do, anymore.

"Okay. Maybe it's best that you only read my draft." Her smile turns slightly sheepish, which seems unlike her. But, perhaps, even Pulitzer-winning Leila Zadeh is prone to doubts. "Speaking of… shall we get on with it?"

I nod and Leila asks me a bunch of to-the-point questions about my youth in Ohio and my family. She's clearly fact-checking more than gathering background information.

"I'm sorry if this seems repetitive to you, but I have my process. It gets a little OCD at times." Another sheepish grin. There's something slightly off about her today, despite her immaculate look. Her demeanor is too professional. After she got so close to me last week, it feels like someone else is interviewing me today.

"Are you okay, Leila?" I ask. Maybe it's none of my business, and I'm sure she'll tell me if that's the case, but I'm concerned.

"Sure. Why do you ask?"

"You seem more... distant than before."

She nods. "I am more distant."

"Why?"

She heaves a sigh. "I—I had a good hard think about my behavior over the weekend. While sipping that truly exquisite Scotch you sent me." Her lips curl into the beginnings of a smile that quickly fades. "I came to the rather ghastly conclusion that I crossed a line. I got a bit carried away. I shouldn't have put you on the spot like that when I asked to stay over and I shouldn't have said certain things and I most certainly shouldn't have imbibed that much of your booze. It was not professional, Izzy. I hope you accept my apologies."

I can't believe what I'm hearing. What is she talking about? Granted, her style is entirely different than Bruce's, but I like it. "Did someone give you an earful or something like that?" More than anything, I'm confused.

She nods. "You."

"Me? What did I say?"

"Just before I left last Friday, you asked whether I was befriending you for the right reasons and it made me realize that I was getting a bit too carried away."

"With what?"

"You. No offense, Izzy, but it's easy enough to get a bit dizzy when spinning in your orbit. I don't—"

"Sorry, but..." I interrupt her. "What does that mean?"

"You're Isabel Adler. And there I was... suggesting I set you up with a friend of mine?" She scoffs—at herself, I assume.

"How inappropriate is that? In hindsight, I'm so mortified that I said that. Even before I drank a bit too much of your liquor, I already felt quite intoxicated just being here."

"I thought it very forward, but not inappropriate. You have nothing to apologize for. Really."

"Maybe I'm just..." She pauses. "How to say this. Annoyed with myself for being so impressed with you. I feel like I should be above that."

My confusion only grows. At no point during our time together did I get the idea that Leila was overly impressed with me. Or maybe I was too busy being impressed with *her* to notice. If anything, I loved her straightforwardness. It was one of the things that drew me to her.

"I don't know what to say to that."

"Last night, I watched the DVD of your concert in Madison Square Garden. The *In Too Deep* Tour." For the first time today, it feels like, she rests her gaze on me. "It made me understand better how you must feel now. About what you lost. Because I have never seen anything like it. That concert was pure magic."

Some nights, when I can't sleep, I remember that evening as if it was yesterday.

"It made me wish I had a time machine because I so wanted to be there."

"Thank goodness for DVDs." There's a phrase I never thought I'd say again in this day and age.

"It also made me wish I hadn't pushed you so hard before I left last week. I was being a bit cocky and it made me disrespectful."

I'm not sure I prefer this more reverent version of Leila. I've been showered with reverence for the most part of my life, followed by pity. That's why Leila was such a breath of fresh air. I hope she doesn't break out the pity next.

"I don't mind a bit of cockiness." I attempt a smile, even though her mentioning the *In Too Deep* tour has made me a little sad. "On the contrary."

She mirrors my smile and it's already a lot more confident than the sheepish one she treated me to earlier. "I just don't want you to think I'm a heartless journalist who wants to turn your pain into something sensational. That's not what I do. Respect is always at the core of what I write."

"I never, for one second, felt disrespected by you, Leila." If anything, I disrespected you, I think, with all my veiled glances at your lips and all my thoughts about kissing them.

"That's a relief."

"I know my reputation still precedes me. And, sure, I used to sometimes be a bit of a monster to the press, which I regret. But you're someone else to me, Leila. You're writing a book about me. There's really nothing to be worried about."

"I've just been so fully immersed in all things Isabel Adler." I can see her relax. "I might have lost perspective for a minute. What your voice... could do. It's astounding. Unite an arena full of people. Forge a connection. Spread joy. Ignite emotion. Music can be so powerful and no one was more the epitome of that than you."

"Jeez, Leila." I mock fan myself. "You're going to make me revert to my diva ways."

"I mean it." Her gaze on me is hot. "But I wouldn't want you to conclude that I think any less of you now."

"*I* think less of me now, so I most certainly wouldn't hold that against you."

She shakes her head. "I know it's easy for me to say, but I wish you wouldn't. I understand that it hurts and that it will continue to do so for a long time, but what happened wasn't your fault. The surgeon made a mistake. Why would you feel less about yourself because of someone else's mistake?"

"Even that's debatable. Maybe I shouldn't have decided to have the surgery. I knew the risks."

"A twenty-five-million-dollar insurance payout says differently."

"What's the point of insuring your voice for such a ludicrous amount of money if it means you'll never use it again?" I told Ira not to transfer a penny of that blood money into my personal account. A few years later, I asked him to set up a scholarship fund for young people who can't afford music lessons, but I'm not actively involved in it. I don't want to know anything about what that money has done.

"The irony's not lost on me," Leila says. "Anyway, I won't be offering to set you up with any of my friends again." I see what she's trying to do. She's trying to lighten the mood. I decide to play along.

"What? And I was just going to take you up on your offer."

Something crosses her face, as though a cloud just blocked the sunlight streaming into the window. "Nah, I think we should just leave it at that." She sinks her teeth into her bottom lip.

"Since we're... sharing." Maybe it's not the right word for what we're doing, but Leila has been unexpectedly vulnerable with me. And who knows? Maybe it's just another journalist ploy. But I don't think it is. Either way, I remember Vivian's words: *what do you have to lose, Izzy?* "I would like to state for the record that I quite enjoyed having you in my house for a day." I make sure to look her straight in the eye. For the first time, I feel like I have the upper hand in this thing, whatever it is. Leila's little confession has only reignited my attraction to her. "In that spirit, I would like to invite you to stay for dinner."

"Oh." She looks a touch flabbergasted, but there's something else in her expression as well. "I'm so sorry, but I can't tonight."

Damn. "Of course. No worries. Another time," I blabber.

"I have a... thing." She quirks up her eyebrows briefly. "It's a sort of date. I don't know. I mean, I do know."

Oh, for crying out loud. Way to read a situation, Izzy. She's going on a date with someone else. Tonight. I wish she hadn't told me. But at least now I know where I stand. As soon as she leaves, I'll need to call Vivian—maybe I'll even ask her to introduce me to Ramona.

"Sure." I feel instantly ridiculous for even thinking that Leila might be interested in me. "Someone you've been seeing for a while?" I inquire because, apparently, I'm a glutton for punishment.

"You really want to know?"

"Only if you want to talk about it." I thought I was well past the stage in my life where I mistake adoration for my voice for something else. Especially because I don't have the voice anymore.

"You've been sharing so much with me. Maybe it's only fair to reciprocate." She shrugs. "It's a first date, however, so there isn't that much to say."

"Yet." I have no idea how I manage to sound so chipper, so encouraging of Leila's date.

"I'll gladly take a rain check, if I may. For that dinner invitation."

"Sure." My entire system deflates. I'd been looking forward to Leila coming around today so much. Serves me right for getting the wrong idea. "Look, um..." I don't want her around anymore. "I suddenly don't feel that great. Can we continue another day?" I press two fingers against my temple, indicating a headache. "I get these migraines. They can just come out of nowhere fast."

Leila squints, then slants her head slightly, as though she can ascertain the gravity of my fake upcoming migraine that way. I don't care what she thinks. My head might not hurt, but my ego has certainly taken a hit.

"I can stay a while," she says. "Make sure you're okay."

"I'm not alone in the house," I remind her brusquely. "Please, if you could just go. I'm sorry."

"Of course."

Through the hand with which I half-cover my eyes, I see her jump out of her chair.

"I'm no stranger to migraines myself," she whispers. She crouches next to me. I feel her hand on my knee. "Let me know when you feel better and take good care of yourself, Izzy."

With that, she exits the room. Seconds later, Harry enters. I'm still sitting in the chair with my hand in front of my eyes, not because I can't handle the light, but because of the bottomless embarrassment working its way through me.

"Real or fake?" Harry asks matter-of-factly.

"Fake," I sigh, letting my hand drop in my lap. It's not the first time I've used the migraine excuse and Harry knows me too well.

"Shall I fix you a drink, Izzy?" he asks.

I shake my head. "No. I think I'll do an extra workout." Only Ramona can cheer me up now.

The power of creation is perhaps the most powerful force that we know in life, that we can experience as mere humans. And yes, I can write songs, but let's be honest, which I know all of you have always been with me, my biggest hits were never the songs I wrote myself. It's a fact. But it's also, technically, true that I could still write songs and that I could try to channel my creative energy into that, but for me, doing so is pure torture. To write music I can't perform. I've tried. I really have. The empty feeling it left inside of me is not one I'm looking to experience again any time soon.

The fact of the matter is that I'm done creating. My creation time is over. And the thing is, once you've had the power of creation, once you know what it can do for you, how it can make you feel, how it can make everything better, life without it is too hard. For me, it was never about writing songs, anyway. It was never what I truly excelled at. My power came from performing. From pairing my voice with my dramatic tendencies and turning it into an emotional event. Because that's what every single concert I've ever performed has been to me: an emotive experience. A place where I communicated with the audience in the only universal language there has ever been: music.

Now, I feel as if I no longer have a way out for my emotions. And I have so many of them. But I don't know what to do with them. I'm utterly sick of talking about them, as you all know. And what kind of a life is that? A life where I have to keep all my emotions inside to somehow deal with them? I don't know how to do that. But even if someone could guarantee me that they could teach me to do it without singing, even then I wouldn't want to learn.

CHAPTER 15

I've barely sat down to a dinner I'm eating by myself and that I don't much feel like, when the doorbell rings. It must be Vivian because she's the only one who comes round unannounced. I perk up at the thought. She can join me and I can unload my embarrassment on her.

Harry enters the dining room alone. "It's Ms. Zadeh, Izzy. Should I let her in?"

"Leila?" I check my watch. It's just gone eight. Shouldn't she be on her hot date?

"She wants to know if you're all right," Harry says.

Oh shit. If I'd had a real migraine, I'd be laid up in bed. If Leila is familiar with migraines, she must know that. Maybe that's why she stopped by instead of texting me, because she knew it would be impossible for me to reply.

"What did you tell her?" I ask Harry.

"I said I would check." Everything Harry says is so matter-of-fact. Luckily, I stopped worrying about what he thinks of me years ago. It was either that or go crazy.

"Ask her to come in," I say on a sigh. I'll just tell her it was a false alarm.

Harry nods and goes to fetch Leila. I wipe my mouth and take a sip of water. I try to look casual but as soon as I hear her footsteps approach my muscles tense.

"Can I get you anything, Ms. Zadeh?" Harry asks.

"I'm fine, thank you." She's not staying then. Makes sense. She must be on her way to her date. She looks absolutely stunning. Like a layer of gloss has been added to her entire being. Her hair is loose, cascading down her neck onto her shoulders. Her lips are red as ever. Her eyes smoky and heavy-lidded. Pang. A merciless stab of jealousy shoots through me. Serves you right, Izzy.

"Hey." She fixes those dreamy eyes on me. "I thought I'd check on you." She glances at my plate of food. "You're eating. You must be feeling better." Her lips lift into a smile, telling me all I need to know. She's on to me. I feel even more like a silly schoolgirl with a one-way crush than before.

"False alarm." I smile back. "Aren't you supposed to be on a date?" I give her a once-over—again. *Damn*. Who is this woman she's going out with? She's in for a nice surprise.

"I canceled," she deadpans.

"You don't look as though you canceled."

"Maybe not. But I did."

"Why?" I figure it's a fair enough question.

"I realized something." She takes a step closer.

"What's that?" A shiver runs up my spine.

"I realized several things, actually." She holds up her forefinger. "One: you're a very bad liar, Izzy."

I shrug. I'll give her that.

"Two." She holds up another finger. "I'd rather have dinner with you tonight than go on a date with a stranger."

"Is there a third one?" My heart pitter-patters in my chest.

She nods but doesn't say anything.

"Are you going to tell me what it is?"

She shifts her weight from one foot to the other and the air in the room changes. "I think that you might want to kiss me now."

It's a good thing I'm sitting down, otherwise my knees might have given way. Leila doesn't say anything else. She just looks at me as if, all this time, she's been seeing right through me. As though, from the very first thought I had about kissing her, she could read it right off my face.

I push myself out of my chair. I feel the way I used to right before I went on stage. My belly flip-flopping with excitement. Every last nerve ending tingling with anticipation. I had completely forgotten what that feels like. But here it is. That divine blend of low-grade angst and knowing that an amazing experience might just be waiting for me, if only I round that corner. If only I keep taking these steps.

I head over to Leila. Her lips are all I see. They're what I'm walking toward. My ultimate prize.

My heart does a silly dance in my chest. She came back. I asked her to leave, but she came back. She's standing right in front of me, waiting for me to kiss her.

I grab her hand and look her in the eye. For the first time in years, the thought that has consistently been nestled in the back of my head—the one counting down the days until I die—evaporates. In the face of this moment, this split second I have left before my lips meet hers, it goes away, as if it was never really there.

I bring my other hand to her jaw. I touch my fingertips gently to the soft skin of her cheek. Her lips are slightly parted. She leans into my touch. Her eyes close for an instant, then reopen, her gaze hot and heavy on me.

I want to say something, but my voice seems to have

broken all over again. I do very much want to kiss you, I think. And then I do. I bridge the last of the distance between us and find her lips with mine. God, she smells divine as well. It's not a light perfume she's wearing. It's earthy and musky and it suits her so much. It fits the gravitas with which she carries herself. Leila is by no means young and frivolous. She's mature and wise and, in her own words, knows a thing or two about loss.

Now, she opens her lips to me and I let my tongue slip inside her mouth. I feel her hands on the back of my neck as she pulls me closer. Our tongues meet and dance, then retreat. She pulls back a fraction and looks at me. Her eyes are narrowed and she flicks her tongue along her lips. Is that a hint of a smile? Why wouldn't it be? If she's enjoying this half as much as I am, she must be over the moon.

She tugs me closer again until our lips are but a hair's width apart. I can feel her breath on me. I look deep into her eyes before I close mine and lean into another kiss. The tenderness of it surprises me again. Her tongue is soft against my lips. The touch of her hands on my neck is gentle. Despite her way, which can be blunt at times, nothing about Leila's physical appearance is angular or sharp. She has the kind of body I want to bury myself in, disappear into. I curl my arms around her and press myself to her. I wasn't hungry for dinner but I am hungry for this kiss. For Leila's touch.

Our lips break apart and she kisses me just below the ear. "Are you all right?" she asks. "You're shaking."

Am I? Maybe just a light tremble. My body doesn't know what's happening. It might have completely forgotten what this felt like. My brain sure has. Although both my body and my brain know one thing very clearly: I want to kiss Leila again. I want to feel her soft lips against mine again and again. I want to feel how she wants to kiss me too.

"I'm all right," I whisper. "Just..." A bit overcome, perhaps. *A bit lost in my overwhelming feelings for you.*

"I didn't mean to come on so strong, Izzy." Leila's hands glide up and down my arms. Then her lips curl into a knowing smile. "It's not a migraine, is it?"

I shake my head. "It's you. You're... a lot."

She gives an unexpected hearty laugh. "You know what I've come to appreciate about you?" She slants her head and regards me intently. "Your ability to completely forget who you are and what you stand for." A quick smile. "I should be the one shaking in my boots right now. Because I'm kissing *you*. Not the other way around."

"Maybe that's what I appreciate about you so much, that you don't give a fuck that I used to be Isabel Adler."

"Used to be? Last I checked, Isabel Adler is still your name and she is standing right in front of me."

"I'm just Izzy now."

Her hands have stopped their motion and they lightly grip my shoulders. "And I do give a fuck, Izzy."

"I'm not entirely sure what we're talking about here." My gaze gets stuck on her lips again. That lipstick she wears must be of the highest quality, because it hasn't been smudged a fraction. She still looks as utterly delicious as when she walked into the room. Although something in her eyes has changed. "But I'm so happy you came by."

"Can we sit for a moment?" Leila asks, deflating my hope of kissing her again. "We should probably have talked before I came barging in here."

"I don't need to talk." I pull her close to me again, but instead of finding her lips for another kiss, I wrap my arms around her and push my nose into her luscious mane of hair. I only relax when I feel Leila's arms curl around my waist. Even though kissing her was definitely top of my list of things to do, this embrace feels like what I needed the most. To be held in her arms. To exhale and just be me.

"I do need to talk," she says softly, but doesn't let go yet.

CHAPTER 16

"I'm not entirely sure what I feel," Leila says. "I know what I want, but I'm also wise enough to question my desire."

Desire. Want. Feel. Only a few of her words are really getting through to me. If I'm being perfectly honest, if it were up to me, I wouldn't be sitting in a chair talking to Leila right now. Because my heart rages inside my chest. My blood pounds in my veins while my pulse throbs wildly between my legs.

If it were solely up to me, Leila would be all over me right now, taking care of my desire, which I know is not the same as hers. It can't be. Not only because we are different people but also because we're coming at this from totally different places. What I'm warring with is reconciling our kiss, and whatever might or might not happen after, with ticking off an activity on my final to-do list—sleeping with another woman one last time.

As long as I'm being honest with myself, I admit that, from the moment I walked into her home that night she invited me to dinner, I knew I wanted her to be the last person I ever shared a bed with. My body made quick work of informing me of that.

"This might not be the best idea, Izzy."

"Depends what angle you take."

"Of course, but I have a code of ethics that I've always stood by. I didn't take this job so I could be in a position to kiss you one night. That was never what this was about for me." She scoffs. "Although I'm well aware I could have easily fooled you—and myself."

"What's your code?" I suppose I also live by certain rules now and I want to respect other people's as much as I can.

"I don't use seduction as a tactic to gather information. It's not professional. It's not serious. It diminishes the work."

"If that's the case, then yes, you really could have fooled me, Leila." I try a smile. Maybe she's one of those people who don't know how naturally seductive they are, who change the air in a room without realizing it. But I think she does.

"I'm well aware, but it was never my intention."

I nod. "Look, sometimes something happens when two people get together. Something that's stronger than your resolve. Or any code." Or a long-held belief that all that's left for me is to die in peace and with dignity.

"True, but... I'm not in two minds about kissing you, Izzy. I'm insanely attracted to you. What I'm struggling with is whether I should quit the job or not."

"Please don't. In the end, it's just a book. It's not a matter of life or death." Oops. Wrong choice of words, although she doesn't know that, and I'm trying to make a point. "I know for you this book is work and it's important to you to do a good job. I respect that. But, for me, it's not enough of an argument to not kiss you anymore." I shrug. "If you feel that strongly about it, we can find someone else to finish the job. It's a small thing compared to... exploring what there might be between us. But please don't make any rash decisions."

"Here's my current dilemma." Her voice has dropped into a lower register. "I need to think about this, but I don't want to go. I don't much feel like taking the time that is required to think this through."

I try to suppress the grin that's already spreading on my face. "You must have thought about it on your way over."

"I did, but my rumination was inconclusive."

"What happened to your date?"

"I had to let her down." The skin around her eyes crinkles so deliciously again. "I couldn't bear the thought of sitting across from a woman who wasn't you. Imagine if she asked me about my work, which she surely would have. What would I have said? And how would I have felt? I couldn't do it."

The pure elation that courses through me at hearing Leila's words is like magic. It lifts my spirits to a level they haven't reached in years. Maybe a decade. Maybe since before... *No, don't go there, Izzy. Take what you can from this.*

I decided long ago, once my decision was final, that what I would never do was look for reasons to go on living. By the time I'd made my decision, I had done enough of that. And I won't be reduced to the cliché of having another woman 'save me'. Or even worse, being 'saved by love'. This has nothing to do with love. I just want to spend a night with Leila. Maybe two. Who knows, maybe there are even three nights in the cards for us. Surely, by then, she'll be sick of me. She'll want to move on, like she's wont to do, with her serial monogamy and all that. And I will have the memory of having been with her for whatever number of days I have left.

"I'm putting all my cards on the table here." Any notion of trembling, of shaking at Leila's touch, has left me now. I can think clearly again. "I would very much like you to stay." I reach over and grab her hand. I turn her palm upward and stroke gently along it with my thumb. "But you're the one with a job to do so it's your decision, which I will, of course, respect. But... think of it this way." I find her eyes. "From what you've told me, you're not looking for anything too serious. Neither am I. In fact, it's important that we're very clear about that. Is it really worth giving up this job for? Code of ethics aside, it could be considered as some very... deep research."

She returns my gaze, but I'm not done yet.

"Besides, Leila, you didn't seduce me any more than I seduced you."

She expels a small sigh. "Already, I want to ask you so many questions after what you've just said."

"But I would have never said any of this if we weren't in this post-kiss situation."

"Exactly my point. Where to draw the line?"

"You're not conducting an official investigation into my life. You're writing a book about it. Not some official report for the authorities, but a piece of entertainment."

Her hand closes around my fingers. "This is no longer an issue of whether I will or won't sleep with you, Izzy."

Music to my ears. If I still could sing, I'd want to write a song about it. "Then what have you got to lose?" I repeat Vivian's question to me. Because I now know with complete certainty that I only stand to gain from this. But I'm not Leila.

"I've always found that to be such a stupid question. I don't have anything to teach you about loss, Izzy, nor do I need any lessons on it myself. It's not about that. It's about professional integrity, which is important to me."

I stand corrected. For a minute there, I was under the very wrong impression Leila was a fangirl I could easily talk into my bed. Although it hasn't happened for many years, it wouldn't have been the first time. It's also, mercifully in some ways, a reminder that Leila is not here because of who I am—not tonight.

Then another thought occurs to me. Is she asking *me* to put a lid on this for tonight? Or to at least help her stop this until she figures out what it is she wants? Christ. I couldn't have gone for a less complex woman, of course. It had to be someone with professional integrity and a code of ethics. Obviously. Why keep it simple if there can be complications? It's pretty much the story of what my life has become.

"Okay. Then go home. Think about it. I'm not going anywhere," I say.

"I guess I could fake a migraine." Just like that, she manages to defuse the situation with one single sentence again.

"You can hold that against me until the clock strikes twelve. After that, it's off-limits. You knew how I felt. I was just... saving face."

"Oh, I know. As soon as I figured out you weren't really having a migraine, it was actually rather adorable." She squeezes my hand. "But you see how things between us can shift so quickly? I want to keep this job, Izzy. And I want to be able to do it to the best of my abilities, not just for me, or for the readers, but for you. This book must be a big deal to you as well?"

It's really not, I almost say, but I manage to swallow the words. I want to meet her halfway in this, but it's hard, because it's difficult for me to understand why she's making such a fuss about this.

"Leila." I cup her hand in both of mine now. "I want you to finish the book. I want to work with you. But I also want you..." My mind's racing, trying to come up with a way to get Leila out of her head. The only thing I can come up with is to kiss her again. Surely that should work? I lift her hand and bring it to my mouth. Before I do anything else, before I move this forward, I look her in the eye. Oh, damn.

When I meet her gaze, I realize that it's not up to me to convince her to do this. It should be her decision entirely, no matter her reasons. At least she's being honest. Brutally so, but honest nonetheless. Something I will never be able to be with her.

Gently, I put her hand down. "I'm sorry. Just as you don't want to feel you've seduced me, I don't want to feel I've manipulated you in any way."

"Oh, Izzy." What starts out as a chuckle quickly turns into a low rumble of a laugh. "Do you know what I think it is?" She sucks her bottom lip between her teeth, the way I've seen her do a few times already. It makes her look vulnerable and utterly kissable at the same time. "I think I might be a little bit scared." She might look vulnerable, but she doesn't look scared to me at all. "Maybe even a bit intimidated."

"I'm scared too." I might as well admit it. We might as well admit it to each other. "I haven't done this... you know." And most certainly not with a woman as gorgeous and impressive as you, I think. A woman who might just completely overwhelm me. Maybe what scares me the most about taking things further with Leila is that she is almost exactly, insofar as that is even possible, what I had wished the last ever woman for me would be. Strong but vulnerable. Elegant but never mincing her words. And mesmerizingly beautiful.

"I know," she says. "You've locked yourself away, Izzy. You've made everything and everyone outside yourself, outside the intimate circle you've created around yourself, scary."

"Are you going to put that in the book?" Jesus Christ. I feel like I'm in my shrink's office again. Leila might be right, but this is not the time to be psychoanalyzing me.

"I don't know." She's the one who stands up now. "Do you think I should put this in?" She locks her gaze on me, walks over, and kisses me lightly on the lips.

If it helps with your professional integrity, I think. I can't say it because my mouth is otherwise engaged. My lips find hers again and again. With my lips still glued to hers, I manage to push myself out of my chair.

"How does it work with your staff when you take someone to your bedroom?" she asks as I tug her toward the door. "You haven't even finished your dinner."

"Stop being a journalist now, please." I touch the back of my fingers to her cheek. "Stop asking questions."

She pulls me close to her. "If I don't ask, how will I know what you like?"

"I'll make sure that you do." I run the tip of my tongue over my upper lip.

"I have no doubt about that," she says.

Hand in hand, we walk up the stairs.

CHAPTER 17

I might be pushing sixty, but my doctor always tells me I have the body of someone at least twenty-five years younger. I know she exaggerates—she's the flirty, overly complimentary type, which is why she's been my doctor for so long—but Dr. Fererra's confidence boosting words mean I never have any qualms about undressing in front of someone else. Although, truth be told, apart from medical examinations, of which I've had enough to, literally, last me a lifetime, it's not a very frequent occurrence in my life.

"Why the rush?" Leila asks, after she's given my bedroom a once-over. I can't wait for her to rake her gaze over me like that.

She's right, of course. My self-imposed number of days to live has nothing to do with tonight. In fact, I'd better take my time to enjoy this.

"Come here." She holds out her hand and I take it. She looks deep into my eyes and I wonder if she's like this with everyone she sleeps with or if it's different because she's with me. It's a thought I've never been able to banish fully from my mind, even though it's utterly futile. "It seems I've gotten over my fear." The corner of her mouth lifts a fraction.

I never asked her what she was so afraid of, but it seems foolish to bring it up now. "Leila, you're..." I drop her hand and cup her face in my palms. "You're so fucking sexy." While I kiss her, I hope I don't start shaking again like I did earlier.

"Ditto," she whispers when we come up for air. "Are you okay?" It's not worry I detect in her gaze when I meet it.

I glance at my hands. Only a slight tremble. Maybe I've gotten over my fear as well. I give her a nod.

She covers my hands with hers. The warmth of her touch and the strength of her grip calm me down further.

"I want you," I say. My voice is shaky but that was always going to be the case.

The smile she gives me is full and seductive. Maybe we'll never be able to settle on who seduced whom, but in my mind, it will always be Leila. The way she came into my house with all her confident elegance. The way she shook my hand and looked me straight in the eye, as if to say, I'm here now, there's nothing to worry about anymore.

"Me too, Izzy." Her gaze is warm, brimming with affection. "Oh, me too." She brings my hands to her lips, turns them to her, and kisses both my palms. Then she places my hands on her shoulders, while her own hands get to work on finishing the unbuttoning of my blouse I had started earlier.

Her dark skin contrasts starkly with the pale yellow of my blouse. Leila is not one to delicately undo garments. I get the feeling she'd rather be tearing it off me than fumbling with a bunch of useless buttons.

Seeing her impatience on display makes my own grow. And it's in that moment that I decide to let go of any qualms I might have left. To evict the thought of my days left from my head and not let it matter tonight. To not think of Leila as a means to an end—as the woman I've chosen to spend the night with for the last time ever. Because if I do that, most of the magic of tonight will be lost on me. I need to get out of my head. I need to be here with her to be able to delight in the furtive touch of her fingertips against the swell of my breasts. I need to feel my breath hitch the way it does when she finally guides that blouse off my shoulders, when she finishes her impatient work of ridding me of it, of exposing a bit more of me to her. Because, in the end, that's what she's here for. That's why she came into my life. To expose me. And while I will always keep certain parts of myself hidden, I'm willing to let her see a whole lot tonight.

"Damn," she says on what sounds like a sigh of admiration. "You weren't kidding about working out." She skates a fingertip over the taut skin of my belly.

I can hardly say it's all because of Ramona. Instead, I flex my muscles so she can get a hint of the six-pack I have on a good day. It's only ever a hint. But still. I like to think that Ramona would approve. Leila certainly looks like she does. She casts her gaze to my biceps next.

"Hm," she says, as she traces a fingertip over the swell of my muscle. I'm not sure what the 'hm' means, but I don't have time to contemplate it further, because the next thing Leila does is hoist her top over her head.

With her tan skin and delicious curves, her body is the opposite of mine. Where I'm sinewy and firm, she's soft and voluptuous. Everything about Leila as she stands here in front me is so utterly inviting.

"I don't work out at all," she says, without any apology in her voice.

"Oh, Leila." I can't help myself. I need to feel the warmth of her skin. I bring a hand to her shoulder again and trail a line down, to where her breast curves out of her bra.

She unhooks her bra and reveals her breasts to me. Something inside me, something I've kept a tight lid on for a very long time, unhinges at the sight of her topless. I cup her breasts gently and brush my thumbs over her nipples. They harden against my touch. My own nipples tighten against the fabric of my bra, but I'm much too preoccupied to even think about taking it off. Later. After I've finished worshiping the marvels that are Leila's breasts. They're so exquisitely soft in my hands. It's not only acute arousal I feel coursing through me, although there's plenty of that. Somehow, her baring her breasts to me has loosened something else in me. The need for comfort. For touch. For human warmth. All needs I had safely locked away.

"You're so beautiful," I whisper, wholly mesmerized by her.

Her smile, when I manage to tear my gaze away from her bosom, is like the sun bursting through a cloud. Come to think of it, that's how I'm feeling inside as well. Like the sun has finally found a way to illuminate a darkness I've lived with for too long. A darkness created by neglected needs, by pretending I could live without certain things.

I lean in and kiss her lips before trailing a hot, wet path to her breasts. When I take one of her nipples in my mouth, something inside me further unclenches. And Leila, as if she senses that I need to take this time, just lets me do what I need to do. Allows me to reacquaint myself with the incredible comforting power of the female body.

I hear her gasp and when I look up from her breasts, her head is thrown back, her neck an open invitation to be kissed. I grab the invite with open hands—and very eager lips.

"I want to see you," she says, when my lips have almost reached her mouth again.

It most certainly wasn't a question because her hands are reaching behind my back already. She opens my bra and lets it slide over my arms. Here I am with all my muscle tone but barely any swell to my chest, I think. The bra was just for show. I've never really needed one. I wasn't wearing a push-up bra or some other male-invented contraption. What lies beneath is hardly a surprise—although, in the past, I have come across disappointed glances. But Leila doesn't appear any less enthralled. She looks at me the way I want to be looked at right now. Like she wants to discover every last inch of me.

When she puts her hands on me, my breath stalls in my throat.

"You're beautiful too," she whispers in my ear as her hands cup my breasts and her lips trail along my neck. She walks me toward the bed until my legs bump against the mattress. Before pushing me down, she zips down my jeans and I hastily step out of them.

"This too." She has hooked a finger into the waistband of my panties. Her smile is back.

When I don't budge, just to see how she will react, she lowers my panties herself. By now, Leila's bossy streak is not a surprise to me.

By the time she has divested herself of the rest of her clothing, I'm waiting eagerly for her on the bed. Now I certainly can't keep my eyes off her. I watch as she sits down, ever so gracefully. I have no idea how she can still be so elegant now. Me, who was actually trained in looking elegant on a stage way too big for the wisp of a girl I was back then. There are still many things about Leila I don't understand. But what I do know is that she has me eating out of the palm of her hand. My gaze is glued to her. My ears are fully attuned to the smallest sound she makes.

"Come here," she says, beckoning me with her eyes.

On my knees, and extremely inelegantly, I shuffle over to her. She pats her thighs.

"Straddle me like this," she says.

I maneuver onto her, fully aware of how widely my legs are spread. The free flow of air on my sex is intoxicating.

She wraps her arms around me and grins. "Exactly where I want you."

Exactly where I want to be. She kisses me on the lips and my mouth opens for her. I let my hands run wild over her soft, warm skin. I let them drift into her hair, which looks so lovely when it's loose like it is tonight. I push myself against her, into the inviting heat of her body, the warmth of her skin, the sexy pout of her lips.

"Never in a million years," Leila says, when we finally break apart for some much-needed air, "could I ever have imagined this happening."

I pretty much wished for it from the moment I first met her, but I'm not going to tell her that now. I'll save that for later, for when she's gone back into journalist-interrogation mode.

When she speaks, I just want to kiss her again. Everything about her, including her words, spurs me on to touch her, to feel more of her, to become one with her.

"Hold on," she says. "I want to see your face." The smallest hint of a smile appears on her face. "When I do this." Her fingertip traces a circle on the inside of my thigh. She keeps her gaze glued to mine. Inadvertently, I emit a small groan. Christ, Izzy. Get a grip. She's inches away from my clit. Or is she? Her other hand rests on my opposite thigh. Her thumb presses into my flesh. She's so beautiful. Still so poised. Like she knows exactly what's going to happen next and she's fully in charge of everything. It's a look I very much like on her. Her dark eyes are magnetic with warmth and want. Even if I were too bashful and I had to avert my gaze, I wouldn't be able to. Her lips are slightly parted. Her head is tilted back somewhat. Her breasts jut out, as though reaching toward me. Seeing Leila like this is by far one of the most gorgeous sights I've had the pleasure to witness in recent memory.

Her fingertip is inching closer. It's no longer stroking my inner thigh. It slides through my wetness. Once. Twice. She avoids my clit, which only makes it rage more. All the energy I have in me pulses between my legs. Every cell in my body is already screaming for her to touch me more, where it matters.

From her glance, I gather that her finger won't be doing what I want any time soon. Because Leila isn't done looking at me yet. She regards me so intently, as though by looking at me while doing this, she can see straight into my soul. Yet her look is not invasive. It's comforting and hot and intimate. It's also wholly unexpected.

What is most exquisite of all is the expression on her face. It's one of wonder and utter delight. It makes me feel that she, too, has been dreaming of a moment like this since the instant we met. It makes me feel desired by every last inch of her.

Her finger keeps teasing me and avoiding my clit, but I'm so aroused by her gaze on me, by everything that has come before, that, when her fingertip slides inside me for the briefest of moments, I want to hold onto it with all the muscles I've trained over the years.

Her smile widens a fraction. Her eyes narrow. She might be reading me, but I'm reading her too. Although my faculties are being severely impaired. Still, it's easy enough to see what kind of kick she gets out of this, out of being in total control over me, of having me at her mercy, of me acquiescing to her so easily.

My breath stops in my throat as her finger dips inside me again. It lingers a bit longer this time, but nowhere near long enough. She skirts the edge of my clit now and desire jolts through me. My eyes fall shut, but I quickly reopen them. Every hint of smile has disappeared from Leila's face. She means business now. We've shifted into a higher gear—the one that will take me to my climax.

She edges around my clit with small, controlled motions, that are in stark contrast with how I feel inside. Nothing about me is controlled any longer. Under Leila's gaze, at the mercy of one single fingertip, that seems to direct all my desire, my heart beats like a herd of galloping horses. My skin is tight with goose bumps and moist with sweat. How is she even doing this? Is this some sort of witchcraft?

"Leila." I start chanting her name. It comes from all the way deep in my belly, emanating into a low rumble in the back of my throat. It's not even so much because of the action of her finger, which is divine and increasingly more geared toward what I want—what I need. It's about her gaze on me. As though she expects to glean something unsayable from my face when I come. Something I can't express in words. Something that can only be read from someone's features in their most ecstatic moment. If it's lust for life she's after, I'm sure she'll see it. Because I haven't felt more alive in years than I do now, teetering on the brink of climax. The sparks that fly through me, the electricity that runs beneath my skin, the charge in my muscles are all things that do not rhyme with my desire to die. They're the opposite.

I dig my nails into the soft flesh of her thighs. In response, it seems, she brings her other hand into play. She must have. I'm not looking. I'm trying to keep my gaze on her face. It contorts a bit, as though she's making some sort of special effort. Oh, but she is. A finger slips high inside me, while another circles my clit much more insistently now.

It's all I can do to hold on to her. Seeing her is no longer enough. I need to feel her skin under my hands. I want to kiss her, but I can't move. The heat inside me has turned into a landslide of ecstatic fire. And if she was hoping to meet the truest version of Isabel Adler in my eyes as I came, Leila will be disappointed, because I close my eyes and let it all wash over me as I exclaim her name again and again, as if the sound can somehow prolong my pleasure. Although, if it did, I'm not sure I'd be able to take it. It's almost too much. Everything about what just happened is the exact opposite of how I live.

"Hey, come here," she whispers as she pulls me close. She presses me against her warm skin and wraps me in her arms. "Damn, Izzy. You're fucking spectacular when you come."

I let her hold me and it feels so incredibly soothing, as though she's also cradling all the pain I've held inside me for so long in her warm embrace. Why did she have to look at me like that? If she hadn't, I tell myself, I wouldn't be falling apart like I am.

"Let's get under the covers," Leila says. "You're cold."

But I'm not cold, although I am shaking. My body's betraying me—and I thought it would be my eyes. I'm empty and only a long bout in Leila's arms can restore me. Or maybe it can't. I don't know. All I know is that I don't want to leave her embrace. And just maybe, the emptiness I feel is the sudden absence of pain. The shock of no longer unequivocally clinging to what I lost. Just for a few moments. It scares me more than the most petrifying thought I've had since my surgery.

CHAPTER 18

"Better?" Leila asks. I've had to leave her arms only for the few moments it took to throw back the covers and crawl into bed properly. I'm tucked into the nook of her shoulder and I feel safe in her arms. My hand rests on her belly. My energy is starting to come back.

"Much. Thank you," I mumble. "That was quite... intense." At least I didn't cry. It wouldn't have been the end of the world if I had, but I might have had more explaining to do.

"It's not the first time I've been described that way." My head bounces on her chest as she chuckles.

Her saying that makes me think of the date she was supposed to go on. Of all the women she's been with, though faceless and nameless, and all the ones she will be with. After me. After this. After I'm no longer here. It also makes me feel like I have a point to prove, lest she think that sleeping with Isabel Adler is a one-sided pillow princess experience.

I draw a circle around her belly button and it takes me right back to the motion of her finger around my clit earlier. It reignites the fire in me. It stokes my energy to a level that will make her squirm under my touch.

My hand is drawn upward to Leila's breasts, as though they're exercising the same kind of magnetism that her gaze did earlier. From my vantage point on her shoulder I can see her nipple. It's already reaching upward, but I want to find out what other reactions my touch might elicit. Slowly, I trace my finger over the underside of her breast, lingering on every inch of skin I encounter.

Deep inside me, something sparks again. The flicker of aliveness that has shone in me since Leila touched me earlier. Unsure of what to do with that, and intent on giving Leila my full attention, I push the thought away. I focus on her nipple instead. Skating my fingertip over it, however divine, is nowhere near enough. I need to taste it, taste her. All of her.

Beneath me, Leila emits a small sigh. The low growl I coax from her sounds divine—better than any music I ever made. It's neither soothing nor comforting. It's inspiring and arousing. I remember how forlorn I felt after she left earlier today, to get ready for her date. How foolish it made me feel. How utterly silly. Because this is what I wanted from her all along. Sometimes in life—not often—a woman comes along who shakes everything up. Leila is definitely a woman like that.

I push myself up and twist so I can look at her face. Her head is thrown back, her neck an open invitation again. But I have my sights set on another of Leila's body parts. Ever since she took off her bra, I've been wanting to run my tongue along her nipple, suck it into my mouth. So I do.

Yep, still a breast woman, I think, as my tongue dances over her nipple. I cup her other breast in my hand and shower her with open-mouthed kisses, lavishing so much attention on her nipple, losing myself in my desire to taste every last inch of her skin, that by the time I can finally tear myself away from her breasts, my clit is having a party of its own again between my legs.

I honestly can't remember the details of my last few sexual experiences, but all I can think is that if they felt anything at all like this, I wouldn't have stopped seeking them out. Being with Leila gives me back something I didn't know I'd lost. The intimacy of intertwining my limbs with hers, of feeling her warm skin all over mine, of taking her nipple into my mouth, reminds me of what it feels like to be truly alive. To know what it's like to want to do something over and over again.

"Please, Izzy." Leila pushes herself up on her elbows and glances down at me. I hadn't expected the plea. It fires off another round of manic pulsing in my clit. "Lick me."

She doesn't specify where or what, but of course I know what she means. For someone who was so scarce with her ministrations, she's asking a lot. But it's hardly something I can hold against her. I might tease her with it later, though. Leila's voice is made of nothing but raw arousal. Her gaze conveys the acuteness of her desire. Oh, and I thought I felt alive earlier. This, the way she's looking at me now, is the very stuff life is made of. To have a gorgeous woman look at me like that. All I can do is obey her request.

I take her nipple into my mouth one last time, for good measure, before kissing my way down. Her legs are spread wide already. Her sex glistens with lust. I like to think it's doing so solely for me.

A jolt of desire shoots through me again at the sight of her. My reaction to Leila feels a bit out of proportion. Like she's some sort of magic woman with special powers over me. Or the first woman I ever made love with. The wonder of it all and how everything suddenly all made sense. The novelty and the knowing how everything worked at the same time. That sense of coming home, of knowing that, yes, this was what I'd been looking for all along. This elusive thing I'd made myself believe that might not even exist in the real world.

I kiss her inner thigh and it feels as though I'm being kissed right back. One of Leila's hands is in my hair, the other claws at my shoulders. I need to stop myself from letting my tongue run wild all over her arousal. I want to give her a taste of her own medicine. I want to tease her the way she teased me earlier, how she drove me mad. How she made me come while barely touching me.

Ever so lightly, I skate the tip of my tongue along her sex. Her smell is so intoxicating, I almost lose myself again. My self-control is in serious peril when confronted with the force of nature that is Leila Zadeh. But I get a grip. It's something you learn when you take to the stage as often as I have. Learn to deal with the overwhelm. Enjoy it but don't let it knock you sideways. You're here to do a job. You're here for the audience. The real satisfaction always comes from going through the process, of breathing in the right way, through the roar of applause, so I can hit the high notes. So the applause multiplies and the process is repeated again and again until I've worked both myself and the people listening to me into a frenzy that I can feed off for days to come.

The tip of my tongue slicks through Leila's wetness, but I avoid touching her clit. My own clit is about to explode between my legs, but I resist the urge to attend to myself. This is my very first time with Leila. I want all my focus on her. When I take an instant to just look at her, to take her in, to drink in all her magnificence, she pushes her hips toward me impatiently.

Before I finally bestow some much-needed attention on her tortured clit, I suck her lips into my mouth. This elicits a different kind of groan from her. Much more high-pitched than I thought she was capable of. Almost a mewl. There's definitely some desperation in there.

"Please," she says again. At least I think she does. It's barely audible. I kind of like it when Leila begs for it.

Then, I bring her torment to an end. I let my tongue dart along her clit softly, still teasing her, because, by now, I can't help myself. Teasing Leila is my new favorite thing to do. To have her squirm beneath me like that. This proud woman with all her confidence. It almost makes me forget about my own growing arousal.

I apply some more pressure. She bucks toward me more. My tongue sweeps over her clit more insistently. I suck her into my mouth, tasting her most intimate flavor. Everything about Leila is so divine, it's no wonder she tastes so incredibly moreish. This is what I want to do with the rest of my life. Get so intimately acquainted with Leila that all my senses are saturated by all things her. *Ok, Izzy. Time to get a grip again.* Next time—and there'd better be a next time—I'll try to be a bit less dramatic about this in my head. But this is the effect she has on me. And it's not as if I can still sing the drama off me. This is all I have now. Or again. Christ. Why did I deny myself this?

"Ooh," Leila moans. Her fingertips dig into my scalp now. "Oh, oh, I'm coming." She's an announcer. Wonderful. I revel in the sound of her groans, in the pressure of her fingers, in her smell in my nose, and her taste in my mouth. Next, she whispers something wholly unintelligible. I'm not even sure it's in English. Then, she stretches her legs. I hurry to her.

She grins and, with her thumb, wipes some of her arousal off my chin.

"And to think I had to be somewhere else tonight," she says.

Another thing I like about her. Her devilish sense of humor.

"Did you cancel or postpone?" I quash any notion of jealousy. Leila came back for me tonight. That's all that matters.

"I was vague, but I think I'll cancel now." She runs a finger through my hair.

"Does that mean you want to be exclusive already?" I joke.

"Like you're juggling a dozen women." She chuckles.

"Not *me*." I lift my eyebrows. "And I fully understand why. You're such a catch."

"And you..." She pulls me back into the crook of her shoulder, where I lay before. "Are exceptionally gifted with your tongue." Again, I feel her body shudder beneath me as she laughs heartily.

CHAPTER 19

Leila's already awake when I open my eyes. She's looking at me as though she can't quite believe it's my bed she has just woken up in. For some reason, maybe because last night was so devastatingly glorious, the first thought that pops into my head at the sight of her is: oh damn, was this really a one-night stand?

"Good morning." Her voice is extra low and gravelly. The duvet is half-draped over her, exposing her magnificent chest.

As much as I want to enjoy this moment, this morning with her, and despite only having just opened my eyes, this is quite the mindfuck already.

At least Leila had the decency to tell me, beforehand, what she's like. It might be a one-night thing, although I sure as hell hope not. It might be a three-night dalliance. Or it may even continue until she's finished working on the book. And that's absolutely fine, because it's exactly that honesty that made me capable of doing this. But I haven't been as honest with her and it makes me feel like the world's biggest fraud. It makes me feel like I just lip-synched an entire concert and the audience never even noticed. It feels like I got away with something while at the same time betraying my truest self.

I might have been able to banish the thought from my mind last night, but now, in the cold hard glare of a new morning, despite the fact that I just woke up beside her, it's firmly back at the forefront of my mind. 170 days left.

Wanting to die has become such an essential part of me. It defines me much more than having been a singer ever did. I'm always scribbling notes for when I sit to work on my letter, like I used to do when I was still a musician. Will I have to include her in it now? Not after just one night with her, although I can't possibly pretend she never existed, that last night didn't happen. Last night and all that led up to it.

"Izzy?" She narrows her eyes. "Last night was pretty spectacular, but I do hope it hasn't rendered you speechless." Her smile quickly fades. "Sorry. Oh, shoot, I'm sorry. Does your voice require some sort of warm-up in the morning—"

"I'm not speechless," I quickly say. "I was lost in thought. Sorry."

"How did you sleep?" Her smile is back. Her eyes glimmer like hot coals. God, those eyes. The way she looked at me last night—looked right through me. But there are things that eyes can never see. Looking at her now, I fear I might have let her come too close.

"Fine," I say.

She scoffs, but gently. "I won't pretend I'm an authority on all things Isabel Adler just because I'm writing your biography, but... something about you seems off this morning. Or are you not much of a morning person?" She tries another grin.

"I'm sorry." I pull her into a hug so I don't have to look at her face. "I'm just..." I'm falling apart. If I had known that sleeping with Leila, no matter how incredible it felt at the time, would make me feel like this afterward, I wouldn't have done it. Maybe she was right to question her professionalism. I should have done the same with my sanity, but it's not really something you can bring up in a conversation that is also foreplay.

"Talk to me," she says against my neck. "Tell me what's going on inside that pretty head of yours."

I can never tell you and that's the problem. "I think I just need a moment." I hold her close, though. I have an inkling this might be the first and last time we wake up next to each other. I didn't know sleeping with Leila would take such an emotional toll. I'm not sure I can do it again. I'm not sure I can ever hold her in my arms again. I feel like I've given away something of myself that I shouldn't have. As if allowing her to look at me so intensely when she brought me to climax exposed my true self to her, the irrevocably injured part of me that can never be healed. The part of me that wants nothing more than to stop existing, stop being. The part of me that's been in charge for a long time. I'm afraid that if I even allow her another glimpse at that hidden part of me, she'll manage to undo something about it, and I can't have that. Where would that leave me? In limbo again? No, thank you. I've been in limbo, in a kind of super-extended purgatory, for the past ten years. I'm not going back. Not even for someone as magnificent as Leila. "I'm going to take a shower."

"Shall I join you?" My erratic behavior hasn't squashed the mischief in her voice.

"Not today." For a split second, the image of Leila underneath a cascading flow of water pops into my head. Oh, to lick the drops off her as they stream down her luscious breasts. No, Izzy. Put a cork in it. The deal was that you got to enjoy last night. Today is another day.

Oh shit. It finally hits me that I'm being a massive bitch to Leila. I take a breath. "I'm sorry. I..." I need to give her something. Not an excuse, but a sincere emotion. After last night, she deserves it—and so much more. "Being with you has destabilized me. Sorry for being such a pain about it."

"Why has it destabilized you?"

"It made me feel some—" I stop myself.

"Hey." She takes my hand and puts it on her chest. "I felt it, too. I was there."

"I know, but... I'm going through something right now and I can't share it. I'm really sorry, but I can't."

"That's okay. You don't have to share everything with me."

"Only what's ready for publication." I take the opportunity to throw in a joke, no matter how lame, with both hands.

"I hope you know you can share much, *much* more with me than that."

"I do." It's hard not to when you've looked into someone's eyes while having the most earth-shattering orgasm. For a split second, I imagine Leila being the one—and the only—I share my deepest secret with. While it's impossible to gauge her reaction, it still scares the living daylights out of me. "Maybe later," I lie. My stomach growls, reminding me that I hardly ate last night. I extend my hand to her. "Why don't you join me in the shower, if you still want to."

She takes my hand. "I want to," she simply says.

CHAPTER 20

This time, Leila seems to know exactly what she wants for breakfast. As though she has given it some serious thought beforehand.

After Rian has gone into the kitchen and Harry has made himself scarce, she looks at me intently. "I'm not sure I could live like this."

"Like what?" I know what she's getting at. I had to get used to it myself.

"Always having people around. Take last night. Surely Harry is no fool and he knew very well what was going on."

"It didn't stop you from announcing your orgasm." I can't help myself. The memory makes something mellow bloom in my belly.

"I wasn't thinking about Harry at that exact time."

"I know it's weird at first. But you get used to it. And trust me, once you're used to it, you're *used* to it."

"You mean that you get accustomed to never having to do anything for yourself again?"

I shrug. "I've lived like this for two thirds of my life. I know it's indulgent and I know it has made me terribly complacent when it comes to household tasks." It's been a while since I've thought of doing a chore. "And administrative ones," I add.

"And you've never considered the value of those tasks?"

"What do you mean?"

Leila drinks from her coffee, then says, "Our lives are made up of what we do every day. For most of us, that includes at least a minimum of mundane tasks like grocery shopping or doing the dishes. Or making our own coffee, for that matter. For me, it's like a morning ritual that I couldn't live without."

"I'm willing to bet a lot of money that you could." I throw in a smile.

Leila just shakes her head. "A lot of life is made up of in-between moments like that, when we do a routine task and allow our mind to wander."

"I admit I'm spoiled when it comes to these things. I never have to think about what I'm going to eat or whether I called the plumber. But I like it that way." As if on cue, Rian brings out our breakfast. Smoked salmon, avocado, and poached eggs for Leila. Pancakes and fresh fruit for me.

"Oh, I'm sure you like it, but... I don't know." Leila seems to have lost her train of thought. She looks at her breakfast in the same way she looked at me last night. She must be starving. I know I am. Without saying anything else, she digs in. All I hear from her side of the table for the next five minutes are a few 'hmmms' and 'aaaahs.'

I watch her eat and even that she seems to do in a sensual way. It's also really nice to have someone around to have breakfast with. Especially someone as lovely as Leila. I wish she could stay all day. We didn't have an interview session planned for today, but, of course, so much has changed between us since those plans were made. Maybe everything is an interview session now.

"What are you doing today?" I ask.

"I had planned to start working on some of the rewrites of Bruce's draft, but I can easily change my schedule." She raises her eyebrows. "I'm very amenable to accepting better offers."

"I guess all the time you spend with me can be considered work."

"No, Izzy. That's not how I see it." She puts down her fork. "I hope you don't think I slept with you to obtain better information for the book. Even though I'm the one writing it, or at least finishing it, I don't consider it *my* book. It's your book."

That damned book. I wish I could tell Leila how little my biography means to me. But then I would need to tell her why, and I would hurt her feelings and her professional pride. "I don't think that's why you slept with me. Neither do I think you slept with me just because I'm Isabel Adler."

She chuckles. "Although, you are, of course, Isabel Adler."

"Always have been and always will be."

"This is so good." Leila goes back to eating her breakfast. It's clearly the most important thing on her mind at the moment.

Her absorption gives me time to really consider if I want her to stay today. I go over my schedule in my head. Daisy always sends a summary the night before. She must have noticed that most days it's barely worth summarizing anymore. Since I set 'the date,' I've scaled down my activities to a bare minimum. As if I'm already dead. But I feel very alive this morning. It must be because I ticked a massive item off my final to-do list.

Images of last night catch up with me again. And not just images, but the memory of how Leila made me feel. The way she looked at me. Then, I remember how I behaved upon waking, and I realize I need some time to process. Sleeping with Leila is a huge deal. I need to find a way to give it context, to find out what it means. In a way, this was a first for me. The first time making love to someone while knowing I was going to die soon. It certainly made it more intense, but it also gave the whole night a melancholic quality I wasn't expecting.

"I have some things I have to take care of today, but..."

Leila has polished off her breakfast. She licks her lips like a cat licks its whiskers after a satisfying meal. "You made me hungry." She casts her gaze to me and, for a few moments, I feel bashful. Like I have something to hide—something to be ashamed of, even. "Sorry, continue." Even without makeup, she looks glamorous. She doesn't need the red lipstick to bring out the sparkle in her eyes. She definitely doesn't need it to enhance the beauty of her smile.

"Can I see you tonight?" I ask, my heart pounding as though she might say no. As though there's still a distinct possibility that she will go on the date she missed last night.

"I would love to see you tonight, Izzy." She runs a hand through her hair. "Do you want to come to my place? Give your staff some time off?" She bursts into a chuckle. "Maybe Harry needs some processing time on his own after last night."

"I'll be there."

"I promise I won't make you do any chores." She gives a hearty belly laugh now. I guess I deserved that.

As if on cue, Rian comes out of the kitchen to clear our plates.

CHAPTER 21

After Leila has left and Ira has done his daily check-in, I sit to continue my goodbye letter. It's important to me to work on it today, after my night with Leila, so that I can make clear to the loved ones I intend to leave behind that I'm not doing this on a whim. And that sleeping with another woman, no matter how spectacular, is not something that will change my mind. Of course I won't tell them about Leila. I will keep it vague. There's no need to torture them with details.

When I sit in front of my laptop, my screen is no longer blank. This is turning into an epic farewell note. I let my fingertips hover over the keyboard. Once I got myself into the groove of writing this very difficult letter, the words just seemed to come to me, as if they were sitting at the ready in the surrounding air for me to just pluck them and arrange them in a fashion that made sense. Today, though, I come up completely empty. I can't express what it is I want to say. That could mean my letter is done. I've said all I had to say. I check the word count again and it's already over four thousand words. I've never been economical with language. It's one of the reasons I never became a great lyricist. The songs I wrote would have been ten minutes long at least, if I had my way. When it came to the output of music, many people, for whom I was a money-generating machine, made sure I never had my way. But this is my final letter. I can write whatever I want in it. Today, my thoughts keep drifting. I keep starting a sentence, then deleting it.

But that's all right. I have time. 170 days. The letter will be ready. I will be ready. The difference with when I started this letter, however, is that if I had the option to take my life tomorrow, I wouldn't be able to do it. I need the time I have given myself to let this thing with Leila play itself out.

At the thought of seeing her again tonight, my heart does a little leap. My cheeks flush. My skin heats up. Because I want her, and she wants me too.

I will not be the kind of person who is saved by another woman, the sort who finds herself redeemed by love. On the contrary. I'm glad I get to experience this one last time, but the ferocity of it all is also defined by its limits. Whatever kind of affair Leila and I embark on has a very definite end date. She doesn't know this but that's the beauty of doing this with someone like Leila, someone who doesn't believe in endless, long-term love. Maybe that's part of what drew me to her as well.

I close my laptop, resigning myself to the fact that I won't add any new words to my goodbye letter today. Maybe I won't be able to do so for a while. Not until this book and my time with Leila are finished. But I'll have plenty of time after. For now, I will enjoy my dalliance with Leila as much as I can. I will, literally, make love to her as though it's the last time I will ever do so.

I reach for my phone and check Ramona's schedule. She

has a live running class in two hours. "I'll be there, Ramona," I say into the empty room.

I drift through my house with a spring in my step. I call Daisy and ask her to check in with Bruce's family and see when I can go visit him. Instead of asking Harry to fetch me a bottle of wine from the cellar, I go down myself and pick one to take to Leila's tonight. I hang out with Rian in the kitchen and ask if she can make tahdig sometime this week so I can reminisce about my first dinner at Leila's.

I end up in the music room and sit in front of the piano. My fingers are as hesitant as they were on my laptop earlier. I start and three times I fail to remember the intro to "Somewhere I've Never Been", one of my biggest hits. On stage, I always let a professional, much more gifted piano player than me, accompany me so I could focus on the high notes. So I could do what I loved to do more than anything. Sing my heart out. But I can play this song on the piano. I must have played it thousands of times, but my fingers are rusty. My muscle memory seems to have vanished. I try again and again, until it comes back to me. Until I can make it through half the song. Then I start again. Until I make it all the way through. The movement of my fingers over the keys brings back a certain sense of freedom, of expression, that I've missed so much. I might not be producing this music with my favorite instrument, my voice, but I'm producing music nonetheless.

It's not that I have avoided this room. I come in here quite often, but my lack of inspiration usually squashes my desire to keep on playing, to make the number of restarts—to make actual music. As though my fingers knew it was a lost cause.

Today is different. After a while, there's the same lightness to my fingers as there was in my step. And I'm no fool. I know it's because of Leila, because of how she made me feel last night. And this morning. And when she kissed me goodbye, her lips lingering like a promise of much more to come.

Next thing I know, I look around for the notepad I keep next to the piano, and I find myself jotting down a few lines of potential song lyrics.

CHAPTER 22

As soon as I walk through Leila's door, she pulls me to her and kisses me. The way her tongue sweeps into my mouth makes my legs go a little shaky.

"I'm happy to see you too," I say, through the enormous smile breaking on my face.

I hand her the bottle of wine. She studies the label with arched eyebrows.

"Wow," she says, then leads me into the den. "You're right. I could get used to this." She casts another glance at the label before putting the bottle on the table and coming for me again.

"It smells divine in here," I say.

"It's not just me," she jokes, before planting a kiss right next to my lips. "I'm making an old family recipe."

"Can't wait," I manage to say before Leila kisses me on the mouth again.

"You're going to have to wait a little while longer." Her lips trail a moist path to my ear. What has gotten into her? Not that I mind. I've been starved of this kind of touch—any kind of intimate touch, really—for years. I throw my head back, giving

Leila full access to my neck. Her hand catches in my hair. Her lips roam across my skin. The long dormant engine of desire she fully awoke last night is roaring into life again. I want her too. Everything about her is so very wantable, if that's even a word. But it describes her so well.

"Oh, Izzy," she moans into my ear. "You've barely walked in the door and all I want to do is rip your clothes off."

"I have no objections," I groan.

"I've been cooking all afternoon. I can't let my dish burn just because you make me as frisky as a teenage boy." She chuckles heartily. "Please tell me you're staying the night."

Try to kick me out, I think, after that hot and bothered welcome. "Depends how the evening goes, I guess." I try to sound a touch aloof but fail miserably.

"Sit. I'll make us an amaretto sour." She kisses me softly right next to my mouth and then finally puts a small distance between us. "I'm not sure I can do it as well as Harry, but I've been practicing." The flush on her cheeks is so adorable, I need to stop myself from reaching for her and pulling her close again.

"That sounds wonderful." The heat of her is overwhelming. I distance myself farther and take a seat in the plush green velvet couch. She grabs a bottle from the drinks cabinet and takes it into the kitchen.

Once she's out of sight, I take a breather. I hadn't expected Leila to be all over me like that from the get-go. Saying that she looked happy to see me sounds like the understatement of the century. I'm very pleased to see her as well, but I can't be as forward with my emotions.

I look around Leila's living room. The green couch I'm sitting in contrasts with the earthy beiges and dark oranges of the rest of her interior. Everything about it is just like her, though: warm and inviting. In hindsight, it now seems to me that Leila was impossible not to fall for.

"It's a little drier than I'd like it to be. I blame the kissing when you arrived," Leila says when she serves the food. "It's *fesenjān*. Pomegranate and walnut stew with chicken."

"It looks great."

"I'm sure your bottle of vintage wine will pair well with it." She grins at me. "Do you still know how to open a bottle of wine? There's a corkscrew behind you."

I roll my eyes at her dig. "I'm very skilled at it, I will have you know."

I manage to uncork the wine smoothly and pour us each a glass. Leila raises hers and tilts it toward me. "To..." She fixes her gaze on me. I feel it everywhere. "Us."

I clink rims with her while I consider what that means. Us? We shared a night together. Although there's much more to it than that. So I feel like I need to say something heartfelt as well.

"Do you want to join me for dinner at Vivian's on Friday? She's introducing me to her new girlfriend." It's all I can think of in the moment. And I texted Vivian earlier to ask if I could bring Leila. They need to meet soon, anyway.

Leila regards me with a funny expression on her face.

"What?" It isn't that odd a question. Leila has asked to meet Vivian.

"I would love to, but... I was just wondering how to classify it. Is it you introducing me to your best friend because we've slept together or is it you introducing me to someone I need to interview for the book?"

"Does it need to be one or the other?" The book is what

brought us together and it will keep us together until it's finished.

"No, but I was just curious as to how you saw it. It would be quite telling in many ways." She sips from the wine. Her full eyebrows lift. "Oh my god." She nods. "At the risk of repeating myself, I could so definitely get used to this. This wine is spectacular."

I take a sip. Maybe I should add drinking the best bottles from my wine cellar to my final to-do list as well. It hadn't even occurred to me. Maybe I can leave whatever's left to Leila.

"Izzy?"

"Yes?"

"Where did you go just now?" Leila asks.

"What do you mean? I'm right here."

"In your mind." She slants her head. "You do that sometimes. It's like you just check out for a few moments. It's a little disconcerting to witness."

"I'm sorry. I didn't realize. I was casting a mental glance over my wine cellar."

Leila's lips curl into a smile. "Please promise me you will take me into your cellar at the earliest possible convenience."

"Sure." I make a mental note to not look as though I'm 'checking out.' No one has ever mentioned me doing that before, but I don't spend that much time with anyone these days. Or maybe Leila just notices it more because it's her job to observe me. "Have you written any new chapters?" Unlike with what Bruce has written about me, I'm dying to know what Leila has come up with.

Leila picks up her cutlery. "I've made a lot of notes, but I haven't actually started writing yet. I've been working on Bruce's draft. I'm trying to get an appointment with him, but he's still not well enough. I don't want him to feel completely shut out of the project he's been working on for so long."

"Yeah. That's two years of his life."

"Still, maybe he can put it in perspective," Leila says. "The poor guy was in a coma. From what I hear, he has a long recovery ahead. Maybe he just feels lucky to be alive."

"It's so different with you, Leila." A blush rises from my neck to my cheeks. Damn it. "Not just because we slept together, but... your approach is so different."

"I'm a different person." She looks expectantly at the food on my fork.

I take a bite of rice and stew and the flavor explodes in my mouth. "Take it from someone who employs a professional chef, this is so tasty."

"I know. It's my grandmother's recipe. One of the very few things I managed to salvage from my family." There's so much confidence but also a hint of sadness in her tone. "I made this with her for the first time when I wasn't even ten years old."

"No wonder it's so good." I shovel another forkful into my mouth.

"Is now a good time to ask you about the surgery?"

"Really?" It's my first knee-jerk reaction.

"I have to ask you, Izzy." Leila doesn't sound apologetic at all.

"I know, but..." I want to say that the timing of this question tonight comes across as slightly manipulative, but I also know she's right. And does it really matter how we got here?

"Maybe it will make you feel better to talk about it."

I look at the scrumptious food on my plate and try to push away the queasiness in my stomach. It's been ten years, Izzy. Woman up. Besides, there are no secrets here. Leila has copies of most of my medical files. She just wants to hear me say it in my own words.

"I had nodules on my vocal cords. It was supposed to be a

pretty routine operation. But let's just say the surgeon had a really bad day."

Leila nods. She keeps on eating. Maybe the food was meant to be comforting. Maybe that's why I'm here tonight. That's why she greeted me so lovingly earlier. To get me in the right frame of mind to share with her.

"He managed to remove the nodules, but he had to work on a bigger part of my cords than expected. The resulting scarring was much more extensive than anticipated. Even though the medics said the initial operation was pretty routine and standard, there were always risks, of course. I was made aware of that, but I didn't really think about the risks that much at the time. I only focused on being able to sing properly again. Only, I never could."

"Ten years later and it's still beyond repair?"

I can see why Leila has won so many awards.

I nod. "If there was the tiniest chance of fixing it, I would know about it. I just got extremely unlucky. It's the only explanation. There was a ninety percent success rate. I'm part of the other ten. I saw just about every specialist in the world after the surgery, in the hope they could do something. But even if they removed the scarred part of the cords, there wouldn't have been enough left for me to ever sing again. At least not like before." I shrug. "I guess I should consider myself lucky that I can still speak. It can always be worse, right?"

"Not if you're Isabel Adler." Leila's voice is warm with empathy.

I try to eat a little more. To my surprise, it's not that hard. Maybe I don't feel that sorry for myself anymore. Besides, all this will be over soon. This might very well be the last time I tell the story. And Leila's dish is delicious.

"How did you feel when you were told?"

"Like my life was over. Like I wanted to die right there and then. Like I wished the surgeon had nicked an artery instead and I had bled out on the operating table." It sounds a bit too gloomy for the occasion. But it is the truth. "I know I've always been privileged, but no longer being able to sing... it's like endlessly prolonged torture."

Leila doesn't interrupt. She just lets me speak.

"I went through all the regular stages of grief. In the end, I had no choice but to accept it. All the money in the world wasn't going to bring back my voice."

"Sometimes it's hard to believe it's been ten years."

"Time flies... even when you're not having fun."

"Does it, really?" Leila asks.

"God, no. The past ten years have just been..." A grueling slog. A constant reminder of what I used to be able to do and will never do again. A downhill slide from being someone at the top of her game to a pathetic has-been. An ever-increasing drift into loneliness. Until I first had the idea to no longer live like this. That I don't have to go through this any longer if I don't want to. "It's been hard," I say drily.

"Thank you for sharing that with me." Leila puts her fork down. I drop mine as well. She should have waited to ask me about my surgery until I'd finished eating. The emotion has fully caught up with me and settled in my stomach, filling it to the brim. "You must have received a lot of support from your fans," she says.

"Sure, but it didn't change anything. And once you realize that the singer you've always loved will never sing for you again..."

"But your fandom is alive and kicking, Izzy."

"Only as a nostalgic tribute to my former greatness."

"I can see why you would look at it like that, but that's not the impression I got when I joined a few of the hundreds of Facebook groups dedicated to you. You're not just anyone, Izzy.

The music you made has been there with people at their weddings, birthdays, even the funerals of loved ones. You sang the kind of songs that were made for important moments. People always stay attached to that in some way."

"That might be true and I'm grateful for that, but it doesn't change the fact that I will never sing any of those songs again." More than half of Daisy's time is taken up with replying to fan messages in my name.

"What do you miss most? The stage or the actual singing?" Leila asks.

I huff out some air. "Both. The combination of the two is unbeatable for the best natural high. The energy you can get back from a crowd of people singing along to a song you're performing..." I pause to shake my head. "There's nothing like it. Absolutely nothing."

"Better than sex?" she asks.

I chuckle, because I think it's a joke, but when I look at Leila's face, I can't find a smile. Not even one of the mischievous grins she specializes in. Is she really being serious? "Well, I mean..." I feel like I have some explaining to do, even though, deep down, I do know better. "You can't really compare. It's—"

"I'm kidding, Izzy." She leans forward and reaches out her hand to me. "I've been part of that crowd and it was magical for me as well. Bruce described it so vividly in his first draft. I haven't touched those chapters."

I should really read Bruce's draft. Vivian's been raving about it in a bunch of text messages. I take Leila's hand in mine and the comfort is immediate. She closes her fingers around my palm and we sit in silence for a few moments.

"Earlier today..." I whisper it instead of saying it out loud. Leila's looking at our intertwined hands, which makes it easier. "I was playing the piano and some new lyrics came to me."

In response, Leila's hand intensifies its grip on mine. "Maybe," she says, "when you have music inside you as some kind of primal energy, it never really goes away. It can hide, but it will never fully disappear." Her voice is so soothing. Her hands are so soft.

"Maybe." I lift her hand and plant a soft kiss on her palm. "Or maybe what we did last night helped free some of that hidden primal energy."

"Maybe sex can be useful in that way." She smiles but her voice is low and solemn.

I lock my gaze on her and, as I do, suck her fingertip between my lips.

"How about we put that to the test again?" something changes in Leila's eyes. We both know what's going to happen next: I'll swiftly be introduced to her bedroom.

"Work up a bit more of an appetite as well." I'm the first one to rise. I keep Leila's hand in mine, but I let her guide us. After what we just talked about, and the ball that settled in the pit of my stomach, I hadn't expected to be up for this so quickly. But that's what Leila does to me.

I was right this morning when I concluded it couldn't possibly be a one-night stand. It's already so much more because of what I've just told her. All of it is already so intertwined. Could I have told her if we hadn't slept together? Could I ever have told Bruce? I will never know. All I know, as Leila leads me to her bedroom, is that the days I have given myself seem to be running away from me at a much quicker pace than ever before.

CHAPTER 23

I haven't woken up in someone else's bed in a very long time. It must still be dark outside because I can't see a thing. I feel Leila's presence beside me. I hear her soft breath. Once my eyes get used to the darkness, I can't help but run a finger over her upper arm, as though the force field between our bodies is too strong to withstand. I need to touch her.

I also need to end this soon. Or I need to work out some sort of protocol for myself. Draw a line. It can go this far, but absolutely no farther. I need to find the boundary that I can't possibly let her cross, and then stick to it. I very much wanted to sleep with Leila and she made herself the ideal candidate to be my final bed partner because of how she presented herself to me, as someone who enjoys a loose fling, someone who's up for a few nights together before moving on, but also someone who, ultimately, prefers her own company most of all. But how she makes me feel is unsettling. On top of that, I don't want to be unfair to her. At the very least, we need to have a conversation about expectations.

I push myself up and look around the room. She doesn't have an alarm clock and I don't wear a watch. I'm suddenly overwhelmed by the urge to get out of Leila's bedroom, out of her apartment. Maybe even out of her life, because being here, now, is bringing up some complicated emotions I'm not sure how to deal with.

On the other hand, maybe this is exactly what I need to be sure of what I want to do. I've been certain about my future path for such a long time, I haven't questioned it. I haven't felt the need. The prospect of dying always felt like such a relief. Nothing much has changed. Sure, I like Leila, but she isn't going to give me my voice back. Sure, I might even be capable of falling in love with her, but that will only become another emotion I can't express. Sure, starting something with her that lasts beyond a few nights together, if such a thing is even in the cards for us, may offer me some temporary relief from my demons, but they will always come back. Fundamentally, even being with someone as glorious as Leila won't change anything about why I have chosen to die.

I'm wide awake. There's no way I'm falling asleep again any time soon. I consider my options. Waking Leila for another round of earth-shattering sex and then, exhausted, falling asleep in her arms. Or making a quiet, quick escape. It shouldn't take my driver that long to get here in the middle of the night, even though I didn't ask him to be on standby, so certain was I of spending the entire night with Leila. However, the thought of her waking up to an empty bed later doesn't appeal to me very much. I want to be here when she opens her eyes. When she stretches her body after the gymnastics I put it through earlier. I want to see that smile on her face explode into a grin when she looks at me. Damn. It might very well be that this is exactly what I need to fully test myself one last time, but nevertheless, it's a pain in my ass. It's an unexpected hurdle—it's the perfect example of how life is.

I slide back under the covers. When Leila turns on her

side away from me, I snuggle up to her. I press myself against her warm, soft body. The comfort of it is almost enough to chase the morbid thoughts from my mind, but I'm so used to dealing with and accepting my own mortality by now, that I end up ruminating for the next hour. I don't let go of her, though. I listen to her breathing. It's punctuated by a gentle snore every so often that delights the hell out of me.

The next time I open my eyes, sunlight peeks beneath the curtains, but Leila's still asleep. How I envy her talent for sleeping. I must have caught a few more winks myself because, while I don't feel super refreshed, it's as though my brain has worked through some stuff during the night and I have a better idea of how to let this play out.

I'll just enjoy it while it lasts.

Now that I've started telling Leila about my botched surgery, I'm fairly certain I can give her all the information she needs to finish my biography in the next few weeks. After which, I suspect, she'll work on the book for a few months—an ideal opportunity to restore the distance between us.

I also realize I'm not the only person in this bed. I will ask her what she wants and whether she has any expectations at all. I can adjust my plan to whatever it is she has to say about how she sees this thing between us evolve. My days are numbered, but I can still be flexible.

"The options for breakfast are rather limited," Leila says. "And we have to prepare it ourselves." She shoots me a wink.

We polished off most of the food Leila prepared last night between bouts of lovemaking, so I'm not that hungry.

"Or... we could go out. There's this place just around the corner where I often go for a croissant and a coffee. The croissants are so buttery, you'd think you're in Paris when you bite into one."

My ears perk up. Is she testing me? Or does she really just want to go out, not caring that she'd be walking around with me and attracting the kind of attention I very much try to avoid.

"Just coffee is fine for me."

"I don't want to push you, Izzy. And I don't mean to imply I know what it feels like for you to step outside the safety of your house, but this is New York City. People just go about their business. I bet no one will even look at us twice. And as I said, it's very close by."

"It's not that," I lie, although I get a feeling that venturing outside with Leila by my side would make me feel less exposed than I usually do. "I'd like to talk to you about something and I need it to be in private."

"Okay. Let me make some coffee first then."

I watch her shuffle around the small kitchen. She's barefoot and dressed only in a nightdress. It's pale pink and it makes her look like she's come from another world to tempt me—to change my mind about the most important decision of my life.

Once we're both huddled around the kitchen table with steaming mugs in our hands, I start, "I lay awake last night wondering... what your expectations are. Of this. Of us."

"We slept together twice." She locks her gaze on me. "It's really hard to say at this point. I like you. A lot. I love being around you. I love getting to know you better. I love seeing the real you. But as far as expectations go... I don't know if I have any."

"I'm not asking you to predict the future, but..." As far as I'm concerned, there is no future to predict. "You told me certain things about yourself which led me to believe you're not really looking for anything too serious. Which is fine. I'm not looking for that at all. Maybe... we should see this as a time-constrained fling. Something that lasts only as long as you're working on the book."

"Okay." She puts her mug down and tilts her head. "Are you asking me if that's what I want or are you telling me that's what you want?"

"I just don't want there to be any upset between us because we raised our expectations too high." I'm getting an inkling that I went about this all wrong. Maybe this is what happens when you push people away for years, when you don't let anyone in or, heaven forbid, come too close. Until someone does manage to sneak in, past all the walls you've put up.

"Why don't you tell me all about your *low* expectations then." Leila's tone isn't as warm anymore.

Partial honesty is all I can give her. "I haven't met anyone like you in a long time, Leila. Being with you has... overwhelmed me. I'm not used to this anymore. Therefore, I don't think I have any expectations. I guess I just want you to know that I don't expect anything from you."

"Oh, Izzy." She shakes her head. "This isn't about expectations. We're just two women getting to know each other and enjoying the process. Why does it have to be anything else? Why can't we just see where it goes naturally?"

"Because..." I look away from her burning gaze. I can't say any more. "I have my reasons."

"Is it the thing you told me you were going through but you can't talk to me about?"

"Yes."

"You don't have to tell me everything." She cups her hands around mine. "You've already told me so much."

"I can never tell you everything," I blurt out.

"That's perfectly fine, Izzy." Leila squeezes my hands.

"Although the journalist in me does find it extremely intriguing."

For the first time, I dare to look her straight in the eye with the thought of my death so prominently at the forefront of my mind. I can only hold her gaze for a second. The two are incompatible. The sight of Leila's delightful features and the number of days ticking away in my head. The seconds I have left seem to go faster when I'm with her. At the very least, I'm going to have to write her a letter. Or I will have to try, because I'm not sure whether I can.

"I wish I could explain it to you, but I can't."

"Maybe now that you've jotted down those lyrics, you could try writing a song about it." Leila's hands are still wrapped around mine. I'm still connected to her warmth. Yet what she's saying makes me want to pull away. She doesn't let me, though. She keeps her hands firmly entangled with mine.

"What would I do with a new song?"

"I have a few ideas about that, but I'm not sure you're ready to hear them," Leila says.

I quirk up my eyebrows. "Seriously?"

Leila nods. Then a grin appears on her face. "You will need at least a dozen more orgasms before I can tell you."

I burst out laughing. "Maybe we should go back to bed then."

"As much as I would love that, I have a meeting in an hour and a half." She gazes deep into my eyes. I couldn't turn away from her now if I tried. "But I promise you that we'll get to it very soon."

CHAPTER 24

Jade looks even younger in real life than in the picture Vivian showed me. She hugs me like I'm a long-lost friend. Her energy is relaxed and friendly. Long dreadlocks cascade down her back. She gives Leila the same warm greeting.

"Jax is sleeping over at Shawn's," Vivian says, her tone tinged with a touch of nerves.

"Too much female energy for a boy his age," Jade jokes. There's almost thirty years between her and Vivian. Although she seems kind and lovely at first sight, it's hard for me to see this ending well—because I've seen this kind of thing between Vivian and a much younger woman go south a few too many times.

"Check this out, Iz," Vivian escorts me and Leila to the bookshelf in the den. She points at a finely carved wooden sculpture of a naked woman in an exuberant dance pose. "Jade made it."

"Wow," Leila says. "That's stunning. Can I touch it?" She glances at Jade and they share a look.

Jade nods. Leila picks up the carved statue and runs her

finger over the fine grooves that are carved along the woman's body.

"I'd like to buy one of these," Leila says.

"Aw, you don't have to say that." Jade stands there beaming with pride.

"I'm serious. I want one of these in my home." All of Leila's attention seems to be absorbed by Jade and her sculpture. It must be the journalist in her. Maybe she's already preparing a piece about Jade in her head.

Vivian pulls me away from them a fraction. "What do you think?"

I chuckle at her eagerness, even though I could ask her the same question about Leila. "First impression is certainly great," I whisper.

Vivian smiles from ear to ear. She really does have it bad. It's plastered all over her face. I wonder if she can see anything on mine regarding my feelings for Leila.

"Not doing too badly yourself," Vivian whispers back. "Such presence." She nods approvingly.

"They're judging us," Jade says. She and Leila have turned back toward us. "Like we're pieces of steak at the meat market." Her smile is the kind that can light up the darkest room. I searched for her classes on the Olympian app but I haven't been able to find any. I make a mental note to ask her about that later.

"Who can blame them," Leila says, in that self-possessed way she has that, somehow, never comes across as conceited.

Giggling like schoolgirls, we sit while Vivian pours us her favorite sauvignon blanc.

"If I may address the elephant in the room," Jade says, pinning her gaze on me. For a split second, I think she means the age gap between her and Vivian. Maybe it's because I'm out with Leila that I feel less self-conscious, and that, for a few instants, I forget who I am—or used to be. "I don't mean to go all fangirl on you, Isabel, but I literally grew up on your music. My mom may very well be your biggest fan in the whole wide world." It's one way of addressing the age gap, I guess. Jade's mother must be the same age as Vivian, Leila and me. "She may pass out if I send her a selfie with you."

"Sure. Anything to help a mother lose consciousness," I quip, while hoping that Vivian has instructed her latest conquest to not quiz me about 'what happened'. Knowing Vivian, I'm sure she will have.

"It's truly an honor," Jade says while tapping her hand against her chest. "When I met Vivian, I had no idea she was *that* Vivian."

"You wouldn't have played so hard to get if you'd known," Vivian says.

"No, darling. I could so tell you were getting off on it." Jade returns her full focus to Vivian.

I exchange a glance with Leila who sends me a small smile. As always, I can never tell if she's enjoying this on a purely personal level or if she's secretly stashing away every experience she has with me to use in the book later. Probably a bit of both. It seems to be the undercurrent of our affair.

"It's been very hard keeping this one away from Bruce's draft." Vivian points her thumb at Jade. "At one point, I thought I would actually have to lock it in my safe." She snickers.

"Don't worry. I know it's top secret," Jade says seriously. "And I reckon I will get an early copy once it's ready." She turns to Leila. "Has it been hard for you to step in this late in the process?"

"I wouldn't say hard." Leila puts her hand on my knee. "It's been nothing short of exhilarating."

My heart couldn't melt any more than it just did. I

remember what I said to Vivian the last time I was here about not wanting to fall in love. Maybe it's already too late.

"That time when you brought Bruce around for dinner, he most certainly didn't speak about you in this way, Iz," Vivian says. "Nor did he put his hand on your knee."

There are chuckles all around and for the next hour, as we lounge in Vivian's den and chat about this and that, just four women talking, something happens that has, so far, only occurred when I have found myself in bed with Leila, totally under her spell. I forget how many days I have left. I forget about my plan to die altogether. When the notion hits me again, it's so disconcerting, I go quiet for a while.

"Who's Ramona?" Leila asks. "Izzy?"

"What?" Why is Leila asking me about Ramona?

Leila leans into me and whispers, "You did that thing again where you space out."

"Sorry." So much for paying attention to no longer doing that. "I'm back." I give them all my widest smile.

"Ramona?" Leila's full, dark eyebrows are raised all the way up.

Vivian and Jade are the very personification of glee.

"She's my fitness instructor. On the Olympian app," I stammer.

"You're very H-O-T fitness instructor," Vivian adds.

"She's my former colleague *and* friend," Jade says. "I concur that she's rather pleasing to the eye."

"Is that why you're so fit, Izzy?" There's definite amusement in Leila's tone.

"One of the reasons, I guess. It's not because the instructor is hot that you don't have to put in the actual work. It's just... extra motivating." There's an easy way to divert the attention from the blooming blush on my cheeks. "Jade, when I looked for your classes on the app, I couldn't find any."

"Oh, yeah, they've been taken down. They prefer to only offer recorded classes with current instructors."

"Really?" Maybe I should have hidden the panic in my voice a bit more. "Why?" Then it hits me that it doesn't matter. By the time Ramona ever leaves Olympian and her classes disappear, I'll be long gone as well.

"It's policy," Jade says. "Maybe you should ask Ramona." She follows up with a grin. "I told her you were a, uh, *fan* of her work. She got a real kick out of that."

"Next time you do a workout, I think I'll watch." Leila's grip on my knee intensifies.

"Nuh-uh." I give her a defiant look. "You can only be in the room if you join in." My mind drifts back to my workout earlier today. Ramona doesn't teach a live class every day, so I had to settle for a previously recorded one. I picked an interval running workout I've done dozens of times because of how Ramona addresses us in it, with such lust for life and vigor. The irony of that is never lost on me, but I can't help returning to it, as though Ramona is somehow helping me to squeeze the very last drop of juice out of life before I shuffle off this mortal coil.

Leila waves off my comment. "I'd rather take a walk outside than run myself ragged on an indoor treadmill."

"I'm with you," Vivian says. "Maybe we can take a walk together some time, while these two sweat indoors."

"I would love that." Instantly, Leila's tone of voice changes. I'm starting to pick up on it. It's not just her voice that changes. Something in her demeanor changes as well when she goes into investigative mode. "How does Monday sound?"

I let Leila set up a rendezvous with Vivian while I glance at Jade. If only Vivian didn't have such a bad track record with these twenty- and thirty-somethings she keeps having flings with. If only I could have the certainty of leaving her with someone I know won't break her heart. Although I guess that's never a certainty. At least she'll always have Jackson. And who knows, maybe things with Jade will be different. They seem very smitten with each other, but I've seen that before. I return my attention to the conversation before I space out again, feeling very pleased with myself for having the awareness to do so.

Before dinner, Jade and I take a few pictures on her phone, and I make her promise the snaps will only be sent to her mother, even though I know it's not something I can control. Her mother might send them to her friends or, even worse, post them on social media. But I can at least ask.

"Oh my god, I shouldn't have sent this to her now. I'm so sorry." Jade's phone keeps lighting up with messages. "Mom's going nuts."

"We can call her if you like." Maybe it's the wine, or another effect of having Leila by my side. Or maybe I just want to put a stop to it. Or, just maybe, I'm ready for some enthusiastic adoration, even though the reason Jade's mother adores me no longer exists.

Both Vivian and Jade's eyes grow wide. "For real?" Jade asks.

"Sure. If she's such a fan, I owe her a lot."

"You're going to make her year." Jade is already reaching for her phone. "Her decade. Possibly her life. I'm not kidding you with this shit, Isabel. She asked my dad to play your music while she was giving birth to me."

"Well, then do tell her we'll call her after dinner." I throw in a smile. It's not the most far-fetched event where my music has been played.

"Thank you so much, Isabel."

"Please, call me Izzy."

"Is that true?" Vivian asks after Jade has given her mother

the news of our impending call via text. "That Izzy's music was playing when your mother gave birth to you?"

"You bet your sweet ass, babe. I've only had to hear about it a million times. Obviously, I don't remember, but 'Right Here in My Heart' was the very first song I ever heard." She sends me a crooked smile.

"'Right Here in My Heart'?" I ask. "That's an old B-side from back in the day when B-sides were still a thing."

"I told you, my mom is your biggest fan. She knows every song you've ever recorded. She has been to at least two concerts of every single tour."

I haven't been faced with that level of fan devotion for a long time. But I'm also bracing myself for what will, inevitably, come next. *She was devastated when she heard you lost your voice.*

"She's looking forward to your biography so much. If I can get her a signed copy, I think she might give me my inheritance early." Jade chuckles. "Honestly, sometimes I think the woman loves you more than she loves me, her own daughter."

"Her love for Izzy hasn't faded over the years?" Leila asks.

"Hell no." Jade shakes her head. "Not one single bit." She looks at me for a beat. I brace myself for *that* question again.

"I told you." Leila turns to me. What is she doing?

Opposite me, I notice Vivian stiffen.

"I told you that your fandom is alive and kicking," Leila continues.

"Of course it is," Jade adds. "It's not because you're no longer recording that..."

Vivian must have nudged her foot under the table, because she stops speaking abruptly.

"I'm sorry." Jade averts her gaze. "Anyway, Mom will be thrilled to her very core."

"It's okay." Maybe it's because I've had the conversation about losing my voice with Leila, but I actually mean it. "Your mom will get her signed copy of my biography as well, of course." I lean into Leila a little. "If you play your cards right, maybe you can even get the author to sign it."

Leila chuckles. "I know my place when it comes to this. Nobody will want *my* autograph."

"Have you written any other biographies?" Vivian asks, and with that, the moment of possible tension passes. If I had decided to flee the table because of Jade's harmless remark, it wouldn't have been the first time. But I stayed. I didn't run from what her remark inferred. I didn't relive the devastation, all those years of pain crammed into a few seconds as I remember what my voice sounded like the last time I tried to sing.

The rest of the evening is more than pleasant, what with making Jade's mother's year and having Leila by my side. Vivian and I haven't been on a double date in a very long time and it somehow feels right. By the time we leave, I have even changed my mind about Jade. Maybe her relationship with my best friend will last. Maybe Vivian won't need a shoulder to cry on after I'm gone.

CHAPTER 25

Leila and I settle into the back of the car.

"Yours or mine? Or do we go our separate ways for the night?" I ask her.

"Yours," Leila says without hesitation, as though it was always a done deal that she would come back to mine tonight.

"Getting used to certain luxuries?" I joke, after I've asked the driver to take us to my house.

"More like addicted to your company." Leila slips a hand between my thighs—high enough to make all my nerve endings stand to attention, but not touching me too inappropriately yet.

With the press of a button, I close the tinted glass panel that separates the driver's seat from the back.

"I like Vivian and Jade," Leila says. "Thank you for taking me to meet them." Her hand snakes up a little.

"What are you do—"

Leila doesn't wait for me to finish my question before moving her hand decidedly toward the apex of my thighs.

"Just checking in." She sends me a wicked grin. "It was fun

to see you in the company of other people. It always sheds a different light."

I can't help but spread my legs a little wider. Leila is not someone I can deny access to that part of me.

"It was very sweet what you did for Jade's mom." A fingertip slides along the crotch of my pants. "I honestly hadn't expected you to do that." Leila slants toward me and her lips find the skin just below my ear. "I thought you were more of a diva." I feel her chuckle more than I hear it—a warm expulsion of breath on my neck.

"My diva days are long gone."

"So you keep saying." Next, she sinks her teeth gently into my earlobe, while her fingertip keeps meandering back and forth. "Now tell me all about Ramona."

I'm the one who chuckles now. I'm happy to release some tension. "Are you jealous of a woman I only see on a screen?"

"Not jealous, just curious." Her finger retreats a little. "What does she look like?" She kisses my neck softly.

"I'll show you when we get home." I turn my face toward Leila and pull her in for a kiss. Whether it's jealousy or curiosity doesn't matter. What it tells me is that she must feel the same way about me that I do about her.

"I'll show you something else first." When we break from our kiss, Leila smiles, but only briefly, before her face goes all serious and solemn again and she kisses me deeply. Her fingertip means business as well as she circles it around my throbbing clit. There's too much fabric between us, but I'm not the kind of woman to take her pants off in the back of a car. Or should I add climaxing in the back of a car to my bucket list? The thought disappears automatically because I couldn't care less about my final to-do list right now. I just want to feel more of Leila's finger. I want it high inside of me while her tongue dances in my mouth.

Mercifully, the car comes to a complete stop. Thank goodness I didn't unzip my pants.

"We're here," the driver announces, his voice muffled from behind the divider.

Leila bursts into laughter and it's contagious, as is so much about her. As I exit the car, I realize that what Leila does like no other, like no one else has done for me over this past decade, is, very simply, make me feel good about myself. She makes me see the joy in small things, like slipping her hand between my thighs, like teasing me about Ramona.

I'm not sure how we make it to my bedroom without tearing each other's clothes off—maybe Harry opening the door to us has something to do with that. Leila chats with him for a bit, while all I want is to drag her upstairs.

"Time to finish what you started," I whisper in her ear.

"Maybe this weekend I can have a chat with Harry," she says.

I stand in front of her and place my palms on her temples. "Turn off your work brain. Now."

"You are my work, Izzy. Let me do my job, please." She grins and pulls me near for another kiss. The next thing I know, I'm half undressed in my bedroom and Leila's finger is back at it, with much less fabric as a barrier this time.

She draws lazy circles over my panties. When I tried to tug them off me earlier, she wouldn't let me.

Her lips find my nipple—my bra was allowed to come off —and she sucks it deep into her mouth. One of my knees is sandwiched between her legs, giving her unfettered access.

Her body glued to mine is all soft warmth again. I could call it heat but it's not the same. It's more than that. The way in which I want Leila is more than years of pent-up friskiness being let loose. It's not just her glorious body I want. It's all of her. Her conversation. The way she gently needles me. The way she dares to confront me even though she's only known me for such a short time. The way she can seem in awe of me sometimes but also treats me as if I was always just Izzy, and not Isabel Adler. The way she goes silent sometimes, maybe to consider her own pain and the people she has lost.

"Leila, please." I know that she likes it when I beg a little. She gets off on that feeling of control, that much I've learned. "You make me so hot."

"Let's see exactly how hot." That's another thing about Leila. The confidence with which she carries herself in the world effortlessly translates into the bedroom.

Finally, she lowers my panties. She glances down between my legs. Her mere gaze sends another round of furious throbbing through my clit.

I can see her swallow hard. I love how she's never shy with her emotions. She's so unafraid to show herself to me fully.

At last, after the torture in the car and on the bed, I can feel the magical touch of her finger against my heat. With her other hand, she pushes up my knee so my leg is bent, exposing me to her farther.

Her finger slides through my wetness, up to my clit. I exhale sharply when I feel her finger touch me there. It's a sigh of relief at first, but not for long. The fire inside me—the fire that died a long time ago—lights up again at her deft touch. It's as though she already knows how to play me so well. Like when I play the piano and muscle memory kicks in. But Leila plays me much better than I play an instrument.

I might no longer be able to sing with my voice, but my heart sings when she touches me like this. When her finger slips down and skirts along my entrance, before pushing high inside of me. She goes so deep from the get-go, and because my leg is bent, it's as though I can feel it even deeper, I can feel more of her. Her finger retreats briefly, only to be replaced with two of them. Again, they slide inside me slowly but oh so deeply. As Leila's fingers fill me there, I feel another part of me fill up as well. The part of me that doesn't want to die. I don't know if it has been here all along. I don't even know if it's real. As long as Leila's fingers are inside me, it doesn't matter, because she's with me—she's in me—and I'm not alone. When she's with me, I don't have to face my biggest demons. Life is infinitely lighter with Leila by my side. I feel so light right now, it's like I'm floating. Her fingers stroke me and my whole being lights up.

"I want you to come for me, Izzy," she whispers. Her voice is low but insistent. "For *me*," she says, emphasis on the 'me'. When she has her fingers inside me like that, there's nothing I wouldn't do for her.

I don't know how Leila got this inexplicable power over me, but, for her, right now, I will come. It's hardly a big ask. I was already so revved up from when she touched me in the car, but still, for me, it's a lot. Not so much physically, but emotionally, to react to another woman, another human, so eagerly, so willingly, so in need of this intimate connection.

My head is thrown back, my eyes shut with pleasure, so I don't see how she bends toward me and kisses the inside of my thigh. I feel it though. The touch of her lips sends me right over the edge. With all I have, I clench myself around her fingers, clasping them in the spot where it feels so good, where they make me think that this is something to discard all my plans for, because isn't this the very stuff that life is made of? That makes it worth living, no matter what has happened before?

I come hard around her fingers, my body convulsing as if in pain. But this is not pain. The muscle tremors are caused by an onslaught of tears. Oh, for crying out loud—quite literally. Not now. But if not now, then when? My emotions are all over the place. Because as much as I want to pretend I don't, as much as I want to bask in Leila's attention, and that lovely smile on her lips, I do have a decision to make. One that's already ripping me to shreds inside.

She wraps me in her arms, holding my head against her breasts. "Hey," she whispers. "It's okay, Izzy."

It's not, I think. I can't fall in love with you. Even if I were to ultimately decide to not go through with my plan to die, it still wouldn't be fair. What kind of start to a relationship would that be?

She kisses me on the top of my head and rocks me back and forth a little. "What is with you and orgasms?" she says more than asks. "That they make you fall apart like this?"

It's not the orgasms, I think but can't say. It's you. Then I shuffle upward until my lips find hers so I no longer have to be subjected to questions I can only answer with lies.

CHAPTER 26

That night, despite Leila exhausting me, I don't sleep a wink. Once I'm certain Leila's asleep, I get up, throw on some clothes, and quietly sneak out of the room.

I go into my office and re-read the letter I've been working on. Every word I've written—and I've written so many by now, although I haven't added any since Leila and I first slept together—still rings true. My reasons for wanting to end my life haven't changed. Right now, it feels like I'm falling in love, but am I even still capable of that? I am, after all, a woman who has been plotting her own death for the better part of the past five years. Even if I were able to develop those kinds of feelings for someone else, it wouldn't matter. Falling in love isn't going to bring my voice back. It isn't magically going to give me back my creative expression—the one thing I crave like no other.

When I reach the end of the letter, I heave a big sigh, because I know what I have to do. I have to end it with Leila before it goes too far, before I fall too deeply. For both our sakes.

It doesn't mean I have to tell her about my plan, about the days ticking away in my head. About how the mere thought of that, ironically, makes me feel more alive. I will need a plausible reason, however. Leila's not the kind of woman who will settle for some vague explanation.

The only thing I can think of is to tell her that I'm not enjoying her company in that way. That I'd like to go back to the more businesslike subject/biographer relationship we used to have, if we ever had that at all. I immediately dismiss this as the least plausible of excuses.

A knock on the door startles me.

"Izzy?" Leila appears in the doorway, her face sleep-wrinkled but as gorgeous as ever. "Are you okay? What are you doing?" She rubs her eyes. "Are you writing?"

I quickly close my laptop. "No, just... um, no."

Leila walks farther into the room. "You couldn't sleep?"

I shake my head. "Not really used to sharing the bed just yet." The kindness in her eyes is already breaking my heart. If I'm going to do this, maybe I should just do it now. Get it over with. Rip off the Band-Aid. I point at the armchair next to my desk. "Can we talk?"

"Always." She pulls the robe she must have found on the back of the bedroom door tighter around her. I can see the curve of her breast peek through the opening at the top.

"I've hinted a few times at something that I'm dealing with," I begin. "Something I'm going through at the moment."

She nods thoughtfully, her chin resting on an upturned palm. She looks very engaged for someone who just woke up.

"It's because of that, that I..." Oh Christ. This is so hard to say. But I need to push through. It will only hurt for a little while. In any case, no longer than 168 days. "I can't do this with you, Leila. I'm sorry."

"Can't do what? The biography? Or… be with me?"

I don't care about the biography, I want to scream, but that would only hurt her more. She's proved to be very invested in my life story. "Be with you. It's…" It's absolutely impossible for me to lie to her face and tell her that I don't have feelings for her. She would see through that in a heartbeat.

"Correct me if I'm wrong, but that's not the impression I got," she says.

"I don't want to hurt you, Leila. I don't know how to explain this, but I know, more than I know anything else, that you and I shouldn't be together."

"With all due respect to whatever it is you're dealing with, but you owe me more than that as an explanation."

I swallow the emotion out of my throat. I have all the words I can't say to her in a document on my laptop and my laptop is sitting right next to me. I reach for it. I hold it against me for a moment. Am I really doing this? Right now, it feels like I have no other choice. Sharing my letter with someone else before my death was never the plan, yet here I am. Yet another event in my life that didn't go according to plan.

"On this laptop, there's a letter." My voice breaks. "It explains everything." I hand Leila the laptop. I might as well be handing her my life. "I'll be in the music room next door." I stand. "After you've read this, you may want to leave. I will fully understand." My heart beats furiously in my chest. "You don't owe me anything, Leila. Don't feel as though you do because I'm sharing this with you."

I watch her as she glances at the laptop. Then I can't take it anymore. I need to get out of this room.

Gently, I close the door behind me and go into the music room. I sit on the piano stool, but I don't play. Making any sort of noise feels inappropriate. My gaze falls on the notebook I scribbled some lyrics in the other day. I fight back the impulse to just crumple up the paper and toss it away. From years of performing, I know what nervous stress is and that's exactly what's coursing through me right now.

I try to calm myself by calculating how long it might take Leila to read and process the letter. Ten minutes? Fifteen? And once she's done, will she actually leave? Do I want her to? Do I regret this already? A little bit. But I don't regret meeting Leila. Hard as it may be, having to come clean to her about wanting to die was worth every second with her. She wouldn't be reading that letter, the most intimate, vulnerable thing I've ever written—in a way, perhaps, my final emotional performance—if it wasn't.

I cast my gaze about the room. On the walls, there are pictures of me from every one of my tours. In every single one of them, I look happy. Satisfied. Ecstatic. Because I was doing what I loved and did best. At least with Leila reading the letter, I won't have to use my voice to explain it all to her. One small mercy.

Only a few hours ago, my head was buried between Leila's legs. Another high followed by another low. That's exactly the emotional roller-coaster I'm trying to get off of. There's a noise. Is that her moving about in the next room? My throat goes dry. It would be helpful if I could somehow determine what I really want at this very moment. I figure it could be very telling. It could guide me in making my decision. Because, and this I can admit to myself, my decision does feel less final now. But I can't let it depend on Leila. That's not the kind of pressure to put on someone I like.

Why did Bruce have to mount his horse that day? I shake my head. Poor Bruce. I still haven't been able to see him.

What happened to the noise next door? I strain my ears. I sit stock-still and hold my breath. I don't hear anything. Then, making me start although completely expected, the softest of knocks comes on the door.

"Yes," I try to say, but my speaking voice doesn't seem to be working anymore either. I clear my throat. "Yes." It comes out all croaked but at least I made a sound.

The door opens, and Leila's there. Tears are streaming down her face. Her arms are clutched around the laptop.

"Izzy," she manages to say. "I had no idea you were in such pain." She wipes the back of her hand across her cheek.

The sight of her crumbling like that breaks something inside of me. No, no, no. This was never my intention. But of course this was going to hurt her.

With the last ounce of energy I can muster, I hurry over to her. I wiggle the laptop out of her arms and put it to the side. "I'm not in pain," I say. If this is her first reaction, maybe I haven't adequately explained that in my letter. Maybe I need to rewrite it a few more times.

She brings a hand to her mouth. "I wish I knew what to say, but..."

"You don't have to say anything." A large part of me is glad she's still here—for now.

"It's just that..." She gives a small shake of the head. "The woman I've come to know over the past few weeks absolutely does not come across as someone who wants to die. It doesn't compute for me."

"I know." I grab her hand. "You... were unexpected."

Her fingers curl around mine. "Izzy," she says. "I can't let you go through with this. I need you to know that. I need you to fully understand that."

Here we go. My instinct to not tell anyone was correct after all. But Leila's not anyone. "I need you to promise me that this will stay between us, Leila."

"That's not a promise I can make. That's not something you can ask of me."

"And yet..."

She lets go of my hand. The tears have all but dried on her cheeks. Her eyes are red-rimmed, but the life that had seemed drained from her limbs a few minutes ago is coming back. "I won't pretend to understand the full despair of what you've gone through and I don't want to be insensitive to that, not after you've let me read your letter. But the very fact that you let me read it tells me something very important, something I can't possibly ignore." She brings her hands to her side. "Also, if you think, for even one second, that I'm going to let you kill yourself, let me tell you right now that you are very mistaken."

"It's not for you to decide."

She huffs out a breath. "Can I at least give you my opinion?"

"I'm not sure I can stop you at this point." It's not the moment for sarcasm, but the words just escape me.

"I absolutely hate that you've been going through this." Her voice has softened again. "It's not right. What happened to your voice was a tragedy, I get that. But it's not the end of the world. It doesn't have to mean the end of your life. You need to talk to someone. You need to get help."

"I've talked to so many people. I've gotten all the help I could possibly get." Granted, it feels very strange to be fighting for my death—for my right to do with my life what I want, even if that means ending it.

"But the value of life is... it's everything. Literally, everything. If there's no life, what is there?" Leila takes a few paces away from me.

"I don't expect you to understand this. Not immediately after reading the letter."

"To grow old is a privilege, Izzy." She ignores what I have

to say. "To look back on a long life, all the good things that happened and the bad things. To relax with the wisdom your life has given you. Don't you want that?"

"I've had enough privilege in my life. And look where it got me."

"That's right. You've hit the nail right on the head. You've had your privilege. You had the use of your magnificent singing voice for, what, forty or so years? You lost it and that was hard. But that doesn't mean there can't be something else instead." She actually rolls her eyes at me. "Maybe you've been surrounded by yes-men for a bit too long. You've been coddled by your manager. You have everything done for you. No wonder you can't find pleasure in small things, because that's where life can be truly beautiful. In those small, unexpected moments of simply being at peace. It doesn't all have to be endless applause on a stage. Ninety-nine percent of the people on this planet live effortlessly without that. And you know what, most of them are doing just fine. Most of them want nothing more than to live."

She glares at my laptop. "That letter, to me, is proof of someone who has made up a plausible narrative for herself in her head, without the input of anyone else. You hide away in your house. You don't do anything. No wonder you want to die. No wonder you miss the connection you once had. Of course, your life is empty, because that's how you've made it." Her voice has gone up a few decibels. "You're still young, Izzy. So many wonderful things can still happen to you."

Every single thought Leila expresses is something I've thought myself. What I had first deemed a selfish impulse turned into a five-year long quest to find fundamental, unobjectionable reasons not to go through with it.

The only new thought that flashes through my head, the

one reason why I might change my mind, is the woman standing in front of me.

"I know all of that. This is not a whim. This is not something I thought up yesterday. I know that many people can only make true sense of the course of their life, of all the things that have happened to them, when they're at the end of it. Well, I am at the end of mine. And I have the great privilege of being acutely aware of it. Because it's my choice. I've made my peace with what has happened—"

She opens her mouth to speak but I stop her with an upheld hand. "Look, you're right. I haven't been fully alive these past few years. I do hide away. I do live the kind of life that is not acceptable for many, but it is for me."

"It's pretty clear I'm not going to get through to you tonight." Something passes over her face. "When—" Her breath stalls. "When were you planning on..." She tries again but she can't say the words. But I know what she's asking.

"168 days," I say.

"So you can promise me that you're not going to kill yourself tonight."

I wish she wouldn't use the phrase 'kill yourself'. It sounds so harsh. It comes with so many negative connotations. I've chosen to end my life. That sounds so infinitely different. "Of course."

She sags into the nearest chair. "I sure as hell did not see this coming. No wonder you keep bursting into tears." Her eyes glistening with tears, Leila looks at me. "Can you understand why this infuriates me?"

"I can."

"I don't know what to do. I literally have no idea what my next step should be." She swallows hard. "I'm not sure I trust you on your own, even though you said, well, you know..." She holds up a finger. "But that doesn't mean I don't have a million things to say to you, because I do. But you won't hear them properly tonight. And I don't want to bombard you with them right now, when I'm in this state of... shock." Her eyes narrow. "You've shocked me, Izzy. And I've seen a thing or two in my life."

"I realize it's shocking. And selfish of me to include you in my plan."

"The way I see it, because you've included me in it, there is no more plan."

I expel a deep sigh. Of course I know where she's coming from. If the tables were turned and Leila confided in me that she wanted to die, I would react in the same way. The very essence of being human is fighting for survival. Anything that goes against that instinct will set off a bunch of alarm bells—or, in Leila's case, will infuriate.

Leila rubs her palms over her face. "It's certainly a more than valid reason for us to stop seeing each other."

I nod, even though it hurts me—although not on the same scale as I've been hurt before. And shouldn't that tell me enough? Or is it utterly silly to compare degrees of hurt?

"If you want to get out of writing the book, I'll make sure Ira and the publisher don't make things difficult for you." My voice breaks a little—it's only apt, I guess.

"We'll see. I need to think." She locks her gaze on me, her eyes wet but piercing, as though by doing so, she can gauge whether she can trust me.

"Maybe my word isn't worth much to you right now, but I'm giving it to you nonetheless. I'll be here tomorrow."

She huffs out some air, the gesture filled with disdain. "You'd better fucking be," she hisses more than says. She rises, gives a slight shake of the head, and exits the room.

I listen to the sound of her gathering her things in the bedroom. Her stomp down the stairs. Voices in the house.

Harry must have woken up. I wait for the front door to fall into the lock. Only then do I exhale, do I allow myself the tears I've been fighting back.

It's over. It's what's best, I tell myself, although it doesn't feel like anything I would ever have wanted.

CHAPTER 27

When dawn breaks, I'm still in the music room, trying to figure out my level of regret at sharing my plans with Leila. Whereas my intention to die is anything but impulsive, letting her read the letter very much was. And one thing she said last night has stuck with me.

Because I've included her in my plan, there is no more plan.

I'd be lying to myself if I didn't admit there was some truth to it. Even though my only other option was to lie to Leila. Or worse, keep sleeping with her and end my life regardless. There was no winning solution. Just like I will never get my voice back.

Then there's the memory of her. From what she told me about herself, I gather Leila will be fine now that we're no longer seeing each other. I'm not sure I can even call it a break-up because it's unclear whether we were even together. We slept together a couple of times. And I only shared my biggest secret with her. It doesn't get more intimate than that. Of course we were together. And now we're not.

I miss her already. I've missed her all night. I couldn't face going back to the bed we slept in before. My back hurts from sitting in this chair all night, thinking about how this is going to play out. Because another thing has become abundantly clear: Leila will not let me do what I want to do. Of course she won't.

Even though it's futile, I can't stop trying to guess what she's thinking. What she's doing. How she's spending the rest of the night after the bombshell I dropped on her. The agony in my head has multiplied as the night slowly progressed. I try and try to find some sort of comforting thought—like the thought of dying comforted me when my pain was at its peak—but nothing has materialized.

When I really can't take it anymore, I push myself out of the armchair and sit on the piano stool. I need to do something. I need to hear some music. I could put on a record, but hearing someone else's music—or, heaven forbid, my own—might make matters worse. It would only make me think more about what I'm no longer able to do. And isn't that the crux of why I've been sitting in this room all night?

I place my fingers on the keys of the piano, just brushing them left and right to feel the texture. Then, as if they have a mind of their own, my fingers start pressing down. I play some scales first, just to warm up and to occupy my thoughts with something other than the prospect of never holding Leila in my arms again. Soon, the scales turn into a simple lullaby. One I've been able to play since my very first piano lessons when I was six years old.

My first piano teacher, Mr. Clifford, was so gentle and affable and sly in a way that my six-year-old self could never fathom, but I see it now. Bruce reminds me of him. I wonder what happened to the horse Bruce fell off. Did it get injured? Is it still alive? And why would my life be so much more valuable than an animal's? Because I have consciousness? The very thing that's making it impossible for me to find any joy in what is left of my life. But, of course, with Leila, I did find joy.

I go from the lullaby to "Right Here in My Heart", in honor of Jade's mother. When Jade was born, this song was the soundtrack to a brand-new life. Again, the irony's not lost on me. Because I'm not thinking about the music and the notes, because my thoughts and my hands are operating on two different levels, it's easier for me to play the song. There's no pressure. It's just me in this room. Just me and my thoughts and my sadness.

My fingers must be feeling frivolous because I start to freestyle, playing a melody I'm not sure I've ever heard before, until it dawns on me that, if I'm not subconsciously repeating a song I know or have recently heard, which is very unlikely as I avoid music, I must be composing a song. Maybe it's my grief trying to find a way out. Maybe this has been a long time coming—about ten years, I would guess. Maybe this is my inner voice, the one that's been silenced for a decade, screaming its way out, because I had to push Leila away.

I let my fingers take me through the melody a few times. If this ever becomes a proper song, if I can even remember it after today, I will call it "Leila". Or "Red Lips". Or "Beguiling Smile". Or "Tear-inducing Orgasm". The titles I make up become so silly I find myself snickering. I might as well crack a joke at my own misery. Who else is going to do it for me?

There's a knock at the door. It's unlike Harry to disturb me when I'm in here, so I figure it must be some sort of emergency.

I stop playing and open the door. I stopped wondering what I look like to Harry, or anyone else who works in my house, a long time ago. They're paid handsomely for their work, but even more so for their discretion.

"I'm sorry to disturb you, Izzy. It's Miss Zadeh. She

urgently needs to speak to you." He holds up the landline phone.

Leila. My heart does a double take.

"Izzy." She breathes heavily into the phone, taking my mind on a route it really shouldn't go. "Thank goodness. I couldn't get through to you on your cell phone."

I've been in the music room all night. I have to think hard to remember where my cell even is. Probably still in my bag from last night, what with the way Leila came for me in the car and then our absorption in each other once we got home. Because I got sucked into playing the piano, I didn't hear it ring. Oh damn. She must have been worried.

"I'm so sorry. I was playing the piano. I didn't hear my phone."

"Oh, Izzy." Leila's voice trembles. I don't think it's because of a bad connection.

"I'm really sorry, Leila. I lost track of time." And I had no idea you'd be checking up on me.

"What were you playing?" Although shaky, Leila's phone voice is even more sultry than her live one.

"Just some scales and easy stuff."

"And you got so caught up in it that you didn't hear your phone?"

"I guess."

"Okay." As lovely as Leila's voice sounds over the phone, I wish I could see her face—so I could see what she's really getting at. "Sure."

"Did you call to check up on me?"

"I texted you three times first. Then I started calling. Then I tried your landline." She pauses. "Look, Izzy, it's not because I left in the middle of the night that I'm leaving you alone with this. Nor am I abandoning the book. I care about you. While I agree we shouldn't see each other socially anymore, I will finish this project and I'm here if you need to talk. In fact, I want to talk to you. Not only for the book, but because I need to say some things to you that I really need you to hear."

Socially? Nice one, Leila. Nevertheless, I'm touched by what she says. In not abandoning work on my biography, she's also not abandoning me. Not completely. "Whenever's convenient for you," I say.

"Because you're always home," she says matter-of-factly.

"I am." Already, I can't wait to see her, even though I won't be able to touch her. I'm also glad she has decided to finish the book. It saves me a lot of grief with Ira, because there's no way in hell I'm letting a third biographer take over now. It's Leila or no one at all.

CHAPTER 28

Leila looks as tired as I feel. Maybe she has slept for exactly the same amount as I have, which is zero minutes. She hasn't even bothered to apply any makeup, not even her signature red lipstick.

When her gaze lands on me, her eyes go moist instantly. "Can I hug you?" she asks, in stark contrast with how she left last night—for which I don't blame her, of course.

Even though I'm not sure I can handle a hug from Leila, I nod. I walk over to her and she wraps her arms around me. I bury my nose in her hair and inhale her scent. It might very well be the last time she lets me come this close. I need to remind myself that I'm the one who wanted—needed—the distance. I'm the one who broke us up.

She takes a few deep breaths while I stand in her embrace, as though bracing herself for something. When we break apart, there's a moment, a fraction of a second, when I think I might kiss her, but I register the graveness of her expression and the moment quickly passes.

"Are you ready to talk?" she asks. "It seems silly to engage in any kind of small talk now." She huffs out a nervous chuckle.

"Yes, and thank you for coming." I don't tell her that the prospect of never seeing her again might have enticed me to move up my 'end day'.

"I'm not a monster." She attempts a smile but it's wry and forced. "I'm not going to leave you alone with this. I can't do that." Paradoxically, being left alone with my plan is all I want, but then I wouldn't see Leila anymore. For crying out loud, Izzy, I scold myself. Make up your mind about what you want already.

After I spoke to Leila on the phone this morning, I tried to get some sleep, but the melody I'd created earlier kept playing in my head, and I went back into the music room to fine-tune it. It's Leila's melody now. It's inextricably linked to her. Playing the piano doesn't have the same restorative power as sleep, but it has given me some unexpected fresh energy. And I need that energy now as talking with Leila like this is very hard. But I have no choice.

"For the record, I'm not asking for your help," I say.

"Then why did you let me read that letter?" Leila's response comes lightning quick.

"Because... I wanted you to know why I had to stop seeing you."

"But surely you can't have expected me to find out that you plan to commit suicide, say, 'oh, okay', and leave you to get on with it? What did you think would happen? I can really only interpret this as a cry for help. As you letting me know that what you really want is to live." I can see the toll this is taking on her. Her skin has a gray tinge to it and her eyes are red-rimmed. It's beginning to really dawn on me how big a mistake letting her read my letter was. I should have made up some excuse. People do that all the time when they're trying to get out of some dead-end romantic entanglement. I've certainly done it before. But I couldn't lie to her any longer.

"It was an impulsive decision. I'm sorry. I really shouldn't have involved you. I thought that what I was doing with you, whatever was growing between us, was unfair given my plans, but in hindsight, ending it the way I did was much more unfair. This is not something that should have landed on your shoulders."

She heaves a sigh. "Can I give you my opinion?" It doesn't really sound like a question.

"That's why you're here."

"I think that you value yourself by the strength of your voice, that you completely identified with being Isabel Adler, the singer and performer. When you lost your voice after that surgery, your entire world came crashing down, because for the longest time, you've equated your self-worth with the powerful instrument you used to have. But you are so much more than your voice, Izzy. The woman I've gotten to know is... Well, you must know how I feel about you since we've been sleeping together. Didn't that make you feel something else other than the despair that has been slowly destroying you?" Her voice shakes like it did on the phone this morning.

"Of course, it made me feel so much. Too much. But I can't have a woman swoop in and change a plan I've been hatching for the past five years, a plan I've clung to for dear life. Planning my death has given me a sense of freedom to do whatever I want. It has allowed me to see what and who's important." It's all in the letter, I want to say. That's why I wanted you to read it. I understand again why I asked her to read it. This stuff is almost impossible to have a proper conversation about. Too many emotions are involved.

"But isn't that entirely beside the point?" Her voice sounds strained now. "You are a strong, beautiful, talented woman.

Yes, you lost something. And yes, clearly, that has devastated you to the point where you think you shouldn't be alive anymore. But I see the life in your eyes. I see you, Izzy. And when I do, I do not see a woman ready to die."

This is the very thing I've wanted to avoid. I don't want to argue for my death—especially not with Leila. Of course she has seen a spark of aliveness in me. But it doesn't change anything about my reason for wanting to die.

"I understand that this is what you saw in me. Because, Leila, you're... I wanted you. So much. There isn't a thing about you that doesn't seduce me. I've been so utterly enthralled by you, which was never part of my plan."

"What was your plan? A quick fuck and on with it?" Her tone of voice skitters all over the place, making me realize, once again, that even though I understand why I let her read the letter, it doesn't stop being unfair on her.

"I hadn't expected to have so many feelings for you." There. Because isn't that what all of this has been about? I felt like I needed to end it because I was convinced I was falling in love with her. I was starting to find it impossible to stop myself. "When you told me about how much you enjoy being single, it turned you into an ideal candidate for me to have one last fling with."

"Holy shit," she mutters under her breath. "You are a piece of work." She pinches the bridge of her nose—or wipes a few tears from the corners of her eyes, it's hard for me to see because it's hard for me to look at her. "Did you really think I had no feelings? Did you not feel that when we were making love?"

My eyes are welling up. Maybe this is not the time to try to be strong, anyway. A tear slides down my cheek, landing on my lips. "Oh, god, Leila. I'm so sorry."

"I don't want your apologies." She reaches into her jeans

pocket and pulls out a tissue that she wipes underneath her nose. "I want you to see that you still have so much more life to live." She crumples the tissue in her hands and looks at me. "There is only one Isabel Adler in this world. Is that really the legacy you want to leave? Have you thought about the ramifications of taking your own life? People look up to you, Izzy. If you kill yourself, fans of yours who've been emotionally fragile or have been struggling with mental health issues might just see your suicide as legitimization for their own."

I might have thought of that at one point, but for my own sanity, that was an idea I had to dismiss quickly. "Come on. I don't have that kind of responsibility." It sounds weak and I know it.

"Of course you do. It's part of the exchange between performer and fan. Your career exists by the mercy of your fans. They don't only pay for your records and to attend your concerts. They pay for what you mean to them. For the image you cultivate and the message you convey."

"I strongly disagree."

"You more than anyone, Izzy, stand for emotion. Because isn't that what music is? Emotion? Isn't that what you said in your letter? And emotion is the way in with people. Like it or not, but your songs and the emotions they evoke, have given you a place in millions of people's hearts. You can't play fast and loose with that."

I shake my head. It's all I can do to not let it hang in despair. Is Leila really not getting it? Or is she trying to play every last trump card she can think of?

"Yes, I do mention the emotional power of music in my letter, because I no longer have that power. And I think it's wholly unfair to hold little old me responsible for what anyone else might do after I die."

"Little old you?" She shakes her head now. "There's no such thing when you're Isabel Adler."

"Of course there is. I'm no different to you or anyone else, not when I had my voice and certainly not now, when I no longer have it."

"But what you mean to people is very different, Izzy. Think about what you could mean to your fans if you don't give up. If you continue to be the survivor they see you as."

"What are you talking about? I'm not a survivor."

"You are and you could be much more than that, if only you'd let yourself. If only you stopped clinging on to who you used to be. Isabel Adler Version 1.0 no longer exists. We both agree on that. But there could be a next version."

"Usually new versions of things are vastly improved," I sneer. "The latest version of me would hardly be an upgrade. In fact, it would be inferior."

"Do you know what my life motto is?" Leila ignores my sneer. It's probably the only way to deal with it. "Every single day, I get a little bit better at being me. Because of that, every single day, my life gets a little bit better. Which is why I would never want to miss out on the grand finale. That time in my life when I look back and I can see all the events, all the pieces of the puzzle, that have brought me there."

"Exactly." Finally, I hope, something we can agree on. "But I'm not getting any better. My voice is fucked forever. And this is where I look back. This is where I weigh what my life means to me. This is why I've decided that I'd rather be dead." Of course, when I put it like that, so brusquely, it sounds like an aberration—like something that should never be said out loud.

And then there's the image of Leila, who already seems so full of wisdom to me, twenty or more years into the future, looking back on her life. I will have just been a minor blip in the vast expanse of it. An event quickly to be forgotten. It hits me that that is the absolute last thing I want to be to Leila—someone she needs to forget about as quickly as possible.

"You know..." She plays with the tissue in her hands, which is all but torn to pieces. "I don't think we can reason our way out of this. Not right now."

I have to concur, but I also don't want her to go.

"Would you agree that you owe me a favor?" For the first time today, her lips lift into the beginnings of a genuine smile.

"Wholeheartedly so."

"Good." She pushes herself up. "Can we go to the music room?"

Oh damn. But I do owe her. So I stand as well, and we climb the stairs together.

CHAPTER 29

"Play something for me on the piano," Leila says. "Anything. Scales. Whatever you got so lost in this morning that you didn't hear your phone when I called."

"I'm sorry about that." I can hardly tell her that I came up with the beginnings of a song I foolishly called "Leila". It would only get her going even more. "I didn't mean to scare you into thinking that..."

She briefly taps a hand to her chest. "In case you're wondering what it will feel like for the ones left behind after you kill yourself, the people who care about you, I can and will give you a detailed description of that gut-wrenching horror later. You can count on it."

Again, there's so much to unpack from what she says. But I'm tired. And she asked me to play the piano. It feels like something I can hide behind for a while. A safe space where I'm no longer subjected to her questions and statements. Although I do linger briefly on the thought that she puts herself in the category of people who care about me.

"Of course I wonder," I mutter. Some days, it's all I think about. Before I met Leila, my only doubts about going through with my plan at all, were fueled by the pain my death would cause my loved ones.

"You should." She looks away. With her face turned to the window, and the light streaming in from outside, she suddenly looks so pale, so utterly exhausted. She looks like she's in pain. I feel a strong sense of duty to cheer her up. I know just the thing.

Despite myself—it seems to really be becoming a thing with Leila—I say, "A melody came to me this morning." I take a seat on the piano stool.

Leila remains standing, her hands gripping the windowsill. She gives me a nod that's neither encouraging nor dismissive. Maybe she's already getting tired of trying to save me. Or maybe she's just plain old tired. At our age, a night of not sleeping will always take its toll.

The first two times I try to remember the melody, my fingers refuse to cooperate, but I keep going. I keep trying, until it comes back to me. Until I can play it to her in full.

I finish the final note with a flourish, and my finger lingers on the piano key much longer than necessary. I glance at her.

"See," she half-whispers. "Why would you willingly deprive the world of that?"

And *I* thought I had a flair for the dramatic. Leila knows her way around some hyperbole as well.

"Will you play it for me again?" She moves away from the windowsill and sinks into the armchair I sat in all night long.

I play for her and, as I do, as my fingers get used to roaming over the cold piano keys again, as they find a deftness —a lightness—that comes from both muscle memory and the small joy of playing something for Leila. A lightness blooms inside me as well. Even though I can't accompany the music with my voice, the mere act of playing, of filling the room with a tune, lights me up from inside.

"It's beautiful," Leila says. "I could listen to you play that for the rest of the day."

Without being prompted, I launch into "Somewhere I've Never Been", a song with a melody so strong it holds up without vocals. When the song is finished, I'm ready to play another. Not only because I want to keep this momentum going, this wonderful sensation of playing a tune for someone else but me, but also because I'm well aware that Leila asked to join me in the music room for a reason. She has another point to make—another argument I will need to defend myself against.

"I brought a CD," she says, surprising me. "Is it all right if I put it on?"

"A CD?" I haven't used the CD player in years, and not just because I haven't been listening to any music.

"I noticed that particular relic of ancient times in here last night." She grins as she reaches into her bag.

"Which CD do you want to play?" Please, oh please, don't let it be one of mine. It would be hard to refuse her, but I will have no choice. There's no way I'm going to be sitting in this room listening to Isabel Adler songs with Leila. If I want to be in the middle of a living nightmare, I'll go to Times Square and walk around without sunglasses and a hat, inviting all sorts of questions from strangers that I don't have an answer to. Rather that, than sit here and be reminded of what my voice used to sound like while Leila studies my face.

She shows me the CD case. I don't recognize the cover art. Thank goodness.

"Bianca Bankole," Leila says. "There's a song on that album called 'None More Foolish Than Me' that is, for me, one of the most beautiful songs ever written. I'd like to listen to it with you."

"Sure." I've never heard of Bianca Bankole, but that will

soon be rectified. I give Leila the CD back and she pops it into the player. Even though it hasn't been used in years, it still works. I suppose Harry makes sure that all appliances, no matter how last-century, keep on working in my house. Leila presses play and sits back down. Slow, heavy bass notes fill the room. Then Bianca Bankole's voice comes in. She whispers more than sings, yet there's a certain dynamic to the song. When she does hold a note for longer than a split second, it's not in the pure, pitch-perfect way that singers of my ilk are used to doing. It's a touch off, but not in a disconcerting way. By the end of the song, I can sort of see why Leila would like this song so much. Despite its lack of vocal acrobatics, it has plenty of drama and style.

"Aaah," she says on a sigh. "So fucking gorgeous." She grins at me and asks, "What do you think?"

"Yeah." I'm trying to guess at what she's trying to achieve by listening to this song with me. "Lovely. Great lyrics as well."

"When you first listen to it, it almost sounds like a flimsy song. It's so quiet, so sparse, yet there's so much emotion. It's a small song with such great impact."

"Bianca is obviously very talented if she needs so little to convey so much." I genuinely mean what I say. I've always been the 'more-is-more' type, inclined to show off my range with as many spectacular runs as I can manage.

"The reason I wanted you to hear this, Izzy, is to show you that there isn't only one way to put emotion into a song. There are so many different ways of making music." She reaches out her hand a fraction, then retracts it. "Earlier, when you were playing, I felt it. Do you know why? Because I could see you were enjoying it. What makes 'None More Foolish Than Me' so beautiful is that it's so heartfelt. You feel all the intention behind the song, despite its smallness. And isn't that the very essence of music? That you feel it?" She taps just below her sternum. "That it moves something inside you here?"

"I completely agree." But I won't be going on a piano concert tour anytime soon. Sure, I could get better at playing the piano, but it would only remind me of what I can no longer do: sing along to the notes the piano produces.

"You're not catching my drift, are you?" Leila says.

"I guess not." Perhaps because I'm not that keen on doing so.

"Bianca Bankole doesn't have your range. She doesn't even come close. Nor does she have the power behind her voice that you used to have. Yet, she's perfectly able to sing this masterful song. To move something in us while she does."

"You think I should try *singing* like that?" I remember one of the first conversations I had with Leila, when I told her in very clear terms that she should never challenge me on my ability to ever sing again. I suppose too much has changed between us since then for her to keep the promise she made.

"I've done some research," she says, "based on your medical notes I have access to. I've talked to some specialists—and before you ask, I did not give out any information that might identify you in any way." She pauses for a second. "They all said there was no real risk of any extra damage to your cords by doing some gentle singing. So yes, I think you should try."

I shake my head. "No. That's not what I do."

"I hadn't expected you to agree right off the bat." She all but rolls her eyes at me. "A woman as stubborn and defensive as you." The words are insulting but Leila's tone isn't. "A woman who has gotten so used to saying no, at not seeing any chance of getting better, to the point that she's willing to give up on everything completely..." She reaches for her bag and unearths a plastic folder. "But, you agreed that you owe me a favor, so here you go." She hands me the folder. "Sheet music and lyrics to 'None More Foolish Than Me'. I'm sure you'll figure out a way to play it on the piano. Cover this song. For me. That's all I will ever ask of you again."

"Are you kidding me?"

"Absolutely not." She arranges her purse over her shoulder. "I'm asking you, Izzy. I read your letter. It was a fucking hard thing to do. It was a very difficult ask on your part. Now I'm asking you to do something in return. The way I see it, it's the least you can do. What have you got to lose? You, a woman who is willing to lose her life?"

I have no arguments. It's not as if Leila's going to be in the room with me—it's not as if she can check up on me actually putting in the work. Her bag is already slung over her shoulder. She's clearly leaving.

"Fine. I'll try, but that's all I can do. *Try*."

"That's all I ask of you. That you try." She squares her shoulders. "Let me know when you've mastered it. I'll come over and be your audience of one."

"You don't need to interview me anymore?" My heart sinks all the way to the floor.

"I think I have enough information to start on the last few chapters of your life story, Izzy. More than enough." She pins her gaze on me and keeps it there, as though debating with herself whether she should hug me goodbye. Maybe I'm imagining things, but I swear I see her hesitate, until she doesn't, and leaves.

CHAPTER 30

I haven't seen or heard from Leila in almost a week. It's Friday again and I'm getting ready for my weekly dinner with Vivian, without Leila this time. Although I genuinely wish nothing but the best for Vivian and Jade, I hope it will be just Vivian and me tonight—and Jax, if he deigns us worthy of his teenage company.

I'm not sure I can handle the displays of affection that come with the early stages of a love affair. I'm not even sure I can handle the barrage of questions Vivian will fire at me after I tell her that Leila and I are no longer an item, let alone reply to them under the love-drenched gaze of Jade.

At least, from her silence, I know that Leila was serious. The ball is in my court. I'm to contact her when I'm ready to sing her the song. The thing is that I'm not sure I'll ever be ready. If she thinks she's the first person to suggest I change my style of singing into something less powerful and breathier, she's very much mistaken. There might be a teeny tiny chance that she's the first person I could accept the suggestion from, or consider it for more than a minute, but I'm not even sure about that yet. I've listened to the song over and over, more than I've listened to any song in the past ten years. I know the lyrics by heart now—there aren't that many.

Bianca's producer has made smart use of backing vocals. Bianca herself knows how to breathe and talk-sing her way through a song. Leila's right. It's a beautiful, heartbreaking song that accomplishes a lot with only a few select ingredients, but the big difference between me and Bianca is that Bianca can still sing. She has the pipes to back her up, I can tell. She might not use them very often—I've listened to the entire album a few times and she hardly ever goes all out—but her voice is there for her if she needs it.

What I have almost done is penned some lyrics about the emotional blackmail Leila is saddling me with. If I want to see her, I need to be able to sing the song for her. In order to do that, I will first need to try to get a melody past my vocal cords. And that's the one thing I'm not capable of. I can recite the lyrics, as if they're poetry, but that's not the same as singing them, not even in that minimalist style of singing that Bianca has adopted. When you sing, you put emotion into the words, and that's the very skill I've lost along with my voice.

In the car on the way to Vivian, I remember, fondly but also with regret, how Leila's hand snuck between my legs last week while I sat in the same spot. How afterward, we made love for the last time. Does she really think it's as easy as asking me to sing a particular song? I've raged at her. I've cursed her. I've despaired. I've cried a lot, especially when I reread my letter. She shouldn't have had to read that. For that, I do owe her. Because of that, I can't dismiss her request completely. I will try again. For her.

When I arrive at Vivian's, it's just her in the house, and my first thought is that she and Jade have broken up already. I quickly correct myself. Vivian looks the opposite of sad. As though she has spent the past week at a spa and got daily facial treatments, such is the glow coming off her skin.

She doesn't merely kiss me when we greet but gives me a lingering hug.

"Just you tonight?" I ask.

"Yeah, Jade had a thing. She's working on a joint piece with this wood-carver from Haiti. She's very secretive about it."

"Sounds exciting." I force a smile on my lips. Vivian looks the way I felt all of last week, when it was all still flirting and orgasms between me and Leila.

"No Leila?" she asks, although I warned her beforehand that I would be coming alone.

"She's working on the book," I say. It's not a lie. It's exactly what Leila told me she'd be doing.

"Ah, the difficult chapters." Vivian pours sauvignon blanc. "She's really lovely, by the way, Izzy. Both Jade and I wholeheartedly agreed. We should do a double-date again soon."

Because I don't know what to say to that, I ask, "Where's Jax?"

"A party." Vivian's face changes completely, like a dark cloud is progressing overhead.

"He really is growing up too fast now."

"Christ. Tell me about it." My deflection worked seamlessly. Asking a mother about her child will do that. "It feels like only yesterday I brought him home from the hospital. This tiny little creature with those miniature fingers and toes. Now he's all gangly limbs and mood swings. And he goes to actual parties."

"You can't stop time, Viv."

Vivian takes a sip of wine. "He'd better make his curfew, or I'll go over there and march him home myself."

I chuckle at Vivian's words. "You never said how he and Jade got along."

"Swimmingly. They'd barely met and they were already shooting hoops. Jade played basketball in college. I think she may be Jax's new favorite parental figure."

"At least you let him go to the party."

"Not least because I was also under pressure from Jade. She has a very laid-back approach to child-rearing." She tuts and smiles at the same time. "She's only seventeen years older than him so..."

"No wonder he's nuts about her."

"Oh, Jax thinks he's won the lottery."

"I bet you do too."

Vivian lets her head fall back and exhales loudly. "Oh my god, this woman, Iz. She's so fucking amazing." She rolls her head forward and looks at me. "I want this to last so badly."

I set my skepticism aside. I don't feel like I have any right to it. "Anytime you need me to call Jade's mother, I'm here for you."

She fixes her gaze on me. "Leila must have some sort of magic power over you already. I truly hadn't expected you to do a video call with Jade's mom."

Tears push their way into my eyes. Oh no. This is not the time. I inhale deeply, hoping they will somehow retreat. "Leila and I are... no longer seeing each other."

Vivian's eyes grow wide. "What? Since when? Why didn't you say?" She shakes her head. "I wouldn't have gone on about Jade like that if I'd known." She reaches her hand over the table. "What happened?"

I take her hand because I can use all the comfort I can get. "I—" I can't give Vivian the full truth. I'm not making that mistake again.

"Did you end it? Or did she?" She squeezes my hand.

"I can't fall in love, Viv. I just can't do it."

"What are you talking about?" She pauses. "You both looked quite smitten already last week."

I quickly wipe the tears from my eyes. I can't have moisture gathering there if I'm going to quickly regroup. "I told you before that I wasn't looking for anything serious. And it was getting a bit too serious too quickly for me. For that reason, I had to end it."

"You're not making any sense. Why would you end things with a woman like Leila? She's gorgeous, intelligent, ambitious and she clearly made you feel like a million bucks. What aren't you telling me?"

"I'm afraid of falling in love," I manage to say.

"Why?"

I hit the same wall with Vivian as I did with Leila. To make her understand my reasons, I need to explain my plan. But I won't do that. Not again. I won't hurt Vivian the way I hurt Leila. "Leila knows... things about me. She's been delving deep into my life—into my psyche. It's all been extremely unsettling."

"That's her job, though. You can't hold that against her. I get that she's very different than Bruce. A lot more attractive as well." A quick raise of the eyebrows. "But what on earth are you so afraid of? Leila has been digging deep but it clearly hasn't stopped her from developing feelings for you. Isn't that the best feeling of all? Especially for you, Iz, who's been so... shut off from everything for so long." She catches her breath. "Oh, is that what it is? With Leila, you can't hide behind your fortified walls anymore?" She nods, clearly not needing me to confirm. Whatever she's willing to believe is fine with me.

"I can see that. I can see how she would push your buttons." She squeezes my hand again. "Of course you're not going to let her do that. Of course you're afraid."

"She wants me to..." I can barely get the word past my throat. "...sing."

"Oh wow." She wraps my hand in both of hers. "Izzy, you know I love you and I have always supported you, but I have to say... way to go, Leila."

I pull my hand from her grip. "Please, don't you start as well. Don't you see? She wants me to do the one thing I can no longer do."

"Give me the details," Vivian says matter-of-factly, as though, with her also, I've reached the end of my sympathy credit.

I tell her about the CD Leila brought. About the song I played for her on the piano. About the challenge she set me.

"Leila isn't just all the things I said about her earlier. The woman is a miracle worker as well."

"No, she's not. Just because she wants me to do something doesn't mean that I can miraculously do it. There are no miracles."

"But don't you see, Iz? She has gotten so much farther with you in the course of a few weeks than any of us, your doctors, your friends, have gotten for years. You played her a song on the piano. Don't you see the significance in that? You have to do what she asks of you. It doesn't matter what it sounds like. What matters is that you try."

"I can't."

"I'm sick of hearing that you can't. You're Isabel fucking Adler. Of course you can. You have music in your bones. Music that is just dying to come out. Just let it come out now. Ten years is long enough to hold on to all of that."

"Don't you think I've tried already? I can play the song on the piano, but I can't..." There are those tears again. "I can't sing. You know that."

"You can't sing like you used to, that much I know. That I

accept. But you are a very skilled musician, Izzy. You know what a voice can do. If your voice could sing songs like 'Somewhere I've Never Been', surely it can find a way to vocalize a different kind of song." She puts her hand on the table again. "Come on. Take my hand." She wiggles her fingers.

I do as I'm told.

"You said it yourself earlier. You're afraid. Of course you are. This life you've built for yourself is all you've known these past ten years. It's your comfort zone. I'm not saying it will be easy to step outside of it, but don't you want to try? For Leila? Don't you want to conquer your fear for her?" Viv's fingers curl around mine. "For the record, it wouldn't be just for her. It would be for me as well, Iz. I want nothing more than for you to find your way back to the stage, where you belong. Because it's what you do. It's who you are. It's your very essence."

The stage? What is she talking about? Leila said she'd be my audience of one. Even that, I'm very uncomfortable with. "No Isabel Adler fan would ever accept me singing in the same way as Bianca Bankole. She does what she does beautifully, but that's not what I do."

"You're getting way ahead of yourself," Vivian says.

"You're the one who said I should find my way back to the stage."

"Eventually. Maybe." Vivian's thumb skates over my palm. "Okay, I got ahead of myself as well. I'm sorry. I take it back."

For a split second, a vision of me on stage pops up in my mind. I've lived a lot of my life on hundreds of stages around the world. I've experienced so many emotions on stage—enough for a lifetime, I told myself after the surgery. I've always dreamed of being back on stage, but as me. As the technically gifted singer with a magnificent voice. Not someone trying to find some of her former glory again. Someone who only manages to whisper a melody. Suggest it with some clever breathing tricks. That wouldn't be me at all. Why does no one get that?

"Don't think of anything else other than making your very own version of that song," Vivian says. "Only focus on that for a while. Nothing else. See where it takes you."

Great. Now I have both Vivian and Leila on my back. At least Leila will leave me alone until I let her know I'm ready. Vivian, on the other hand, will very much be on my case about it. She's had to hold back for so long and now, thanks to Leila, she can finally tell me all the things she's had to swallow, for the sake of our friendship, for the past ten years.

I owe it to Vivian as well now to try again with the song.

CHAPTER 31

The next four days, I spend my mornings in the exact same way. First, I play the melody I wrote for Leila on the piano, followed by "Somewhere I've Never Been", as a warm-up. Then I play the instrumental version of "None More Foolish Than Me", which is a breeze because the music is just as scant as the lyrics. In fact, the song barely holds up without the words because, no matter how minimalist, the words carry the melody.

Even though the piano notes are practically screaming out for vocal accompaniment, even on the fourth day, I can't bring myself to simply declare the words in a barely audible whisper. It's as though my throat refuses. As though it is the gatekeeper of my fears and it wants to hold them all trapped inside of me.

All the while, I think of Leila. Of how she would smile at me if I could only do this. Of Vivian and how she was already imagining me on stage again. And then, when the thoughts of Leila and Vivian crowd my head so much that there's no room for anything else, I walk away from the piano, frustrated that, for some reason, I simply can't bring myself to do it.

I listen to the song over and over again. I know every last inflection of Bianca's voice in the song by heart. I hear it in my dreams. The lyrics float around in my head all day. The song is in me. I've absorbed it as though it were a part of my own repertoire. But as with all my other songs, it's not finding a way out. Not anymore. Not even Leila's anticipated smile or the relief I owe my best friend can push me over that invisible edge holding me back—that's stopped my life in its tracks for ten long years.

It's only when I venture into my office and open my laptop, where my goodbye letter always looms, and I dare to go over it again—dare to imagine what Leila felt when she read it—that I know I can't sing the song for her. Nor can I play it to make Vivian or anyone else feel better.

I can only ever do it for myself. Only I can free myself from the prison I've locked myself away in.

By now, I can play the notes by heart and I start the first chord over and over again, my gaze focused on the sheet of paper with lyrics in front of me. The sheet of paper Leila gave me—all her hopes, and mine, although I didn't know it yet, tangled up in the flimsy material the paper is made of. I start again and again, until I whisper the first line of the lyrics. Until my whisper finds strength and morphs into a declaration. Until I make it through the song while also reciting the lyrics. Maybe to someone else, it might have sounded like singing, but to me, it didn't even come close. But it doesn't matter. I uttered words while I played the piano. I made music. Not the music I used to make by a very long shot, but music nonetheless.

Ignoring the ball that's building in the pit of my stomach, I try again. This time, I put some inflection into the words here and there. My voice dips low at the end of a phrase. It goes a bit higher again at the beginning of the next one. I know the words so well, it's starting to feel as though I wrote them myself, although I've never been much of a wordsmith—and Bianca Bankole is much more talented in that department than I am. In the CD sleeve, I read that she wrote all the music and lyrics herself.

Last night, when I couldn't sleep—when my brain was too saturated with images of Leila in my bed—I looked up some clips on YouTube of Bianca performing live. I was surprised by the drama in her performance. I also understood why Leila said she was a fan. I almost texted her, but I didn't in the end, out of fear that all I would get back was a deafening silence—unlike the silences that Bianca uses in her songs, which are pregnant pauses full of emotional tension.

As I finish my spoken word version of "None More Foolish Than Me" and give my fingers a stretch, I wonder if this would be enough for Leila. I tried. It's all I've been doing. Should I record myself while I play the song to know exactly what Leila will see? Or will the contrast with how I've always thought of myself on stage—loud and larger than life—break me all over again? Because doing this, while it gives me a small sense of relief, hardly feels like me. That's how I know I'm not ready for my audience of one. Not until I feel like myself again when I do this. Although I fear I might have a long road to go, and I won't be able to see Leila while I'm on this journey, I'm a touch hopeful. Because today I've made it farther than I did yesterday. Who knows what tomorrow will bring?

The next day, Vivian comes over uninvited. The glow of newfound love about her has dimmed considerably. Could she and Jade be on the rocks already?

"Full disclosure," she says as soon as she walks in. "I've been in touch with Leila."

My heart skips a beat. It's been almost two weeks since I've seen her. "You have?"

"She called me, asking if I wanted to read her new chapters."

"She finished the book?"

"I don't think it's finished, but she has been working on it at full speed. She must have felt inspired." Vivian narrows her eyes as she locks her gaze on me. A thought hits me. But, no. Leila wouldn't have written about my plan to die. She wouldn't break my confidence like that. Although she did clearly state that she couldn't promise not to tell anyone. But telling someone, like my best friend, is something else entirely than including it in my biography.

"And?" I squeak.

"And? She's a fucking great writer, Iz. So good, in fact, that it was hard for me to read. To go there again. To live through it again. After the surgery. The agony, followed by the hope, followed by the dashed hope again. That endless cycle of grief that kept repeating itself." Vivian swallows hard. "It's been a long time since I really considered it, you know. But the way she wrote about you... about who you are now. It's... kind of gut-wrenching, actually. At least it hit me like a punch in the gut." Her voice trembles. "She must really have delved deep, Iz. She must know... things about you that I've never really had a clue about."

Oh shit. Leila knows everything. She read the letter. Of course she used it in the book. There's no way whatever darkness she weaved into it will make it past me for the final version.

"Look, Iz." Vivian plants her elbows on her knees. "I know it's been hard, but..." Her voice all but breaks. "I'm your best friend and I really need some peace of mind here. Have you ever, uh, been suicidal? Because that's what I got from reading Leila's chapters."

Damn it. I can't bury my head in the sand any longer. I

need to read this book. Bruce's draft and, even more so, Leila's additions. Who else has she sent it to? Ira? Probably not or I would have heard by now. What on earth is she playing at?

"Iz?" Vivian insists. "You never told me. As soon as I finished reading, I rushed over here. If I'd known..." Leila's prose must be very convincing.

"Viv..." I find myself completely unable to lie to Vivian. "The thought has crossed my mind, but that was never supposed to make it into the book."

"But how are you feeling now?" Her words come quick. "I'm sorry, but I need to know."

"Oh, Jesus." The sight of Vivian's ashen face devastates me to the core. "I feel fine. You have nothing to worry about." As I speak the words, I know they are the truth. Not only because I wouldn't lie to my best friend's face like that, but, just before she arrived, pathetic as it might have been, I was making some sort of music. "I promise you."

She opens her arms. I quickly step into her embrace and press myself against her. "Promise me again," she whispers.

"I promise."

"I've always known you to be a woman of your word, Iz, so you'd better not have changed." She squeezes her arms around me a bit tighter. "God, I had no idea."

Because I never wanted you to know, I say to myself only. Vivian's tears trickle down my neck. It's only now, when I stand here in her arms, that the true horror of what I wanted to inflict on her hits me.

156 days and this is where I stop counting.

"We're going to get you some help, okay?" she says between sniffles.

I gently remove myself from her grasp. "I don't need help." I take her hand and lead her up the stairs, to the music room. "I've been playing."

I'm pretty pissed off at Leila and I'm currently unsure whether I'll ever get to play this song for her, so I might as well give Vivian the scoop. She needs some serious cheering up. It's also the first true test for my newfound, still very shaky, voice.

I play "None More Foolish Than Me" for Vivian, and, hoping that it will extinguish the last of her tears, I manage to bring a little bit more emotion to it than the previous time. Because this moment calls for emotion. For conviction. After all, I need to convince my friend that I want to live. That this is enough.

When I'm done, Vivian's crying even harder. Mission not accomplished.

"Fuck, Izzy. I can't believe this." She wipes at her cheeks with the sleeves of her blouse, its fabric too sheer to absorb any moisture. "You're back."

CHAPTER 32

After Vivian has left, I process the last few hours by pacing around the living room. Vivian has emailed me Leila's new chapters. I'm still too afraid to read them. Too afraid that I will feel as though Leila has violated my trust too deeply. Or maybe that's just another story I'm telling myself. Maybe what I'm really afraid of is to see, in black and white, another person's account of the last ten years of my life—a person I happen to care a great deal about.

I ask Harry to fix me a strong drink while I print out the pages. Then I settle into the chair Bruce and Leila have spent so much time in while they listened to the story of my life, and I read what Leila has written.

It's not as bad as Vivian storming into my house asking me whether I was suicidal would have suggested. What Vivian mostly did was read between the lines, because she knows me better than anyone. It's perfectly in tune with what Leila has written in the chapters before about me losing my voice. Like the only logical consequence. Or maybe that's me reading between the lines too much.

Ironically, now that I feel ready to play Bianca Bankole's

song for Leila, I don't immediately contact her. Because, of course, Vivian's reaction to my performance, if it can even be called that, was ruled by emotion. Of course she would say something like 'you're back' after what we'd just talked about. I don't feel like I'm back at all, but what I do feel—strong and clear, like the way my heart has always continued to beat for me, even when I wanted to silence it forever—is that I no longer want to die.

Not because of Leila. Not because of Vivian, although she and Jackson have a lot to do with it. But because I was able to get past myself—my biggest enemy for so long—and actually play her the song, no matter the mediocrity of its rendition.

There are no miracles. The voice I used to sing with is gone forever, the vocal cords I used to rely on to express all the feelings inside of me are forever damaged. But that doesn't mean I don't still have a voice. In that, Leila was right. I may never take to the stage again. I may only ever play to an audience of one—or none—but that's already so much more than I've been able to imagine the past decade. Right now, it's all I need.

So I call her, my finger trembling as it finds her number in my phone. I call her because I'm ready.

I've asked Harry to bring Leila to the music room, where I wait for her, trying to look poised behind the piano. As soon as she enters, I start to play. I can't have a conversation before I get through this.

Playing "None More Foolish Than Me" for Leila is infinitely more nerve-racking than playing it for Vivian. I have to start over two times before my fingers are loose enough to get into the groove. And then there's my voice. It sounds a lot shakier—a lot more shattered and vulnerable. In the audience of one, it matters who the one person is.

When I play for Leila, I don't play with the same intention as I did for Vivian, whom I mainly wanted to cheer up. When I play for Leila, I want to find a way to convey that meeting her, being with her, has changed me. The song lyrics, no matter how gorgeous and heartbreaking, are inadequate for that, so all I have is the emotion that I put in my voice and the way my fingers land on the keys of the piano.

After I've played the final note, my hands fall into my lap. A sudden wave of fatigue hits me, as though I've just spent all my energy. I remember it vividly from my touring days. The deflation that takes over after the adrenaline has worn off. The decompression as the body's chemicals try to find balance again.

I don't dare look at her and I also need to take a moment for myself. A moment to breathe. To assess the condition of my throat and my lungs.

"Izzy," Leila whispers. "Will you please look at me?"

When I turn to her, the smile on her face is the warmest I've ever seen it.

"I knew you could do this," she says. "I knew it as soon as I heard you play for me the other day." She pushes herself out of the chair I asked her to sit in and walks toward me. She crouches down next to me and puts her hands on my knees. "How are you feeling?"

"Ambivalent." My gaze locks on her hands—oh my god, those hands and what they can do. "Like I've lost and gained something at the same time."

"That's definite progress over only feeling like you've lost something."

I nod. I stop myself from covering her hands with mine. "I have a bone to pick with you."

"Hm," she says, as though she knew she had it coming. "I assume you've read the chapters I sent to Vivian?" She arches up her eyebrows. "I'm sorry, Izzy, but I had to do something. That letter... it wasn't a burden I was able to carry alone. I know how close you are with her." Her fingertips dig into my jeans. "And I was getting impatient." Her red lips are so shiny again. "I only sent them to Vivian."

"She was very upset after reading them."

"I can imagine that she was." She pushes herself up. "I was upset. I still am. Did you really think I wouldn't include your death in the story of your life?"

"You might need some rewrites." My voice chokes.

She nods. "I figured you wouldn't be very happy with what I've written."

I stand as well and bridge the gap between us. "I don't necessarily feel like that anymore. Trapped in despair, I mean. The past ten days, all I've done is play and it must have rewired something in my brain. It was hard. The first week, I could only play the piano. I practiced the song over and over again. Until Vivian set me straight and I tried adding the words. Until they felt almost natural coming from my mouth. I know it's not much to listen to, but in the end, it doesn't really matter, because, even though it was hard, I did find joy in playing again. I did find that connection between what's inside me and the outer world. Briefly and flimsily, so maybe more of a promise of something... But I can now see that it might be possible for me to feel differently about my life." It's most certainly not a speech I had prepared, hence its rambling character.

"Oh, Izzy." Leila clasps her hands in front of her mouth. "Oh," she says on a sigh. "Sorry." She catches a tear that threatens to spill from her eyes. "For the record, what you just played, was fucking beautiful. It was... mesmerizing because I could feel your pain. I could hear you trying to expel it. Your voice was small but captivating. It made me want to sit very still and listen oh-so-carefully."

The tears gathering in Leila's eyes must be contagious, because here come my own waterworks again. Her words flatter me in a way I'd never deemed possible again. "You're not just saying that? Giving me a compliment just for trying?"

She shakes her head vehemently. "Izzy, don't you see? You have music in your bones. In your heart and your soul. No wonder you wanted to die, because you denied yourself the very thing that makes you who you are. Ask anyone else to play that song and it will sound infinitely worse. You may no longer have that huge voice you once had, but you still ooze musicality. You still instinctively know where to lean into the words to get the melody across and where to pull back. You may no longer have the range, but you still have pitch. You still have expert phrasing. You have decades of experience in performing. You might have lost part of your voice, but you never lost that part of you."

"Maybe you should put that in the book." I have to say something to keep from bursting into tears completely. Because Leila is right. I locked it all away. The pain of what I lost was too great to consider the possibility of another version of me. Until she made me see.

"There's so much you can still do, Izzy. You have so much more life left to live."

"Thank you," I say, because I don't just owe Leila this first glimpse of what could be a new Isabel Adler. I owe her my life. I hold out my hands, and she takes them. "You've given me something priceless. Something that was beyond my comprehension, beyond my dreams, since the surgery."

"I won't say something trite like it was there all along." She pulls me to her. "Maybe you needed this journey. Maybe you needed the pain in order to make a new kind of music."

"A new kind of music." Ha. "Maybe that should be the title of the book."

"You're the boss. You get to choose." If a mere smile could set something on fire, I'd be in flames right now.

"I'm the boss?" I chuckle. "Maybe your true talent is making me believe that I am."

"My talent must be severely lacking then, because you don't seem to believe me." Her face is so close to mine, I can feel the warmth of her breath on my cheeks.

"Leila," I whisper. "I may not be certain of many things right now, but..."

"Yes?" She inclines her head.

"I'm so madly in love with you." I tear up as I say it. "I've missed you so much." My heart beats double-time. Maybe I've overplayed my hand again. Although all the signs indicate the opposite. But still.

"Jeez, Izzy. I'm crazy about you too. I do hope that's obvious by now." Her tone is anything but serene.

"What with you trying to save me and all that?" Oh, Izzy. I just can't help myself.

"Let's be clear about one thing. I didn't save you. You saved yourself. The last time we spoke, despite your feelings for me, you still wanted to die. The reason you want to live again is because you know, in your heart, that your life is worth living. Because your life is not over. Because you still have so much to do. So much love to give and receive—and not just from me."

"Maybe you should kiss me before I say anything else stupid."

"Sounds like the better plan." Leila sends me that smile again, until it disappears from my field of vision, and I feel her lips press against mine.

And sure, playing the song for her, while it made me feel insecure, might have been cathartic, but this kiss is so much more powerful than playing a song. It jolts the life right back into me, gives me back the energy I spent while singing for her.

As she opens her lips to me, and lets my tongue slip inside, I think that, yes, I might try getting old alongside her. While I was making my plans to die, and I wanted to exhaust every possible avenue of life, any possibility, be it moral or ethical or even just plain practical, I came across a quote from an old lady who said that getting old was like having a delicious dessert after a wonderful meal. If she hadn't experienced what had come before, the dessert would never have tasted as sweet.

Leila's tongue against mine, agile and soft, is what that sweetness tastes like to me right now.

CHAPTER 33

My bedroom isn't far from the music room and we make it there between kissing and manically groping at each other, as though we have to make up for the time we've lost. It's a funny sensation, because instead of losing time—counting down the days—I have gained the rest of my life, no matter how long that might be. I may die tomorrow. I may die in 156 days. I may die in thirty-five years. The point is that I no longer know, that I no longer want to destroy myself—that I choose to continue to exist until my natural time is up.

Although a conscious choice, I can't pinpoint the moment I made the decision, unlike the moment I decided I wanted to die. I'm not even sure it happened over the course of the past ten days. The decision-making process might have been put in motion the minute Leila walked into my house, with all her poise and elegance. It's not important for me to know the exact time. Maybe it's even impossible. Because it's not so much a decision as a brand-new current of energy running through me. Something vibrating underneath my skin. A new wavelength in my brain that has opened me up to the option of possibilities again. Things don't have to be the way I thought they were going to be—the way I convinced myself they would be.

Pain is no longer the only thing that drives me. What drives me right now, what has my skin buzzing with all sorts of energy, are Leila's hands all over me. This woman who came into my life like an angel sent to keep me from killing myself. Even though my rational mind knows that's not what happened at all, part of me does want to believe it. For me, from now on, there will always be 'Before I Met Leila' and 'After I Met Leila'.

She undresses me hungrily—I think she might have even ripped my blouse. The patient lover she was before is overtaken by someone else. Someone so ravenous for me, she can't help but tear my clothes off me.

I can't wait to get my hands on her luscious, soft breasts again. I missed them pressed against my back in the night. I missed her hot breath on my neck. I missed everything about her.

In a matter of minutes, she has me stark naked on the bed. I've managed to at least get her blouse and pants off her. Next, I go for her bra. Oh, to clasp eyes on those breasts again. Maybe I should write a song about them—to sing their abundant praise. Another song to only ever be performed for an audience of one.

As though she's tuned in to exactly what I'm thinking, Leila reaches her hands behind her back to unhook her bra. She lowers it slowly, unveiling one nipple, then the other, before tossing it aside.

I swallow hard at the sight of her. This woman, this beautiful creature. What was it about her that made me forget about myself, about what I had become, so utterly and completely? Her warm gaze? Her sexy smile? The comforting curve of her body? As I lower my head toward her breasts, I know it's futile to even ask the question. Because it's all of her. It's her own journey, her own life, that made her into who she is today, into the woman sitting here with me, the woman who was brought onto my path because of Bruce's misfortune.

I do know one thing very clearly—or maybe I'm already getting ecstatic because my tongue is skirting along her nipple —and that is that when I'm with her, I'm more than the sum of my own parts. I'm no longer the person I was before. That scared, hidden-away woman who let her pain consume her, eat away at her soul, until all it wanted to do was dissolve into nothingness.

I also know that I want her with a ferocity that must be equal to the desire to live. The passion I feel for life matches the passion with which I desire her. Right now, to me, they are the same. I push her down onto the bed, my lips not letting go of her nipple. My hands cup her breasts and I relish their softness. Leila's hands find their way to my breasts. She lightly pinches my nipples while her lips peck at my neck. Soon, she's the one pushing me onto my back. I might have changed but some things never do.

"I want you so much," Leila says, breathing heavily. "I need to taste you."

Music to my ears. I pull her in for a long, hot kiss, before I let her do what she wants, which also happens to be what I want. She showers me with wet kisses all over my body although she has only one final destination. Between my legs. My clit is throbbing wildly, impatiently waiting for her ministrations.

When she pushes my legs apart, I'm engulfed by a new wave of passion. Of love. *I love her.* Her way with me. Her power. Her confidence. Her red lipstick. The curve of her hip as she sits there looking at me. Most of all, I love how angry she got with me when she found out I wanted to die. I'll never forget the tears streaming down her face that night. As I'll never forget how she made me sing again.

She bends toward me, her hands roaming across my inner thighs. Her mouth goes straight for my sex. Her tongue slides through my arousal and halts at my clit. Gently, slowly, I feel her lips gather around me. Her tongue is hot. Her fingertips are like fire dancing across my skin. I throw my head back, eyes firmly shut, and that's when I see it. In my mind, there's an image of me behind the piano, singing a song to an audience of much more than one. The woman I see is not the Isabel Adler from before. It's is me as I am, now, with my new voice.

The rhythmic stroke of Leila's tongue is divine, as is the applause of the crowd that I imagine. That specific sound I've always been so addicted to. Not only because of the praise it signified, but because of what it gave me. Feedback. Respect. The constantly reinforced belief that I was put on this earth to do one thing only and do it well. And I did do it well. Despite the Isabel Adler haters that have been out there from day one, I never had to doubt my ability, until the scar tissue in my throat made me. Then all that was left was doubt.

Doubt is the last thing on my mind right now, as Leila's tongue flicks warmly around my clit. Already I know this is going to be a different kind of orgasm. Born in equal parts from Leila's actions and my attraction to her and something else taking root inside of me. A new belief. Another new possibility. It's no coincidence that it's coming to me now. In Leila's touch, I feel her love for me. It stokes the tiny, dust-like embers of self-love that have lingered somewhere deep inside me. Her touch renews me, her love ignites my own. And as I let her take me to my climax, my body shivering underneath her tongue, I know that, one day, I will be on stage again.

CHAPTER 34

The next morning, neither of us wants to get out of bed, so I ask Rian to bring breakfast to my room.

While we wait, Leila looks at me in a way I can't decipher. I glance back at her and it's almost enough to make me lunge for her again, to kiss her for minutes and minutes, but I don't want Rian to find us in a compromising position and, frankly, I could do with a little break.

"The past ten days," Leila says, "I didn't just write those new chapters in your biography."

"What do you mean?"

"Back in the day," she says, her voice suddenly a whole lot less confident, "from my teens to my early thirties, I guess, I used to scribble a bit of poetry. After you played me that new melody, I, uh, thought I'd try my hand at some lyrics for it."

My interest is more than piqued. I let her continue without interruption.

"They're on my phone." She reaches for it on the nightstand. "Do you want to read them?" Bashful Leila is a brand-new experience. Seeing her like this makes me want to throw my arms around her and comfort her for a change.

"Of course I do." My voice drips with excitement. Is there no end to the delightful surprises with her?

"It's making me a little nervous to let you read them." She clutches her phone to her naked chest. "Then again, you must have been racked with nerves yesterday when you played for me so, quid pro quo and all that..." She taps on her phone screen a few times and hands it to me.

"Wow." My hands are trembling when I take the phone from her. "Thank you so much." Leila wrote me a song? I can't believe this. I've had dozens and dozens of songs written for me, but this one, already, even though I haven't even read the lyrics yet, is infinitely different. Already, it has more meaning than any of the songs I recorded.

I blink the beginnings of a tear from my eye and read.

The title is "A Breathless Place".

The hunger in your eyes
The thirst in your glance
The passion in you that never dies
And the never-ending light you cast

You take me to
A breathless place
Away from this
Endless chase
You take me to
A breathless place
Away from all
The pain I face

The lack is gone
The absence filled
A new day born

A strong trust built

You take me to
A breathless place
Away from this
Endless chase
You take me to
A breathless place
Away from all
The pain I face

Time ticks away
But we have endless days
Between us that we'll fill with love
We might not yet be aware of
Darling, you
Take me to
This breathless place

As my eyes skim down the screen, my pulse picks up speed. If I had the tiniest amount of doubt left about Leila's feelings for me, that has vanished now. When someone writes something like this for you, it tells you everything you need to know.

"Leila," I say on a sigh of pure admiration. "You wrote this for me?" I look at her through moist eyes—it would be futile to even try to bite back my tears now.

With her bottom lip wedged between her teeth, Leila nods. "What do you think?"

"I think you're brilliant."

Leila lets out a nervous laugh. "Let's not get too carried away."

"I'm serious. I want to jump out of bed, sit at my piano, and play this now. That's how excited I am about it."

"I should have only let you read it after we had breakfast." Leila's lips curl all the way into a smile. "You know how much I adore Rian's eggs."

"You can eat your eggs while I play for you." I'm so electrified, my feet get tangled in the sheets as I leap out of bed and I nearly stumble.

"Izzy," Leila says, her voice suddenly grave again. "Take a moment to truly feel the significance of this. To mark the fact that you're literally falling out of bed to make music again."

A knock comes on the door.

"I'll get it," Leila says, as she wraps a sheet around herself.

While she asks Rian to set up breakfast in the music room, I take stock of the moment. Leila's right. Even though the sensation is not novel—I used to experience it all the time—it does feel brand-new. Because it's been years since I've felt like this. It's been a decade since I jumped out of bed buzzing with the prospect of singing a song. This morning, in particular, I can't wait to hear what Leila's lyrics sound like in my new voice.

We have breakfast first, although I'm so exhilarated, I can barely eat—like a child on Christmas morning. It's as though the lyrics I've just read are only the wrapping paper of the real gift Leila is giving me. To have my voice back. To use it in the way it was always intended to be used. In the way that has always made me feel the most alive. To use my voice to sing a song—a song she wrote for me.

"If you could only see yourself right now," Leila says. "It's like I hardly know this person sitting across from me." She cocks her head. "Or no, I know her from Bruce's first chapters.

That eager, overzealous young performer. It's like the person you were at the beginning of your career has come back to life."

"Can you believe I still haven't read Bruce's chapters?"

"I can, I guess. It must be hard to go back to a time when everything was different." Leila's voice is soft and sweet.

"I'll read them soon." After I master those lyrics and have put them to music.

"I know you're dying to play and I'd be a fool to keep you from doing so, but I have been wondering about something..." She puts down her fork. There's not a speck of food left on her plate. "Why did you decide to do the biography? Was it to leave some sort of legacy after your death?"

"I guess." I inhale and exhale deeply to buy some time. "It was partly people-pleasing. I wanted to do it for Ira, because then he would have something to do after I had died." Plus, make a killing off me the way he used to, I don't say out loud. "And for Jackson, so he could read my life story and know about all the things I was unable to tell him while I was alive." My throat constricts. If I keep talking about this, I can forget about singing altogether for the rest of the day—even in my 'new style'. "I also wanted to do it for anyone who would still call themselves an Isabel Adler fan. To give them one last thing, to let them look inside my life as a sort of parting gift."

"And for yourself?" Leila's question takes me right back to the first time we met, when she was all about the direct questions. How much has changed since then.

"Maybe for the process of looking back on my life at the time I had deliberately chosen to end it, although I've never really admitted that to myself until now." I take a swig of orange juice. "Because of my timing, I had never intended to read the end product." It's an eerie thing to say.

"But now you will," Leila says more than asks.

"Now I will," I repeat and look her in the eye, but only briefly. The decision to live is as much a relief to me now as the decision to die was back then. Already, I've gotten a glimpse of what I would have missed. Leila's lyrics.

"Can I watch how you work? How you take my words from letters on a screen to vocals in a song?" she asks.

"They're your words, Leila. We're going to do this together."

CHAPTER 35

A few days later, Leila's sitting across from me in the armchair where she started out. She has asked me for one final 'official' interview session. She needs a few last answers before she can finish my biography.

I couldn't feel more different than the first time we sat down together like this. She knows me inside and out now, and only half her knowledge has come from the questions she has asked me. Most of it, I've told her during in-between moments, over meals we've shared, in a post-orgasmic haze or —the best time to share with her so far—after I've practiced her song.

"Okay," Leila starts. "For the record, it's not because this is our last formal session that it's going to be an easy one."

"Way to get off on the right foot, darling."

"Obviously, *before* you didn't have to worry about this, but have you thought about the party the tabloids are going to have when they find out that you've taken up with your biographer?"

"I never, ever think about any party the tabloids might have at my expense. I don't care." I narrow my eyes. "Is this an official question?" It occurs to me that Leila might be mainly worried about herself.

She shakes her head. "Not yet."

It's not the first time she has tried to conduct my official biography exit interview. The two previous times we drifted into topics that should, by no means, ever make it into a book about my life.

We still have so much to discover about each other, so much to unearth. And then there's the unstoppable desire to kiss her every few minutes.

"Are *you* worried about it?" I ask.

"Your biography's going to propel you back into the public eye. So yeah, because I'm in your life now, I have considered the possibility that the life I'm used to might change a fair bit."

"It will, for a while." I scratch my cheek. "But we can make it so that doesn't go on for too long. Ira and his team have a lot of experience with this." While I understand her concern, I also get the feeling she's tiptoeing around a question she's finding difficult to ask. "Either way, we'll deal with it then and it will absolutely be dealt with. I promise." I send her an encouraging smile.

"All right." She flicks her tongue briefly over her lip. "This is an official question."

"Okay. Shoot." I pretend to be shot down by a gun.

"Oh, Izzy," Leila says in that faux-exasperated tone she adopts a few times every day. "Honestly, I'll be glad when this book is done. When we can just be us. With nothing else standing between us anymore."

"Me too."

I see her hesitate for a split second. She can't slip so easily into journalist mode as she used to. She can't turn that part of her on so easily anymore, because she's no longer only a journalist when she sits across from me. I'm well aware of what

Leila means to me and what she has done for me, and she knows it, too. It's not something effortlessly cast aside.

She clears her throat. "What would have happened if you hadn't had the surgery?"

There's a question I hadn't expected. So there is something of the semi-ruthless journalist left in her. Moreover, this information is in my medical file. As with what happened after the surgery, she wants to hear me tell the story in my own words.

"The nodules would have grown, making it harder for me to sing, but..." I'm surprised by how easily my reply comes. Maybe it's because I feel a hundred percent safe in Leila's company and I know she won't twist my words to fit a sensational narrative. "I would still have been able to sing. Most likely. I would have had to adapt my technique. And who knows what might really have happened? It's impossible to say, of course. But at that particular time in my life, for various reasons, I chose to have the surgery. I wanted my voice to remain the same. The rest is history."

Leila nods and looks at me—really looks at me. As though she doesn't need me to say any more words but can glean everything else she needs to know from examining my face. But then, she does speak again. "I've been thinking, Izzy, and I'd like to discuss mentioning your wish to end your life in the book."

"No." Instantaneously, I shake my head. "I don't want anyone to know about that."

"Why not?"

"Because it would needlessly hurt the people that I love."

"You'd need to tell them in advance," she says. "But don't you think they should know?"

"No." Tension creeps into my muscles. "Because I have the right to change my mind without anyone knowing."

"Of course you do, but... you lived with the intention of

dying prematurely for years. It was such a big part of you. I daresay that having the very prospect allowed you to live longer than you might have otherwise. If you're going to share your life story, don't you think your plans to end your life should be a part of that? Otherwise, it will always be a dishonest document."

"Leila, no, I can't put that in the book. It was you who said I have a responsibility to my fans and thus to the people who will read the book. That I shouldn't put ideas into their head. That I shouldn't glorify suicide because of who I am."

"You'd be doing the exact opposite, though. Because you have chosen to live."

"Maybe. But then everything will be about that and that's not a conversation I want to have over and over again."

"I agree it won't be easy, but maybe it's a conversation you need to have nonetheless."

"Music is my art," I say. "It's how I've always said what I wanted to say. The biography is... it's a book about my life, but it's not part of my own artistic output."

"But it is still your message. I need you to really think about what kind of message you want to convey with your biography, Izzy." She pauses. "We could even use snippets of your goodbye letter... It would be so incredibly powerful."

I can't believe what I'm hearing. "But that's so intensely private. That letter is not something to ever share with the public."

"Think about it. Give it some time to percolate." She tries to find my gaze again, tries to pin it down, but I can't look her in the eyes for more than a second at a time. "I think it would send such a hopeful message, Izzy. It would tell people that everything is always still possible. That it's not because you lose something or someone that is extremely precious to you, that everything needs to end. It's a message that I, personally, would very much like to include in the book because it's something I've always believed in."

"Are you asking me to include it for you?" I'm not sure how I would feel about that if she did.

"No. Even though Bruce and I wrote it, this is your book. Your message. But, well, I'd like to think I have a certain influence over you now." She tries a smile next. It's not sly or meant to seduce. It's all warmth and glorious red lips again.

"You have much more than influence over me." These days, my guard is always down when I'm with Leila. I suppose that's what happens when you let someone read the very last words you ever meant to share with the world. "I'll think about it," I say, because it feels wholly unfair to dismiss her request outright. That's not something I can do to her any longer.

"That's all I can ask for," she says, her smile becoming even more radiant. I'm loathe to see it disappear, but I do have a difficult question of my own.

"Can I ask for something in return?" I mirror her smile.

"It doesn't have to be in return for anything. I told you from the beginning. You can ask me anything."

I nod. "What happened to..." The question's been on the tip of my tongue for a long time, but now that I've finally found the courage to ask Leila, it seems even harder than I had imagined. I'd hoped she would have brought up the topic herself, spontaneously, on one of the long evenings we've spent in each other's company, but she hasn't so far. "Your family?" The last two words come out as barely a whisper.

The smile all but disappears from her face. "I can't believe I haven't told you, Izzy."

"It's kind of been all about me all the time." Being the center of attention has become second nature to me, even after all this time. And she is writing a book about my life.

"You may think so, but it's not entirely true. Besides, it's been a pleasure and a privilege to focus on you, and to still be able to do so now."

My cheeks flush. They always do when she says things like that.

"It's not something I go around sharing." A shadow crosses Leila's face. "My mother and brother were in a fatal car crash. My brother was driving. He'd only just gotten his license. It was in 1978, when the revolution was at its peak. When my father called with the news, I wanted to return home, but he wouldn't let me. He said it was too dangerous. That I might never make it back to the US if I came home." Her voice doesn't tremble. Her tone is steadfast.

"I wasn't there when my mother and brother were buried. For some reason, I complied with my father's wishes. That's what young Iranian women did back then, and what most of them still do now. Obey their fathers. I've regretted it ever since." She does swallow hard now. "It's the biggest regret of my life to not have honored their too-short lives with my presence at their funeral. With the very least and also the only thing I could have done to pay my respects."

"Your father was grieving alone in Iran while you had to grieve for such an immense loss on your own in another country." I expel a sigh. "I'm so sorry, Leila."

"It was a very long time ago, but I still miss them. I spoke to my mother every Saturday morning on the phone. It must have cost her a fortune to call me every week, but I know she happily paid the price just to hear my voice for a few minutes." She clears her throat. "Sometimes, even after all these years, I still expect my phone to ring at 10AM on a Saturday morning. That was her time." She takes a deep breath. "Afterward, I learned to see my father's point. He was probably right not to let me come back home. But at the time... well, we were not on the best of terms for years after the accident." She heaves a sigh. "Also, in hindsight, if I hadn't been able to come back and finish my studies, I wouldn't be sitting here right now. And, let's face it, Iran in the seventies and eighties also wasn't the best place in the world to discover that I liked women. Nor is it now, for that matter." A hint of a smile is back on her lips. "Just like with you and the surgery, it's impossible to know what would have happened if things had turned out differently. That's the point of life. You don't know, which is inherently hopeful. The next big change may be right around the corner." She scoffs. "Although, as you and I both know, the next big change might not always be for the better." She locks her eyes on me. "But it might also very well be."

CHAPTER 36

A couple of months later, I find myself walking through the streets of Brooklyn, on Leila's arm. We're going to see Jackson's basketball game.

"How does it feel?" Leila asks. "To breathe in all this polluted air?"

I would have expected her to be more sweetly supportive, but that's never been Leila's style. She also dismissed my request to have someone from the security service I sometimes still use follow us at a discreet distance as utterly silly. It's my impression Leila allows me less self-pity and needless anxiety as every day passes.

It's no wonder, then, that she's the one I'm walking with on the way to my godson's game. The last time I saw him play, he must have been only seven—his tiny hands too small to wield a ball that big. He's fourteen going on fifteen now and everything has changed.

"I'm not sure it's very good for my health, nor my voice," I reply.

"A walk is *always* good for your health. No exceptions." Leila tightens her grip on my arm.

From behind my oversize sunglasses, I scan my surroundings. No sign of any paparazzi so far. No looks of recognition from anyone we've walked past.

Next to me, Leila's humming a tune I recognize easily because it's one of mine.

"Practicing for a duet?" If she can joke, so can I. It will only lighten my nerves.

"I wish." She sounds as though she means it. "But I have been thinking about whether you could use a sample of 'Somewhere I've Never Been' in 'A Breathless Place'. Wouldn't that be so cool? As a link between the past and the present. Between the old and the new you."

"Maybe." Ever since she gave me the lyrics to "A Breathless Place", Leila has been very invested in the actual production of the song—in its future even.

"Imagine, Iz," she says, "that in twenty years' time, when we're old and gray, we'll be sitting somewhere together and the song will come on."

"Aw." I lean into her a little. "Whatever happened to your serial monogamist ways?"

"That's not a question I can answer right now." She turns to me and flashes me a wide smile.

"Yet you can imagine us together twenty years from now?"

"I can imagine whatever I want. That's the very nature of our imagination." She gives me a quick kiss on the cheek. "I'd never imagined walking down the street with you like this, however, having this conversation."

"Going to one of Jax's games was on my bucket list, but I never actually imagined myself doing it," I confess.

"Forget about your bucket list. Sixty is the new forty." Even Leila doesn't believe that because she chuckles heartily. "Such bullshit. What's wrong with turning sixty, anyway?" She glances at me. "There's so much beauty in aging. Why is the world we live in so intent on making us believe the opposite?"

"You certainly look absolutely gorgeous and not a day over fifty-nine, darling." I return the kiss she gave me earlier.

"All the things you gain with age. All the things you have no clue of when you're younger. Acceptance. Wisdom. Knowing who you are and what you can and cannot do. All the life you have to look back on and from which you can share what you've learned. All the ambivalence you've had to overcome to get there. All the grief you've had to endure and how it can be turned into something positive over time." She looks at me with a glint in her eye. "Are you ready for a Leila Zadeh-ism?"

"Any time." Something warm blooms in my chest at the prospect of what she's about to say.

"Getting older is like the grand finale of a song. It can only be so glorious because of all the things that came before."

"A fine Leila Zadeh-ism *and* a music reference as well." I squeeze her arm.

"I, too, know how to play to my audience." She blows me an air kiss.

"Thank you for that." It hits me that I haven't done a thorough scan of my surroundings in a while. "And thank you for everything else."

She pulls me close. "I've told you that you being here, with me, for a good long while to come, is the only thanks I'll ever need."

"That, and Rian's eggs, Harry's amaretto sour, an endless supply of high-end whisky, and sheets with an infinite thread count."

"That goes without saying."

We turn the corner and head into the street where Jax's school is situated. It's not particularly busy, but still much busier than I'm used to. I have lived pretty much alone in a large house for the past ten years. Any crowd bigger than five people will look busy to me.

Jade sees us first. She waves discreetly from her hip. Vivian waits for us with a large smile on her lips and her arms wide open.

"Oh, Iz. Jax will be over the moon," she says, as she pulls me into a hug.

I'm fairly certain that my godson won't care that much about me being in the crowd, but I know it means a lot to Vivian, who has witnessed my struggle from up close for so long. Me being here is a huge deal to her.

It is to me as well. Especially now that it's no longer an item to cross off my final to-do list. That list ceased to exist when I chose the opposite path.

Then, with the sixth sense I wasn't sure I still possessed, I notice a small shift in the air. A frisson. A tiny disturbance of my fragile peace of mind.

A middle-aged woman with big hair walks toward us. I can read the intention on her face. She's caught a whiff of Isabel Adler in the air.

Leila must have felt me stiffen, because she comes to stand a little closer to me.

"Excuse me," the woman says. "But I would recognize the great Isabel Adler anywhere." She giggles nervously. "I honestly never thought I'd see the day," she whispers, as though it's imperative no one else hears—it kind of is. She keeps a small but nevertheless respectful distance. "How are you?" She cocks her head and narrows her eyes.

I straighten my posture and try to take a deep breath. This is one of the main reasons I didn't leave my house for so long, to avoid questions like this. But I remember what Leila told me before we left. This isn't so much about me. It's about this woman who is over the moon to see me.

"I'm fine. Thanks for asking." It's hard not to sound like a robot. I try a smile, which is much easier than expected. Leila discreetly wraps her arms around me. "How are *you*?" I ask.

"Trying my damnedest to not freak the hell out," the woman says. "I can't believe this." She takes a step closer. "It's so good to see you, Isabel. You have no idea how happy I am right now."

Her enthusiasm brightens the smile on my face. It reminds me of all the times when my mere appearance on stage would freak out every single person in the venue. All I had to do, it seemed, was turn up.

"It's lovely to meet you, um, what's your name?" I extend my hand.

"Rita," she says, and shakes my hand fervently, after which she stares at our still joined hands for a few seconds.

"Lovely to meet you, Rita," I say, releasing her hand. "Enjoy the game."

She all but jumps up and down in front of me. Then she narrows her eyes. "You haven't been coming to the home games all season, have you?"

"No." I send her a reassuring smile. "This is my first."

"We should go in," Vivian says. "It's about to start."

Rita glances at Vivian. If she recognizes her as my ex-partner from a long time ago, she doesn't let on. "Of course. I'll leave you be. But truly, Isabel, um, Ms. Adler, I mean, your music..." Her voice breaks a little. "You have no idea how much it means to me. Thank you so much."

"Thank *you*," I say, and mean it from the bottom of my heart.

Is this what I've been so afraid of? A lovely woman like Rita telling me how much my music means to her? It's not that

I've suddenly stopped understanding my fear. But in this moment, I can also see its utter uselessness.

"Are you okay, Iz?" Vivian hooks an arm inside mine.

"I'm very well." I give her arm a squeeze.

Leila's arm still rests on my back. Jade shoots me a quick wink, as though she knows exactly what I'm going through. Vivian probably told her that I'm not exactly a regular at Jackson's games. "It's good to be here," I say and, again, I mean it from the bottom of my heart.

CHAPTER 37

I stare at the cover. At a picture of myself taken a mere few weeks ago. All my wrinkles are on display. The smile on my lips is tentative at most.

Somewhere I've Never Been: The Official Isabel Adler Biography, the title reads. By Bruce Winkleman and Leila Zadeh.

I read the manuscript Leila sent to the publisher a few months ago, but holding the finished book in my hands is different. I'm glad I'm alone in my office. I need this moment on my own.

This is my life I'm holding in my hands. My story of the past sixty years. Mere months ago, it was my plan to never hold this book in my hands. To let it live a life of its own—to let it live without *and* instead of me.

Then Leila came along and changed everything. She gave me back the one true reason I felt I needed to live, which hasn't proven entirely correct, but I couldn't see that at the time—something I no longer blame myself for. She gave me back my music. So far, I've only performed for an audience of one. For Leila. And Vivian. And for myself. From those tiny performances, many other reasons to live have sprouted.

Love is one of them. The people I care for and who care for me. There are only a few of them, but what a bunch they are.

I cast one last glance at the black-and-white picture of me on the cover. Even though my smile is only hinted at, I do look happy. Fulfilled. Satisfied with how my life turned out. The trick, Ira told the photographer, is to have Leila stand behind the camera. It clearly worked. I can't see Leila and not look satisfied. It has so far proven impossible.

I open the book. I caress the title page with my finger. I slide my fingertip over Leila's name. My gaze lingers on Bruce's. He's doing much better now. He's walking again. He won't be riding a horse any time soon, but he confided in me that he started writing again. Leila told me he'd given her a few notes on the book, but had otherwise respected the changes she made.

I know what I will see when I flip the next page and even though I know, I'm hesitant because of how it will make me feel and it's not a feeling I'm keen to revisit. But I flip the page. I take the next step and am faced with the first few sentences of my goodbye letter.

It's certainly not how Bruce started the book in his first draft. But Bruce fell off his horse. Leila took over. I have asked myself many times what would have happened if Bruce's horse hadn't felt so capricious that day. If he hadn't fallen and Leila hadn't taken over. I wouldn't be dead yet. Day 0 is next week. I only know because it's the day after my birthday. Or maybe that's not true. Maybe I will remember Day 0 forever. Either way, I have something else scheduled other than dying that day.

Maybe if Leila hadn't come into my life, someone else would have. Or something else would have disabused me of the notion that death was the only option left for me. Or maybe everything would have gone as planned. Nobody knows, least of all me.

Maybe Bruce himself would, somehow, have been able to light some spark in me, by shedding light on the life I had already lived. But what happened must have done so for a reason. Just as, I'm beginning to think, the scar tissue on my vocal cords grew and grew for a reason. From my old voice a new one was born. A vastly different one, but still mine. Just as from my ten years of solitude, a new me has been born. A new woman, still resembling the old one, but with a new kind of music inside of her, waiting to get out. With a new outlook on life. With new hope. With new love in her life.

I read the beginning of my letter.

> *At first, this may be very difficult to comprehend, but I'm confident that, in the end, you will understand why I had to do this. Maybe not fully. Maybe not how I feel in my very bones that this is the only way things could go for me. But you will get it. That's why I'm writing you this letter.*

It chills me to the core. These could have been my very last words. I could never have sung again. The irony of that fact doesn't escape me. Because I sang again, the words I'm reading are not my last. While the entire content of the letter is one big complaint about no longer being able to sing and express myself.

Leila and I discussed the inclusion of the letter at length. Not so much me allowing snippets to be used in the book. She convinced me to do that quite quickly after she broached the subject the first time. I could see the impact it would have—and, like Leila said, the message of how hope will always spring eternal. But just as Leila got involved in the details of the musical arrangement of "A Breathless Place", I got involved in the details of my biography. I no longer have death as an excuse. I didn't write the book, but it is about me. It tells my story. And Leila was right. Wanting to end my life was a big part of my story for a very long time.

I let my eyes linger on the first page a little longer. The words have lost some of their meaning. Most of the sting has vanished from them now. They're part of my story but they're no longer the end of it. When I leaf through the book to its last page, a happy ending will await me. My happy ending.

Before I do that, I thumb through the pages until I reach the middle section with more pictures. On the very last page of photos, in the bottom right corner, there's one of Leila and me. She didn't want to include it, but I stood my ground. How could my biography, my life story so far, be complete without mention of her? Without a picture of her marvelous face, her generous smile, the kindness in her eyes.

No one else can see it in this picture, but it's evident to me. The way she fought for me. How she, instinctively, knew how to lure me back into a headspace in which I wanted to live. The tears streaming down her face after she'd read my letter. The music she brought. The Bianca Bankole album. The memory of how she walked into my house the first time.

On the opposite page, there's a picture of me on stage in an elaborate white dress, of which the skirt is so puffy it makes me look like I'm standing on a cloud. It was the dress I put on for the finale of the last world tour I did—although, at the time, I didn't know it was my last. For the last few songs of any concert, I always turned the sentiment—and my voice—up to full tilt. I always sang as if it were my very last time. I always gave everything I had and put all my heart into the notes I held for long, long seconds.

There's a section in the book where Bruce and Leila describe how it felt for me to take the stage and then, afterward, leave it again. I have no idea how they came up with the words to describe that most sublime of sensations. I must have told them at some point, but I don't remember doing so.

Although I know I will never again feel the elation of having hit a difficult note perfectly, I can experience what it feels like to be on stage again. I can and I will. I have to try. It's all I want. I want to be the person with that look on her face that I'm seeing in this picture. I can't be that particular performer again, but I can aim for that smile. I can try to bring across emotion with my voice again. I can try to move the people listening to me the way I was moved when I listened to Bianca Bankole's song. And when I do, I want to see Leila's face looking right back at me.

I cast one last glance at the picture of Leila and me, send her an invisible kiss, and close the book. Next, I head to the music room, where I've been spending most of my time, getting ready for next week.

EPILOGUE

19 MARCH 2021 - DAY 0

Day 0 feels like the first day of my new life. I wait in the wings as I used to in my former life. It may be strange to hold a book launch at a concert venue, but when I suggested it, not one single person objected. Even though, so far, Leila and Vivian are the only two people who have heard me sing.

Ira might regret it later, but I have an inkling that he won't. Not after I had to tell him about my goodbye letter—about my plan to die—before Leila submitted her final manuscript to the publisher. Never before have I seen this vital man turn so ashen, his face so dead, in a matter of seconds. I was right when I thought my manager really cared for me, loved me even. It wasn't that big a surprise, considering he's stood by me since the day I was told I wouldn't be able to perform.

He puts his hand my shoulder. "Ready, Iz?" He gives my shoulder a little squeeze. "Ready for the big time again?"

I want to roll my eyes, but he wouldn't see because he's standing next to me. I told Ira numerous times that the 'big times' are over for me. Performing again isn't about trying to recapture my former glory—because that would be impossible. It's about the simple, straightforward joy of performing. Of touching people with my music. Tonight, I will only sing one song, while I play the piano—something I never did before. But the piano is a safe place for me to be when I do this. Only having a microphone to hold on to would be a bridge too far. I need the reassurance of the keys under my fingers. I've found so much solace in the piano since I started playing again. I might even have gotten a bit better at it, although I will never be a virtuoso. While I adore playing, it's not what I love doing the most.

"Ready as I'll ever be," I say on a nervous sigh.

"You've only waited ten years for this," Ira says. "I, for one, can't wait. I'm so proud of you, Izzy. We've had some rough times, but, um, well…" He doesn't continue. He doesn't have to. I know what he means. Ira with all his bluster and his usual fountain of words is momentarily speechless.

I can sense how the room fills with anticipation. People shuffle in their seats. Some don't know where to look. It's a small crowd tonight, a fraction of what I used to play for. Leila's in the front row. She's all glammed up with her trademark red lipstick. Her hair is loose and voluptuous and shiny. She looks straight ahead, at the stage, at the piano stool where I will sit in a few short minutes.

She offered to stay backstage with me after the actual launch of the book, but I want her in the audience. Because, by now, I'm used to having her there. I'm not sure I could do this if she wasn't in my audience of many.

Bruce sits next to her. He looks almost like his old self again. Like the man who managed to pry quite a few secrets from me. He's entitled to be celebrated as much as Leila for his contribution to my biography, but Leila deserves a slew of medals for all the other things she did for me. Without Leila, there would be no piano on stage waiting for me to come out and play it. There most certainly wouldn't be a microphone waiting for me to amplify my voice with it.

A few minutes ago, I stood in this exact spot while she read an excerpt from the book. I was so mesmerized by her presence, by her command of the words and the stage alike, that what she was reading barely registered. She reminded me of myself, in a way, of how I used to take the stage back in the day, full of confidence because, although nervous beforehand, I always knew what I was capable of in the moment. Leila has always been that way in everything she's done. Maybe it's one of the things I picked up on when we first met. Maybe I caught a glimpse of my former self in her.

That former self is long gone. Tonight, I'm so nervous, my throat so tight, that I wonder whether I'll be able to sing at all. Nerves are a natural part of being a performer, I know that in my bones. But this is a different kind of stage fright. Because I no longer have the pipes. The natural power of my voice is gone. Even though I have practiced for hours and hours—I could perform this song in my sleep I know it that well—I can't possibly access the confidence of knowing, beforehand, that I'll do it well. I can't rely on my past as a performer.

Tonight, I'm presenting a new Isabel Adler. One many former fans will turn their backs on—there's just no other way. But I'm not doing this for them. There are plenty of other singers who can reach the high notes. I'm here to distill every last ounce of emotion from what's left of my voice. From beneath the scar tissue, that not only thrived on my vocal cords, but on my heart as well. While scarring is an inherent part of healing, underneath the unwanted tissue that grew inside me, I forgot what healing was all about. As my vocal cords stiffened, so did my heart. As the unwelcome tissue tightened my most precious organ, it suffocated my resolve. Until there was no room left for hope or love.

Now here I stand, ready to take to the stage, to feel the love from an audience once again. Vivian's chatting to Jade and the woman sitting next to Jade. A face—and body—I would recognize anywhere. Jade has brought Ramona. I will never be able to tell Ramona what she stood for on those days when I hardly spoke to anyone and she was always there. At the very least, Ramona's motivational prowess is responsible for my physical fitness, which has also helped with my return to the stage. My breath is powerful. My muscles are strong. My physical fitness can carry me through a night like this. And, well, Leila's very fond of the bulge in my biceps when I flex for her.

Next to Ramona, there's Jade's mother. I wonder what she will think of my new voice. There's only one way to find out. It's time to take the final few steps. I take a deep breath. Ira's hand is on my back now, supporting me. I need all the support I can get because my legs feel like jelly. But this is the thrill I was after all along. This is what I've been dreaming of for ten long years.

The MC walks onto the stage and takes the microphone.

"And now, ladies and gentlemen, the moment we've all been waiting for." The crowd whoops. "The one and only Isabel Adler, back on stage. Please give her a warm welcome —" His words are drowned out by a huge wave of applause. Every last person jumps to their feet. There's that rush I've missed so much. But it's not the same. I haven't deserved it. I haven't done anything yet. They're clapping, just like before, just because I turned up. Bless them. They have no idea what they're in for. I won't even be playing a song they know.

"Izzy," Ira whispers in my ear. "It's time to go on now." He finds my hand and gives it a light squeeze. "Knock 'em dead," he says, before he nudges me from the curtains.

The wave of energy that hits me as I walk out nearly knocks me to my knees. The applause only swells and swells.

Hold on, people, I want to say. I don't need to be applauded just for being here. Or maybe I do. Because if things had gone a different way, I wouldn't be here at all. This could have been my funeral. Now, it's my resurrection. They haven't read the book yet, so they don't know about that yet either.

I walk to the edge of the stage. First, I find Leila's dark, smoldering gaze, which calms my nerves and lights a brand-new fire in me at the same time. Then I send the other people in the audience a warm smile. I bring my hand to my chest and give them a small bow. Surely, I'm not ready for the big one. It still remains to be seen whether I ever will be.

"We love you, Isabel," someone shouts.

The warmth with which I'm greeted eases my nerves further. I walk to the piano. I take my seat. I adjust the microphone. I let my fingers hover over the keys. In my head, I hear the first chords. In my head, it's already happening. I find Leila's face again. I take a breath and I play. That's when I know, no matter what happens next, I've found my way back home.

But playing the intro on the piano is easy compared to what I'm about to do next. Compared to defying the audience's expectations. So I stop. Not to start again. Not because I don't think I can actually do it. But because I want to talk to them. I always chatted with the audience. My gregariousness was one of the things I was loved for; I've been told that over and over again.

"Sorry," I say. "How rude of me not to say hello." I wait a beat. "*Hello.*" I lean back and look into the crowd. "It's so good to see you all."

The cheer that erupts fill me with glee. Oh, how I've missed this. Performing is never a one-way street. It's a communal experience, which is why it hurt so much when it was taken away from me.

"How have you been?" I ask.

Maybe, I think, when the applause drowns out everything again, the cheer of a crowd is what I was addicted to as well. Maybe it's that cheer I had come to believe I no longer deserved. Maybe the lack of applause has been an intrinsic part of my biggest fear.

"I know it's been a little while since we last saw each other." I follow up with a chuckle. "And I'd be lying if I claimed I'm really back." A few cheers follow but the atmosphere changes as my words take on more meaning. "The truth is that the old Isabel Adler will never be back. That won't be possible, I'm afraid. But..." I do my best to emphasize the 'but'. "This person sitting in front of you tonight, that's the person you're going to get. We both have to make do with her now." I arch up my eyebrows in apology. "It's not that bad."

A rumble of hesitant laughter reaches me.

"It's been rough at times, over the years, as you will read in my biography." I take another moment to find both Bruce and Leila with my gaze. "On the topic of my biography, please put your hands together for my extraordinary biographers Bruce Winkleman and Leila Zadeh. Trust me when I tell you that they are something else." I beam Bruce and Leila a smile. Hard as it is to look away from Leila, who sits there radiating all her innate Leila goodness, I return my gaze to the audience.

After the applause for Bruce and Leila has died down, I continue, "It may be a strange thing to say about a biography, but it has changed the course of my life. It saved my life, to be honest, but, um..." I insert a chuckle. "Before things get too serious, let's get back to the music, shall we?" I hit a few notes on the piano. "Before I sing you this song, you should know that just as I am not the same, my voice is not the same. It's something else now." I drink in the atmosphere, the energy, the love I get from the other side of the stage. "This song is brand-new and it's called 'A Breathless Place.'"

I start the intro again. The room goes quiet. I bring my lips as close as possible to the microphone. The first line approaches. My heart beats double-time—much faster than the beat of the song.

Then, I sing. I let it all go. The past ten years, the anger, the grief, the fear. I let it all go and I sing. I get my voice back from behind the scar tissue on my vocal cords. I defy that growth inside my throat and sing despite of it. I sing for all the times I was convinced it had gotten the better of me. I sing for all the years that I wanted to die. I sing with all the emotion that I have inside me, that has built up over years of silence, and I lay it all out there for these people who have come to see me tonight.

Only when I reach the final line of the song, when I'm approaching the final chord, do I look at the audience again. They all still seem to be there. No boos are emanating from the darkness the audience has been plunged into when the spotlight was fixed on me. Because of the dimmed lights, it's difficult to make out Leila's face, but I know where she's sitting and I fix my gaze on that spot. I hit the last chord and my pulse picks up speed even more. The jury's out. The verdict's about to be delivered.

"Thank you," I whisper, as soon as the song is done. A habit that has stood the test of time.

For a split second, the applause is hesitant, a few lone claps, but it quickly transforms into a huge roar. When the audience is lit up again, I see that everyone's out of their seats. A standing ovation. It feels like a bit much for what I was able to give, although the feeling I put into the song, into the lyrics Leila wrote for me, was completely there.

The energy that comes at me is heartwarming and, in

some ways, unexpected. Surely, at least a few people must be disappointed. If there are any, they're not making it very clear. I wouldn't put it past Ira to have pulled some managerial magic and made sure that every last person in the audience tonight would behave how he wanted them to—in my best interest.

I look at Leila and then I can't look away. Tears are running down her cheeks. Vivian puts an arm around her and whispers something in her ear. The emotions that sit behind my sternum, that I believed I had loosened by singing, threaten to turn into tears as well. Maybe, instead of crying, I can use them for something else.

"I was only meant to sing one song tonight," I say, my voice shaky, "but it doesn't strike me as though you guys will stand for that." I'm not sure anyone can even see the wide smile that grows on my face. "So how about I play you another one?"

"We want more. We want more," someone starts shouting. More people join in.

Ah, the encore. I always used to save a big belter for that very last song of the night. Neither my brittle voice nor my vulnerable state of mind will be able to handle more than two songs tonight, so I have to choose wisely. Although, really, the choice was made for me when we chose the title of the book.

"You may know this one," I say. "It's called 'Somewhere I've Never Been'." I launch into my current rendition of my biggest hit. It's a strange and exhilarating feeling at the same time. It's a minimalist version, with only the piano and my new voice. But through the words, which are etched in my brain, imprinted on my soul, because I must have sung them thousands of times, I can bring back all the times I performed this song before. All those glorious evenings of singing and sharing and performing flash through my mind as my fingers delicately tickle the piano. My entire life, as described in my biography, is compressed into the four minutes the song lasts.

Whereas during the performance of the first song, trepidation kept me from enjoying the moment in full, now I have pure exhilaration, pure energy running through my veins.

This, what I'm doing right now, is the reason I'm still here.

This is why I'm alive.

AUTHOR'S NOTE

Dear Reader,

After finishing this book, I barged into my wife's office and pompously announced that writing *A Breathless Place* had fundamentally changed something in me. Being quite verbally challenged, I couldn't express to my wife what it was that had happened to me during the writing process of this book. It was only after I sat down to write this note that I managed to explain it, to her, to myself, and now to you as well.

It was while revising *A Breathless Place*, while going over the very last chapters, that I realized I had some demons left to expel—that this book is so much more about me than I believed it to be.

This book bridges a gap of twenty years, between a time I was so lost I wanted to end my life, spanning all the years in between when I felt like I didn't belong, until now, this year specifically, when I've come to terms with my Autism and I've gotten as close to my true self as possible, being fully aware of just how much the power of expression means to me.

It's the contrast between who I was then and who I've become and the message of hope that I want to send with this book. Take it from a person who once truly believed that all hope was lost: there's always something better around the corner.

For many reasons, *A Breathless Place* is not my most commercial book. It's right up there with *At the Water's Edge* and *In the Distance There Is Light* when it comes to theme and darkness, yet it was a joy for me to write.

I'm not a plotter, but I always have a pretty good idea of what I want to accomplish when I start a new book and, perhaps for the first time ever—maybe it takes thirty novels to learn how to do this—I feel like I have succeeded. I feel like I was able to say what I wanted to say.

Even though this is a book about wanting to die and ultimately choosing to live—not the easiest of topics—I came to the page with such gusto every single day because, like performing is to Izzy, writing is what gives my life meaning. I can't even begin to tell you how much the simple act of creating fiction every day means to me. These days, I have to force myself to take breaks between books, because all I want to do is write. I want to go deep into my characters' psyche—all these gloriously gorgeous female characters I get to invent—and unearth what makes them tick. Doing that is what makes *me* tick.

I do want to take a moment to circle back to *At the Water's Edge*, which I wrote six years ago. Technically, it wasn't my first full-length novel, but emotionally, it feels like the first one that truly mattered. Technically, *A Breathless Place* isn't my thirtieth novel either (I've tossed a few in the bin over the years) but it is my thirtieth published Harper Bliss novel and that means something to me.

In my teens and twenties, I only ever had one dream, even

though I always believed it was one that could never come true: I wanted to be a writer. To be a writer now, and to have been for several years, to have published thirty novels, is so much more than that dream I used to have. To be able to live this life of creation and expression, and to be able to share my work with you, often to so much unexpected enthusiasm, is beyond any dream I could ever have had.

This is my dream life. I'm right in the middle of it. And to think there was a time I no longer wanted to be alive.

That is the new meaning *A Breathless Place* has taken on for me—and that is how writing this book changed something so profoundly inside me.

Lately, I've been going on a lot about 'the process being the reward' and how, in that spirit, this book has already given me everything. But that's not entirely true. While I will always write as long as I'm able to, I wouldn't be able to have this dream of a life if it weren't for *you*.

I know my books are sometimes difficult and my stories are not always the easiest to digest, but you, Dear Reader, have always firmly made me believe that what I write matters. That it is worthy of your time. In exchange, I will always give you a little piece of myself, because that's the only way I know how to write.

Thank you for giving me this enormous privilege over and over again. Thirty novels is not nothing. I know some of you have read every single one (more than once.) Some of you have been on this journey with me since *At the Water's Edge*. I hope you will continue to accompany me for the next thirty books.

Meanwhile: thank you from the bottom of my heart.

An enormous thank-you to my beautiful wife, Caroline, who knows all about being married to someone 'difficult but worth it', and who believed in me long before I ever did.

Thank you also to my trusted team of C's (as I like to call them):

- Cheyenne Blue, my editor and friend, in whom I can confide just about anything.

- Carrie Camp, my beta-reader, with whom I share a mutual love of cougars.

- Claire Jarrett, my proofreader who always goes above and beyond, time- and skill-wise.

- All the members of my Facebook Group, whose support has proven invaluable to me. This year, my Facebook Group has really become my online safe space where I can be as pompous, dramatic, and silly as I want to be.

Thank you and here's to thirty more,

Harper xo

ABOUT THE AUTHOR

Harper Bliss is a best-selling lesbian romance author. Among her most-loved books are the highly dramatic French Kissing and the often thought-provoking Pink Bean series.

Harper lived in Hong Kong for 7 years, travelled the world for a bit, and has now settled in Brussels (Belgium) with her wife and photogenic cat, Dolly Purrton.

Together with her wife, she hosts a weekly podcast called Harper Bliss & Her Mrs.

Harper loves hearing from readers and you can reach her at the email address below.

www.harperbliss.com
harper@harperbliss.com

Made in the USA
Middletown, DE
05 January 2024